Red Leaves

Sita Brahmachari is the daughter of an Indian doctor from Kolkata and an English nurse from the Lake District. After studying for a degree in English Literature and an MA in Arts Education she worked in community theatre and in schools, exploring creative-writing projects and plays with young people. Now she writes novels for many of the people who have inspired her along the way.

Sita lives and works in London with her husband, three children and the much-loved family dog, Billie.

...ten book about family, friendship, grief and hope which made me laugh and cry, sometimes at the same time'
Anthony Browne, Children's Laureate (2009–2011)

'A welter of emotions engulf Mira in this touching pre-teen story about secrets and how to keep them and share them'
Julia Eccleshare, Lovereading.com

Jasmine Skies
Shortlisted for the Coventry Book Award and nominated for the Carnegie Medal

'I wish Sita had been writing when I was growing up as this beautiful heartfelt book explores so eloquently the need to find your history in order to find yourself' Meera Syal

'Sita Brahmachari has such a loving touch with the way she delicately and compassionately picks her way through experiences, families and relationships' Jamila Gavin

Kite Spirit
Nominated for the UKLA Book Award

'Brahmachari writes with an incredible grace. She is very, very good at getting to the truth inside her work . . . Reading a book by Brahmachari is a very precious thing indeed' Goodreads.com

'An outstandingly beautiful story . . . Perfectly pitched and written with the utmost sensitivity and truly uplifting charm, this is a book to read and treasure. A moving and unmissable treat'
Lancashire Evening Post

www.sitabrahmachari.com

Sita Brahmachari

Red Leaves

MACMILLAN CHILDREN'S BOOKS

First published 2014 by Macmillan Children's Books
a division of Macmillan Publishers Limited
20 New Wharf Road, London N1 9RR
Basingstoke and Oxford
Associated companies throughout the world
www.panmacmillan.com

ISBN 978-1-4472-6298-5

Copyright © Sita Brahmachari 2014

Extract on page 229 from 'The Moods' from
The Wind Among the Reeds (1899) by W. B. Yeats

On page 320, the character Elder misremembers
'Binsey Poplars' by Gerard Manley Hopkins

The right of Sita Brahmachari to be identified as
the author of this work has been asserted by her in
accordance with the Copyright, Designs and Patents Act 1988.

1 3 5 7 9 8 6 4 2

A CIP catalogue record for this book is available from the British Library.

Typeset by Ellipses Digital Limited, Glasgow
Printed and bound by CPI Group (UK) Ltd, Croydon CR0 4YY

'The ache for home lives in all of us. The safe place where we can go as we are and not be questioned.'
Maya Angelou, *All God's Children Need Traveling Shoes*

Chapter One

'Here I go, up, up above the elder trees to my bird's-eye view. Leaves flying everywhere, red leaves full of passion and anger and sadness. Time to light the fires. The year's turning and the wood's stirring. Time to unravel the vine back through time.' Elder, the ancient homeless woman shook a branch and a shower of leaves rained down. She laughed and threw her arms around wildly as if stirring up a storm.

Aisha placed her key in the lock.

'Sure you can't come back to mine? Mum's cooking,' Muna asked as she leaned on the garden wall.

'Not today. Liliana wants me home. She says there's something she has to talk to me about.'

The girls switched to speaking in Somali, chatted for a while and parted with a giggle.

1

Liliana winced as the door clicked closed.

'Hi,' Aisha called to her breezily and walked straight through to her bedroom.

'Hi love!' Liliana sat at the kitchen table, surrounded by sketching pencils, paper, scissors, glue and a collection of half-drunk cups of coffee. Her hands shook slightly as she smoothed another photo into her foster daughter's scrapbook. *Be rational, be calm, it's only a first meeting,* Liliana comforted herself, but there was nothing rational about the way she felt for Aisha. She set aside the glue and began drawing a detailed pattern of musical notes around the border of the page, stalling again. Perhaps she *should* have let Aisha's social worker give her this news.

Liliana imagined that she was standing with Aisha on a seafront on a cloudless day; Aisha and everyone around looked happy and settled while she alone gaped in horror as a giant wave threatened to engulf them. *It's natural to feel like this,* Liliana consoled herself, for she had been bonded to Aisha since the very first day when the little girl with the saddest eyes in the world had tiptoed through her front door, peering in as if she feared that the flat might explode at any moment.

Liliana clasped her hands together to still them.

'Aisha, come and see! I've added some new photos of you and Muna with your band.'

'What band?' Aisha laughed, stepping into the

kitchen and peering over Liliana's shoulder. 'Singing together once at school doesn't exactly make us into a group!'

'Well, you should be. You were by far the best.'

'You *would* say that!'

'Because it's true!' Liliana shrugged, and smiled to herself as she turned the pages of Aisha's life story book – Liliana had taken to calling it a 'story book' and sometimes 'a scrapbook', because somehow these names seemed less daunting. Every child she had cared for had one. It was a personal history in words and pictures, made so that they, and future carers, could chart their life's journey, record progress and give the children a joined-up sense of their own history.

Some foster-carers she knew didn't bother too much with them, but Liliana always felt that making sure these little details were filled in was the very least that she could do for the children she welcomed into her home.

Aisha's earliest drawings in the book were from the time when she had refused to speak. There was one of Aisha as a baby curled up in a foetal position inside a giant image of her mother. That always choked Liliana up the most. When she had first seen it she'd cried. Who could blame the child for wanting to crawl back inside her mother and be born all over again? Aisha's 'life story' already looked too long and complicated. It was hard to believe that she was not yet even thirteen.

Aisha's description of leaving Somalia and travelling to Britain had broken Liliana's heart. At just ten years old she had managed to convince the authorities that she was twelve. Liliana would never forget the day that the little girl had finally confided in her.

'"It will go better for you if you pretend you are a few years older." That's what the guide said to me.'

'And how did you pretend to be older?' Liliana asked.

'Like this!' Aisha stood taller and made her face into a kind of expressionless mask that no clouds of emotion could penetrate.

It had taken a long time before she let down her guard and removed that mask.

Now Liliana studied Aisha's smiling face. She was in awe of how far her foster-daughter had come from those painful early days. 'Sure you don't want to start writing in this yourself now?'

Aisha shook her head.

If I were to write a life story book for myself, I would make so many things different, she thought. No matter how pretty Liliana tried to make the book, with all her decorations it was a constant reminder to Aisha of all the times that she had been uprooted and torn away from the people she loved.

Liliana glanced at her foster-daughter as she stuck down the last photos of Aisha's 'band' then wrote their names underneath – Aisha, Muna, Somaya, Mariam – and closed the book. This felt like the right moment to raise the subject.

'Can I see?' Aisha asked, leaning over Liliana.

'Of course! It's your story!'

Liliana gently handed the book to Aisha. Maybe she could talk to her as they read over the pages together.

It had been a while since Aisha had really looked at the book, but now she noticed how Liliana had adorned their story so carefully, sticking in little mementos and memories of times they had shared. In fact, Aisha now realized Liliana was working her way backwards through the book, adding her own paintings, sketches and swatches of material from the clothes that Aisha had been wearing in a particular photo on a particular day. Liliana rarely threw anything away. These little scraps of material were the sorts of details that transported you back.

Aisha reached out to touch the piece of red velvet skirt that she remembered wearing, soft and comforting against her skin, and Liliana patted the cushion on the chair next to her. Aisha sat down and Liliana budged up closer so that they now sat shoulder to shoulder.

'I can't believe that I've been here for two and a

half years already.' Aisha flicked back to the formal, typed entries from before she had come to live here and felt relieved that Liliana had not been tempted to decorate these stark pages. *Nothing could be added to that time to make it feel better*, she thought as she read over the facts of her own life.

'Aisha arrived at Heathrow Airport alone.'

'Aisha's first day at Monmouth House care home . . .'

'Aisha's first day at Bishop's Primary School . . .'

'Aisha granted Refugee Status.'

In this section the photos were mostly official passport shots of a shy-looking little girl with long thin plaits who did not want her image captured. Without her hijab, she looked odd even to herself. Looking at her unveiled ten-year-old face, so exposed to the world, so alone, the weight and chill of the cold stone she'd felt lying in her stomach at that time returned to her. Occasionally one of the staff in the home had tried to capture her in a photo with the other children, but Aisha had always stood slightly aside, as if she was living in another dimension. Which was exactly how it had felt as she'd hugged her stomach tight and ached for the heat of home.

'A sad chapter.' Liliana placed a soothing hand on Aisha's back as she leafed forward again to the beginning of their time together and Liliana's own careful handcrafted pages. 'But look at all of these happy memories!'

Aisha hugged Liliana close. 'You made them for me.'

'*We* made them!' Liliana corrected.

In the time that they had been together, everything had changed for Aisha. She had gone from being a traumatized child to a confident young woman, and it was Liliana who had held her hand every step of the way.

Liliana leaned forward and ran her finger over a sentence on the page.

'Remember? Your first words!'

'"I feel safe here",' Aisha read out loud. 'I would never have said that to anyone except you.'

Liliana wiped a tear from her eye. She feared that just bringing up the subject of meeting this family who might adopt Aisha would rock her sense of safety. But maybe she was only thinking of herself. She had promised her own children, now grown-up, that Aisha would be her last foster-child, but in her mind she had always imagined that she would keep Aisha with her until she was old enough to go off to college or university. Liliana had even pictured the graduation photos – '*Such a clever girl*' – and she had no doubt that Aisha would one day fulfil her dream of becoming a lawyer. In her own mind Liliana had decided that the two of them would graduate together: Aisha from university and Liliana from foster-caring into a well-earned retirement.

Liliana sighed deeply. *I should have learned by now that life isn't as neat and tidy as that! But who'd have thought that anyone would come forward to offer a home to a Somali teenager with a traumatic past?* She shook herself. *This is just an introductory meeting. If Aisha doesn't want to go, no one will force her. Anyway, it might not come to anything.* As these arguments sifted through her mind, Liliana felt ashamed of her own selfishness. She attempted to savour the sight of Aisha's serene, trusting face but the spectre of the mask the child had once worn haunted Liliana and the memory seemed now to cast them both in a long brooding shadow.

It'll have to wait till tomorrow. I'll tell her tomorrow.

Chapter Two

Zak slumped down on the bottom step and stared into space.

'Hurry up! You can't afford to be late for school again,' Shalini called to him over the banister. Zak peered up at his nanny's anxious face, then slung his bag over his shoulder and forced himself to stand up.

'Keep distant from the wood. Make sure you stay close by the road,' were the last words that Shalini spoke to him as he walked out of the door.

Or what? Zak asked himself as he entered the rusted metal gates that bordered the woodland. He'd always been happiest in the woods that backed on to his old house, with his dad, hunting for the best place to build a den or pitching stumps for a game of cricket. It hadn't been that long ago since they'd walked hand in hand singing childish songs.

A small red leaf wafted down between the branches. *If I catch that leaf it'll make everything go back to normal.* He rarely missed a catch. He held out his hand, but just as it was about to land safely in his palm, the leaf caught on the wind and floated away.

Zak sighed. *What's the matter with me? How can catching a falling leaf change anything one way or the other?* Except that was just how he felt these days – like a leaf being wafted on winds that other people had whipped up, with no way of knowing where he would land.

Zak watched as the leaf settled on a nearby sign. 'Welcome to Home Wood,' he read, as a ranting voice rose up from somewhere close by. It sounded deranged. Zak ducked behind a tree and held his breath.

'There, my Crystal, don't you cry. My belly's singing you a lullaby! Listen to that hunger-thunder rumble. I'm telling you. It could shake the roots of my Home Oaks.'

Zak tentatively peered out from behind the thick trunk. Touching distance away from him was an old woman, her puckered face all pinched and chafed, her skin like the flaking bark of an ancient tree. He supposed that she could be about his grandma's age when she'd died or older, much, much older even. Her hair hung in a mass of wild frizzy curls down her back and had been dyed flame red. She'd threaded leaves through the top strands like a tangled crown. Zak stared at her clothes. She'd piled one piece on top of the other in an eclectic collection of leaf layers. The overall effect was like the rag rug his mum had once brought home from one of her trips to Africa. It was impossible to tell exactly what the old woman was wearing or how small or large she really was underneath all those petticoats that swept the earth as she walked. Everything she wore seemed to have been chosen to match the russet tones of autumn, like camouflage.

Get a hold of yourself. She's just a homeless old woman. But Zak found that he could not tear his gaze away from her. She was close enough now for him to hear the hollow rumblings of her stomach.

'There, my Crystal, don't you cry. My belly's singing you a lullaby!'

It was then that he realized that she was swaddling a baby wrapped in a crocheted woollen shawl, more holes than blanket. Despite the old woman's hushings, the baby hadn't stirred or made a sound. Zak's heart clamped in his chest. *What's she doing with a baby? Has she stolen it out of someone's pram?*

He was relieved to see a young woman walking her dog up a steep connecting path. The nearer she drew, the louder the old woman's voice seemed to become.

'But here's a wood wanderer coming. Wafting perfume. Not my kind, gets up my nose. Makes me sneeze.'

The woman held the baby close and rocked it. No movement came from underneath its shawl.

'Here she comes. What do you think, my Crystal? Will she walk right past? Pretend we're invisible? How could anyone not take pity on you, my baby?'

11

Then she held the bundle up, like an offering. The dog came bounding over and sniffed at it before tossing its head dismissively. The young woman strained to get a closer look, before she too turned and hurried away.

'Could you spare us the price of a cup of tea? No . . . ? Straight past, eyes glazed over, locking us out. Just an old tree stump with gnarly roots. That's all I am these days.'

And with that the old woman dropped the baby on the ground, where it landed with a thud and slid from its blanket. Zak gave a sharp intake of breath and was just about to spring from his hiding place when a bald plastic head rolled in his direction, its blue eyes wide and unblinking. *What an idiot I am. She's just a crazy old homeless woman wandering the woods with a doll.* Still, Zak felt as if he should DO something. Tell someone. *How can anyone so old be left in that state, with no one to look after her?* There was a homeless shelter just up the road – surely she could go there.

Now the woman slumped down on a tree stump and inspected her bare feet. They hardly resembled feet at all, bulging in unlikely places like fungus growths out of earthy tree hollows. She was close enough for Zak to smell her musty odour. *Was that stench coming from her feet?*

'Count my toes! Make sure they're all still there! Feel the scrunch of red leaves under me . . .' She chatted on to herself, then seemed to notice that her 'baby' was missing and started hunting around on the ground for her. She shoved the doll's head back on to its plastic stump of a neck then stroked its cheeks. 'I didn't mean to drop you, my love,' she crooned, gathering the doll back into her arms and wrapping her tightly in the blanket. The doll's feet protruded and she tucked them in gently.

'Earth's stirring, autumn's coming, winter's just around the corner.' The woman shivered, as if she could already feel the cold biting into her. She turned to Zak's hiding place and sniffed the air, sensing his presence.

Has she known all this time that I've been watching her? Zak shuddered. Then, without warning, the woman was up on her feet and heading straight for him so that he was forced to stumble out of his hiding place. He backed away as she grinned at him, revealing a higgledy-piggledy collection of rotten and missing teeth. She grabbed hold of a low branch and began to climb slowly and steadily up the tree.

'Here I go, up, up above the elder trees to my bird's-eye view. Leaves flying everywhere, red leaves full of passion and anger and sadness. Time to light the fires. The year's turning and the wood's stirring. Hush now, Crystal.' The old woman closed her eyes and lifted her face to the warm sun that fell in shadow-shafts between the trees, bathing the wood in a magical

13

amber light. She was leaning forward now listening intently . . . to the sound of a gentle song that meandered along the path. Zak heard it clearly now as a girl singing in another language drew closer. Her voice was low and mellow.

'Here's a young one coming, but this one's happy as a skylark! Listen to that song, sweet as feathers, soft as honey.' The old woman knocked her hand against her head as if that could make her brain work better. 'Soft as *feathers*, sweet as *honey* – Happiness chimes the same in every language.'

Zak started to back away down the path. He could feel the heat of the old woman's gaze as he collided with a girl in a blue headscarf. She stopped singing abruptly and shot a questioning look from Zak to the old woman who was now scattering breadcrumbs over them both from the branches above. A cacophony of crows swept in. The girl hurried away, brushing her headscarf and shoulders.

'I'm sorry, dears,' the woman called, gathering herself. 'Just feeding the birds. Must feed the birds . . . some have flown a long, long way, further than Elder has ever roamed.'

The girl turned back and exchanged a bemused look with Zak, before shrugging and carrying on her way.

'Sticks and stones and broken bones and even words will hurt you, but sometimes the loneliness is the worst . . . Hey, boy!'

Zak found himself running, but no matter how fast he ran the old woman's chants kept pace, crackling through his mind and refusing to fade away.

At the exit on to the road he brushed the breadcrumbs off his blazer.

Loneliness is the worst . . . Her words continued to echo through his head as he took his first steps up the impossibly steep hill that led to his new school.

Chapter Three

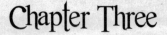

Zak had been at his school for almost a month and he'd decided that it felt weird being among only boys. In primary he had preferred the girls in his year. They were easier to talk to. Now that he went to an all-boys school he felt as if half the world was missing. There was always someone who wanted to prove how much stronger and tougher they were than you. Maybe it was because he was younger than most of the others in his year. And he was definitely smaller . . . as one or two of them had been keen to point out. If they only knew how small he felt inside, they wouldn't bother trying to bring him any lower.

As he walked up the hill a memory of when his dad had still lived with them floated through his mind. The two of them had hooked up a rope swing in the back garden of the old house and Zak had spiralled and twisted so fast that his dad had turned into a spinning blur and it had taken ages for him to form back into the familiar lines of his tall, sturdy body.

Those 'I'll always be there for you' outlines that Zak had believed in, back then, with that big, broad, happy smile that everyone said father and son shared. *Is that what Dad will be to me in the future . . . just a distant, blurred memory?*

He thought of the homeless woman dropping breadcrumbs . . . and of the girl with the blue headscarf singing her way through the wood. There was something about her voice, and the way she had seemed to almost dance away from him, that reminded Zak of what it was to feel happy.

In a courtyard directly outside the school stood a dark granite war memorial. Zak registered the long list of names. 'Fallen heroes . . .' All boys who had once attended the school or lived around here who had grown into young men and then been killed. *What was the point in that? What's so heroic about dying?* Zak thought of his mum over in Syria, and all the other war zones she'd reported from, and not for the first time he wondered what he would do if he was ever called up to fight for something. He felt a great lump of emotion in his throat and swallowed hard to stem the tears. *As if I don't feel bad enough already without that mad old homeless woman and her creepy doll doing my head in. I couldn't even catch that leaf! Maybe it's a sign that something's happened to Mum.* He checked his phone for a news feed. Nothing. No texts or voicemails either. He sat down on the steps of the war memorial and the

17

thought crossed his mind that with both his parents now so far away he was as alone as the homeless woman talking to her doll. *If only when Mum set off she could just tell me the date and time when she'd be coming back. But I can hear her voice now, 'you can't plan anything in a war, Zak.' Well I hate war and I hate not knowing how long I have to hold my breath till she comes home. I hate it, I hate it.*

Zak stood up and kicked the bottom step of the memorial.

'Show some respect!' Mr Slater shouted over to him from across the courtyard. Zak picked up his bag and followed his form tutor through the enormous wooden doors into school. He looked up as he passed the gruesome bug-eyed gargoyles that sat in watch over the archway. *Whose idea was it to put those at the entrance to a school? What kind of welcome is that?* Zak wondered whether they were meant to make him feel watched over.

'Late again, Zak. You're getting yourself quite an impressive record, but I must inform you there is no certificate for one-hundred-per-cent unpunctuality!' Mr Slater attempted to raise a smile as they walked along the corridor together. Zak suspected that his tutor had been informed about his 'family problems' and was attempting to be gentle with him.

Mr Slater brushed the last of the leaf mould off Zak's blazer. 'Come on, Zak, spruce yourself up, best foot forward!' he said, patting him on the back in a comradely gesture as they walked into class together.

Great! Now they'll think I'm teacher's pet.

Mr Slater was reading out a soldier's testimony about conditions in the trenches. Zak sat at his desk and closed his ears to the grimness of it, filling his mind instead with the gentle voice of the girl in the wood, as he began to sketch in the back of his exercise book. First the leaf canopy, then the girl's strong high, cheek-boned face appeared on the page. He drew her large almond-shaped eyes – what colour were they? A sort of hazel-green, he thought. He added in the determined shape of her jaw, framed by the thin silken scarf . . . She reminded him of a girl his mum had interviewed once.

Zak slid his phone slowly out of his pocket, held it under the table and checked his news feed again. Still nothing. He should take Shalini's advice and try to stop this obsession with tracking his mum's movements any time of the day or night.

'So, please make sure that this letter is signed and returned by next week. I've been on this trip to the trenches myself and I can tell you it's an incredibly moving experience. To think that only a hundred years ago 900,000 men, some of them not that much older than you, were killed in just four years. The Second World War memorial at the entrance to our

19

school –' Mr Slater nodded pointedly at Zak – 'is also a reminder of the harsh reality of war. Believe me, this'll be a trip you'll never forget.' Mr Slater tapped Zak lightly on the shoulder. 'But forgive me for boring you, Zak, you clearly have prettier things on your mind.' He picked up the book, catching sight of Zak's sketch of the girl, but before he could examine it more closely Zak snatched it away. His iPhone slid from his lap and lit up. Mr Slater grabbed that instead and raised an eyebrow as if to say, *I'm waiting for an explanation* . . .

'You've no right to take my phone!' Zak shouted as his teacher held it well out of his reach.

'It's confiscated. Mobiles are not allowed in the classroom, as well you know.'

Zak opened his mouth to protest, then closed it again. What was the point? How could anyone here understand what it felt like to have to say goodbye to your mum and not even know when you were going to see her again.

'Have you even heard a word I've been saying about this trip, Zak?'

'Why would I want to go to a stinking graveyard? People die all over the world, every day, fighting and killing each other,' Zak said from between clenched teeth.

'So if you'd been called up to fight, would you have been a conscientious objector?' Mr Slater asked, keeping his voice even so that it was impossible to tell whether he thought this was a good or a bad thing. When he got no response, he prodded a bit further. 'Would you say you're a pacifist, Zak?'

'More like a coward. They'd have shot you, Wimp!' whispered a spiky-haired boy who, in a matter of three weeks, seemed to have decided that Zak was fair game to needle at every opportunity. Zak had already felt the boy's elbow between his ribs a few times and he got the distinct impression that this was just a warm-up. The others called him 'Spike' – probably because of his hair – but Zak had given him a name he thought suited his character much better – 'Spite.' So far Zak had done as Shalini had coached and ignored him completely, but as the now familiar sharp elbow bruised his ribs, something in Zak snapped and he found himself grabbing the boy by his blazer and pinning him to the back wall of the classroom.

Spite was thick set and at least a head taller than Zak, but he'd been caught off guard and, by the way his eyes popped, was clearly surprised by Zak's strength.

'Not a pacifist, then!' Mr Slater struggled to pull the two boys apart. 'That's quite enough. I will not tolerate violence in my classroom.' The teacher raised his voice. 'I'll speak to you later,' he warned Spike leading him, by the shoulders, back to his seat. 'And as for you, Zak.' He marched him towards the door, 'I think you'd better take some time to cool off.'

21

'That *really* makes sense! No violence in the classroom, but we're supposed to celebrate war? I'm not going on any useless trip to the trenches with him or any of you. What do I care? History's a pile of crap anyway!' Zak yelled back.

The general disorder in the classroom was replaced by an ominous hush. As soon as the words were out of his mouth Zak knew that he'd gone too far. *Why am I freaking out at Mr Slater, when he's the only teacher I actually like?* Reading the expression of disappointment on his tutor's face he wished that he could take the words back. He knew that the people he would really like to rant and rave at were his mum, who he couldn't even speak to, and his dad, who was a whole Atlantic Ocean away.

'I've already explained to you. It's not a celebration, or a glorification. We're simply offering you an opportunity to commemorate and pay your respects . . .'

Zak refused to meet Mr Slater's eyes, instead staring stubbornly into the distance.

'. . . Very well, carry on then . . . Ignore me if you want but I can tell you that this is *not the* way to ingratiate yourself with me.' Mr Slater continued, lowering his voice almost to a whisper, 'but I'm sure your father will be delighted to hear your thoughts on the subject. I gather he's a historian.' He placed a firm hand on Zak's shoulder and escorted him out of the classroom.

Chapter Four

After school Zak waited for the others to pour out into the courtyard, to pile on to buses, mucking around, pushing and shoving each other. 'Friendly banter,' the teachers called it. Zak didn't get it. When they had all finally dispersed he made his way down the hill, emptying his untouched packed lunch into a bin so he wouldn't get a grilling from Shalini. She would only worry. But he couldn't eat at school because his stomach felt tight as a drum there, as if it would burst if he forced food into it. At least the tension was starting to ease now. He slung his blazer over his shoulder, loosened his tie and pulled his shirt free from his trousers. The sun had hardly shone all summer holidays, but now that they were back at school the weather was ridiculously hot; a sultry heat that seemed to hold in the pollution and make it hard to breathe.

Despite the late sunshine, the trees were turning an impressive palette of amber, russet and gold. Zak walked past the great line of oak trees, whose branches formed a thick leafy canopy along the road as if protecting the wood from the world outside. He passed through the railings at the entrance where the 'Welcome to Home Wood' sign hung and came to a small clearing. Leaves floated gently down, meandering their way from between the high branches – earthbound. This time Zak did not attempt to catch one. *Who am I kidding? Nothing's going to change. Dad's not coming back. Mum's in some war zone and Lyndon's living it up at uni. It's only poor Shalini who has to put up with me and my moods, and I know she'd rather be back in Sri Lanka with her own son.*

Compared to his morning's walk the light was softer and the shadows longer, but the warm sunlight did at least make him feel welcome as the sign had promised. He threw his jacket on a bed of leaves, flung his school bag aside, rolled up his shirtsleeves and lay down on his back. He stretched out his arms, feeling the light breeze play over his skin. He closed his eyes and let his mind drift through the events of the day. He was in no hurry to face Shalini. The message from Mr Slater to his dad – the eminent Professor Johnson, Head of Contemporary History at Columbia University, New York – would have been transmitted by now, and sooner or later he would have to face yet another 'I am so disappointed in you . . .' Skype. Zak crushed a handful of leaves in each fist, then opened his eyes and caught his breath . . . The homeless woman was staring down at him. Zak sprang up, his heart racing as he backed away and collided with the broad trunk of an oak tree. The woman still cradled the doll in her arms.

How had she managed to appear without him hearing – or smelling – her? She kept approaching until she was close enough for him to feel invaded by her stench, a combination of mouldy damp, urine and something like stale biscuits.

'Thought you were dead.' She held out her hand towards him, to shake. He hesitated for a moment and then felt ashamed. *How can she hurt me? She's just a lonely old homeless woman.* He allowed her to take hold of his hand. She squeezed it in hers for a moment and smiled. At his touch something appeared to clear in her, as if this tiny moment of human contact had brought her back to herself.

'My name is Elder,' she confided in him.

Strange name. Zak felt a sudden desperate urge to pull away from her. But instead he found himself following her lead and mumbling his own name back at her.

'Zak . . . That's a name to keep safe. I'll write it on a leaf and add it to my wreath, like my Crystal's and the others.' She stroked the doll's cheek and creaked her way to kneeling, then lying on the bed of leaves where Zak had been resting. She curled up, closed her eyes and hummed as she cradled the doll-baby close.

'Red leaves flying, earth stars shining, baby crying, hush now, Crystal, don't you cry . . .'

She had blocked him out with her chanting as if there had been no exchange between them at all. As Zak retraced his steps to the path the weirdest notion entered his head. *I shouldn't have told her my name. It's like she's taken a part of me away with her.* It was the first time Zak had really given much thought to a homeless person. He'd passed them often enough in the street, but he'd never actually stopped to think, *How did you get like that?* Somehow knowing Elder's name made it harder to sweep the memory of her aside. It was fine to live outside now, in this warm weather, but where would someone like Elder go in the middle of winter?

When he was at a safe distance he turned and looked back at the woman. The fiery strands of her hair bled into the leaves and she seemed to melt into the earth.

Chapter Five

Zak sniffed his hands and grimaced. The old woman's stale stench clung to his skin. He decided that he would take a shower as soon as he got back – if it was working that is. With the builders in, he never knew when the water would be switched off. Elder, that homeless woman, had pricked his conscience though; every time he felt a grumble coming on, another competing voice entered his head: *Well, lucky you! At least you can take a shower!*

But now a new scent was wafting towards him on the breeze . . . cinnamon, ginger and spice. His belly rumbled and he regretted dumping his lunch. If nothing else, he should at least have given it to Elder. When had she last eaten? Maybe he would do that tomorrow.

Zak followed his nose to another clearing, where a group of girls were sharing a picnic on a huge rug. They all wore headscarves and talked and laughed together . . . *Maybe in an African language?* A plump woman with white-grey hair and a raucous laugh was handing out food in little metal containers. Zak's belly rumbled again, but he felt something else too, a sort of hunger that was not about food. This group looked more like a family than anything he'd experienced in a long time. *What I wouldn't give to be sitting in a wood with Mum, Dad and Lyndon, having a picnic like we used to.* Zak felt his eyes well up with tears. *Try not to think about the past. What good does it do?* Instead he focused on what was going on in front of him.

What he noticed now was that occasionally, as they opened the stainless-steel tins and handed out food, the girls would switch from their own language into English.

'Even Anjero pancakes! Where did you learn Somali cooking?' a girl asked the plump woman with white-grey curls, who was acting as if she was mother to them all.

'From those recipes your mum gave to me, Muna. If I'd done this for all my foster-children I might have turned into an international chef by now! Nothing like cooking from your homeland to make you feel welcome.' As she chatted on Zak warmed to her sing-song voice with its light trace of an Irish accent. 'Now, where's my Aisha got to?'

The woman peered in Zak's direction and spotted him immediately. How embarrassing was that? Zak closed his eyes for a moment. He was sure that it would seem as if he'd been spying on them.

'Hungry?' the woman called over, smiling kindly at him.

The girls looked up and started chatting among themselves. One of them said something in Somali, wolf whistled and then set the others off giggling. Shalini was always saying 'what a handsome boy' he was, that he would 'shoot up taller any day soon', but he didn't believe her. Spite and some of the others had already taken to goading him over his growing Afro. He wasn't really sure about it himself, but he wouldn't give them the satisfaction of shaving it off in case they thought he was only doing it to fit in.

When he looked in the mirror he saw someone who was living in a not-boy-not-man body. *This is all I need now to round off the perfect day, these girls having a joke at my expense!* He went to move away, but then felt someone approach close behind him.

'Ah, there you are, Aisha!' the grey-haired woman called out.

A girl with a blue headscarf walked past him, the same girl he had found himself sketching at school, and just the thought of that made him feel even more self-conscious, as if he really had been spying on them. Once she was back among the other girls, Aisha glanced towards him and he caught the look of recognition in her eyes. Then she turned to the grey-haired woman and back to Zak as if to ask what he was doing here. Now he was this close he realized that his sketch had completely failed to capture her. Maybe it was that expression of determination he had been drawn to. Something about the way she held herself made Zak think that if a gust of wind was to blow through here right at this minute, she would be the one person not to be blown off course. If he told Shalini any of this, she would laugh at him and say he was 'putting the girl on a pedestal'. Maybe he was; after all, he knew nothing about her.

You've got to say something. Zak was desperately searching for a reason why he might be standing there looking so gormless, because the words were out of his mouth before he knew what he was saying.

'The homeless woman . . .' He looked towards Aisha, and she nodded. 'She's over there,' Zak pointed towards where Elder had lain. 'If you've got any food to spare for her, she looks quite weak.' He kicked at the earth for a moment. 'I just thought, if you've got any leftovers . . .' Zak shrugged and then lowered his head and walked away. Behind him he heard one of the girls speak. He thought it might be Aisha's voice.

'Do you know him, Liliana?'

'No, but he's right, we *should* leave some of our feast for her.'

Zak checked his phone. It was already five thirty. He texted Shalini to say that he would be back soon, then returned to his news feed scanning the stories and finding nothing relevant. Zak wondered about Aisha and the other girls picnicking in the wood. His mum had reported from Somalia during some of the civil-war fighting, and he remembered the bloody images of wounded people and starving children, their bellies swollen with emptiness, hungry eyes staring out at the camera. Perhaps at one time or another the families of the girls in the wood had left all that behind, or maybe they had been born here and knew little more about it than he did.

Just as he was approaching the metal railings that led back to the road someone bumped against his shoulder and shoved past.

'Sorry!' Zak mumbled, even though she had collided with him.

The girl had matted blonde dreadlocks and a faint smell, not as potent as Elder's, but stale and damp all the same, wafting from her clothes. On her back she was carrying a guitar. Zak almost tripped as something flashed past his legs.

'Here, Red! Come on, girl!' she called to a dog with a rust-red coat. Her strong, bright accent was uncannily like his mum's. Zak wondered where in Scotland the girl was from. She threw a stick in Zak's direction and he felt as if she meant to hit him, but the dog caught it smartly in mid-air. Then it came nosing up, its tail wagging furiously and looked into him with enquiring

31

eyes as if sensing something of the turmoil raging inside.

'*Big Issue?*' The girl called to Zak, hauling her rucksack off and taking out a magazine.

'Sorry! I haven't got any money on me.'

The girl shrugged and, as she walked away, he heard her mutter, 'Then spare us your pity! Come on, Red – no use sniffing around him. We'll have to sing for our supper!'

Zak paused to scan a sign that he'd walked straight past that morning:

'Home Wood' is named after the oaks that line the paths, some call them Home Oaks. It's an ancient piece of woodland, dating back to the Domesday Book . . . originally part of the wild forest that covered Britain . . . one of the few remaining oak and hornbeam wild woods in the city . . . Plague victims were also buried here . . . It boasts a wide diversity of flora, fauna and bird life. Fungi include the rare 'earthstar' as well as the 'death cap.' . . . It was declared by the Duchess of Albany in 1868 as 'belonging to all the people of the city forever'.

Earthstar? Isn't that what the old woman Elder had said in one of her chants?

Zak looked back along the path and remembered something that his dad had once told him when they'd walked through the woods near their old house together:

'If these old trees could talk they would have

some stories to tell us, hey, Zak?'

When you thought about it, it did feel kind of weird to be standing in a wood that had been here for so long. *It's like I'm a link in a chain that winds way, way back.* Zak liked the idea of this wood belonging to 'all the people of the city', wherever in the world they came from and wherever they were going . . . even the homeless people seemed to feel that they belonged here. Just for a moment, lying in the warm sunshine, Zak had felt at peace too – until Elder's appearance. But at least coming face to face with her and the others had taken him out of himself for a while and stopped him from drowning in his own misery.

As Zak walked past the grocery shop that stood alone on the perimeter of the wood, he was surprised to see a full-sized image of a dog chalked on the pavement. A man wearing a turban was taking a photograph of it with his phone.

'It would be such a shame if it rained before anyone sees this. I tell you, that girl has real talent, if only she realized. Keep buying those art materials for her, Mala,' he called out to someone inside the shop. 'You never know, she could be the next Banksy, and then we'll be digging up the pavement to sell slabs!' The man chuckled to himself as he inspected his photo.

'I just wish she would sort herself out and take my advice! Problem is she has no faith in herself,' a woman's voice replied.

Zak paused as a large woman wearing a bright orange salwar kameez and a flowery pink apron wandered out of the shop sipping a cup of tea.

'She's caught the expression in that dog's eyes perfectly. Strange! She can feel so much for this animal, but she seems so nasty sometimes.'

The woman moved aside for Zak to get past. He glanced down at the drawing. On the bottom was written a signature in large swirly letters: **Iona**.

'You know what she told me, when I suggested she must apply for art college?'

'No, Mala, but I'm sure you're going to tell me!'

'Said I should mind my own business! So I told her straight, I *am* minding my business. *You* are the one sitting on *my* premises selling your magazine, so you *are* my business, isn't it?'

The man laughed heartily. Then Zak felt a hand patting him on the back. 'Ho ho! What have you been up to, son? Rolling in the leaves? Your mother will be after you!'

I don't think so. Zak tried to raise a smile. This must be the Sikh couple Shalini had spoken of – the people who had made her feel welcome on her first day in the area. As he walked away Zak read the shop sign: 'Kalsis Woodland Store.'

'Better shake out that mop of hair too!' Mr Kalsi called after him. 'You're like a leaf magnet!'

Zak meandered aimlessly along the road. *So the*

artist of the drawing is Iona the homeless girl. Her name really doesn't suit her. Zak remembered with a sharp pang his favourite family holiday to Scotland. Perhaps he was idealizing it now, but it had seemed as if the sun had shone every day on the island of Iona. Zak felt like turning around and heading back to his old house where all his happy memories were stored. It had been explained to him a thousand times that after the divorce they would still keep in touch; that his dad would have him for holidays in the States, that he would visit often . . . that his mum's assignments abroad would have long breaks between them and when she was home she'd be around for him all the time. Loads of people he knew had parents who were divorced or remarried, but it still felt to Zak as if he'd been dumped unceremoniously while both of his parents had fled, burying their sadness in their work. *What's a home if the people who are supposed to love you don't live there?*

As Zak waited at the lights for the stream of traffic to stop, the phrase from the sign about the wood 'belonging to all the people of the city forever' kept playing through his mind. *A sense of 'belonging' – that's what's missing,* he realized as he walked towards the house that he was supposed to now think of as home.

Chapter Six

You can't put this off any longer. Liliana printed off some new photos ready to stick into Aisha's book.

Sixteen children she had fostered in these last twenty years, since her own kids had been old enough, and each foster child had taken a little piece of her with them when they'd left. Sometimes she wondered whether her heart had regenerative powers: the more times it broke, the stronger its capacity to love. But after every goodbye there had always been another foster child. Getting too attached was the reason why she'd said that she could take in no more babies. It should have been easier to keep her distance with an older child. But no matter how young or old they were, as soon as she saw them standing on her doorstep with nothing but a teddy or a doll to cling to, they had her heart. She'd learned to steel herself at that moment, swallowing back the tears, because she needed to reassure them that they would be safe with her, wherever and whatever they had come from. And they had been.

Liliana surveyed the flat where she had lived all her adult life. The area had changed over the years and now most of the houses on Linden Road were large family houses, but Liliana felt that she had made her own kind of family home here in these modest rooms that held traces of every child she had looked after. Just this kitchen was crammed to bursting with memories. That little pottery giraffe had belonged to Lydia with her open trusting face, those origami owls were the work of 'folded-hands-just-so Stephan' with his neat, precise ways. Then there was Salma, her eyes like great dark pools, the most beautiful baby anyone could wish to hold. Liliana picked up the cushion that had been one of Salma's comforters and stroked it against her cheek.

'How come you're so into doing all this story-booking now?' Aisha asked as she came in and grabbed a biscuit from the tin on the dresser.

Liliana sighed. Here was the question she'd been waiting for.

'You know, Aisha, every story has different chapters in it . . .'

'Obviously! Why are you speaking all weird? What do you need to talk to me about anyway?' Aisha placed the biscuit on her plate and studied Liliana's face. When her foster mother smiled gently back at her, the expression in Aisha's eyes brightened and she sprang up from the table, holding her hand to her mouth in expectation.

'My abo is alive?' Aisha whispered.

Liliana's heart sank. No matter how many times she, the therapist or the social worker tried to explain to Aisha that there was no hope of her father being alive, somewhere deep inside the girl still believed that one day he would come for her.

'Sit down, my love,' Liliana said gently. 'I need to talk to you.'

Liliana patted the cushion on the chair next to her and began to tell Aisha her news in calm, even phrases that she'd rehearsed many times.

'There's a family been put forward to adopt you. Your social worker has asked us to go to the centre to meet them. It's just to see how you might get on. They're Somali with a daughter of sixteen . . .

Aisha eyed her story book suspiciously and pushed it away as if it had somehow been contaminated.

'Just meet the family and see what you think. Perhaps it would be good to be in your own culture. You keep telling me I don't understand certain things, and that's probably true. It's such a rare opportunity – you should at least give them a chance,' Liliana continued, struggling to maintain her even tone.

Aisha stared at Liliana and said nothing at all.

'And I've been thinking. I'm getting older, Aisha. I have my grandchildren . . .'

Aisha's jaw tightened. She shoved the plate away

from her and it careered over the edge of the table and spun on the tile floor then shattered. Liliana studied her foster daughter. Aisha did not flinch, the muscles in her face remained completely motionless. Here once again was the silent child that had arrived on Liliana's doorstep. *This is my fault* thought Liliana *I've loved her too much, too deeply, and now we're both going to suffer.*

Afterwards, as she swept up the broken pieces, Liliana allowed the tears to fall. She threw the debris in the bin then sat down again and read over the record of the journey that she and Aisha had made together. It had always felt odd to Liliana using her own name so placing herself in the third person in the story and she'd often had to stop herself from writing 'Aisha and I' . . . but she supposed it was a way of keeping a distance. Now it did seem possible that Aisha would one day read her story book and see 'Liliana' as just a stage, a small part in her journey. She scanned the hundreds of entries, resting randomly on a few that caught her eye.

5 *January*
Today Aisha smiled for the first time.

14 *March*
Aisha spoke directly to Liliana .These were her words: 'I feel safe here.'

1 June

Aisha has been drawing pictures with her therapist. She has done a beautiful one of her old home before the fire and another of her father.

5 September

Aisha's first day in Secondary School. She was reluctant to wear her uniform and did not want to speak about her experience at the end of the day.

31 October

Aisha's 11ᵗʰ birthday

A difficult day. Aisha sat and listened to the missing person's register on BBC Somali radio. She said her best present in the world would be if her father was found on her birthday. Aisha hates all the commotion of Halloween. She wanted to stay in and turn the lights off so that no one would call at our door. When asked why she wouldn't join in, she said, 'I have had enough experience of being afraid in real life.' I Liliana made her a cake and handled the ghouls who turned up on the doorstep!

6 November

Aisha is reading fables and poetry in English. She reads the same story or poem over to herself many times, as if she's trying to memorize the words. Her writing in English is amazing, completely fluent, but she's not yet talking much at school.

10 January
Aisha has decided to wear the hijab. Liliana discussed this decision and she said it made her feel closer to friends and family back home.

25 January
Aisha and a group of her new Somali friends sang a traditional song in the school choir today. One line in it was a solo by Aisha. Her voice is exquisite. Liliana told her she could be a singer one day. She says she doesn't want to be a singer - she's going to be a lawyer. That's not hard to believe!

6 May
Aisha has won a poetry competition at school. She recited a beautiful poem she wrote about Somalia and memorized by heart.

2 June
Aisha has begun going along to the mosque with some of her Somali friends and their mothers.

31 October
Aisha's 12th birthday
She has been given a small decorated Quran and a prayer mat by her friend Muna.

Aisha listened to the missing person's register again. She hasn't done it for months, but when she blew out her candles she told ~~me~~ Liliana that her wish was the same as last year – that her father will come to find her on her birthday.

Aisha and her friends composed music to a poem by a famous Somali peace poet called Hadrawi. They performed it at the school concert. Aisha's voice was bold and clear and not to be messed with! Afterwards the girls all came back and had a 'This is not a Halloween' party.

18 January
Aisha was in detention for being 'too loud' in class and chatting to her friends! For Liliana a day of celebration! No more silence.

April school report
Aisha received the award for most improved in English Literature and Language in her year.

15 September
Picnic with Muna, Mariam, Somaya and other friends in Home Wood.

42

Liliana let the book fall from her hands and sighed. She would have liked nothing more than to run upstairs and fling her arms around Aisha and tell her that she would look after her till she was an adult and ready to leave, that she had made a mistake even mentioning the possibility of adoption. But she checked herself because maybe the best outcome for Aisha was to have Somali-speaking parents, to be among people who really understood her culture and religion. It was true that increasingly there had been things that Liliana had struggled with. She had argued with Aisha about wanting to fast for Ramadan. She had worried for her health, such a young girl, working so hard at school . . . Maybe she had been wrong to stop her. Then there'd been this whole thing about wearing the hijab. She could understand that Aisha wanted to identify with the other Somali and Muslim girls in her school, but Liliana couldn't help it, she worried that wearing her hijab might mean that she'd be treated differently. Maybe Aisha would be better off with a family that made her feel more secure in all of these things.

Liliana tapped restlessly on the table as she tried to convince herself that this was the least selfish thing she could offer Aisha. *She will have a sister and a younger mother and father . . . security for much longer than I can offer her. I'm nearly sixty for goodness sake! She'll have a whole new life ahead of her, and in time she'll finally understand that her father's gone. She can always keep in contact with me; she's old enough to make her own decision about that . . .* These were the logical arguments that Liliana laid out for herself as she opened the story book again and turned the pages until she reached the end of her own contribution. This evening, when she'd broken the news to Aisha, had felt like an ending. Liliana's tears landed on a blank page. She wiped them away, but they continued to flow as she thumbed through the thick expanse of empty pages that lay ahead.

Chapter Seven

Linden Road was the kind of endless tree-lined suburban street that Zak imagined hadn't changed much since the houses were built. What were they – Edwardian or Victorian? He wasn't quite sure. But as he walked past the patterned tiled porches and stained-glass windows, something felt different from the morning. Even at this distance he could see that the new house had become a building site. In just one day the scaffolding had gone up and a huge yellow skip had been parked on the road outside. It was ironic really that their new road shared the same name, if not spelling, as his brother but Lyndon had left home for university, and Zak couldn't imagine that he would ever come to think of the new house as having much to do with him. He and Lyndon used to fight about anything and everything, from what programme to watch on TV to who was taking up more room on the sofa! Shalini always said they could find anything under the sun to argue about, but now that Lyndon was gone it felt like there *was* no sun. Zak had tried phoning him, but Lyndon never returned his calls. It was as if he'd disconnected from everything and everyone. Maybe this was his way of dealing with the break-up – to simply leave. *Simply leave – why not? Why haven't I thought of that before? That's what everyone else has done, except Shalini, and no matter how kind she is, she's paid to look after me. Even if Mum's back in the country soon, it'll only be a matter of time before she packs her bags and is off again to another war zone or some crisis.* There was always something and the problem was that every time Zak said goodbye to her a part of him really believed that he would never see her again. The memory of her packing for this last trip was still too fresh in his mind.

Her flak jacket had been lying on the bed and he'd found himself picking it up and trying it on. It was surprisingly heavy.

'I could do with one of these,' he said, and his mum looked at him strangely, then sat down and patted the bed for him to come over and talk.

'What do you mean by that?' she asked gently, but he just shrugged and walked out of the room.

I don't really know what I meant by it, except that I feel as if I could do with some protection.

*

46

As Zak approached the front door of the new house, he found that two large planks of wood had been laid over the garden path. It was like crossing a drawbridge, not to a castle, but to a building yard. When he'd finally balanced his way to the door he stopped and looked up through the fluorescent yellow scaffolding. A tall builder wearing a khaki-green cap was shouting up to another man with arms that looked as if they were made of steel. They shouted back and forth as they set up a pulley with a bright blue bucket attached to one end. Zak wondered what language they were speaking. Bulgarian or Polish maybe? As he stared up, the man with the cap caught Zak's eye and shouted, 'Hi!' Zak waved up to them. Before he could slot his key in the lock, the door swung open. Shalini must have been watching out for him, waiting. Zak looked past her into the hallway. There was rubble and dust everywhere, making his eyes sting. The insistent shrill of drilling sent a shooting pain deep into his ears.

'There you are, Zak.' Shalini had the quietest voice of anyone he knew, but it was high and sharp and it carried above the din of the drill. Zak noticed that her long black hair was speckled with flecks of grey dirt. She was drying her hands on a tea towel that she'd tucked into the waist of her sari. Despite all the rubble, she still wore her traditional clothes; the sari-skirt trailed slightly so that it and her sandalled feet were

47

coated in grey powder-dust. *Poor Shalini having to live all day amongst this.* Zak was glad he had not hurried back to this building site. He had the urge to tell her all about the wood and meeting Elder and Aisha, just as he'd told her about his day ever since he was little, but nothing was the same as before. *Now that Lyndon's gone, who's to say that Shalini won't leave too? Maybe she'll go back home to Anil? I wouldn't blame her if she did. It can't be much fun for her, being away from her own son, looking after me and living in this wreck.*

'I have spoken to your history tutor, Zak. This is no respectful manner to behave in your school.' Shalini squeezed her delicate hands together till her knuckles turned white.

A shower of dust poured from the ceiling and landed on Zak's head.

'Oh baba! This filthy dirt is not good for my asthma!' Shalini attempted to brush the dust from Zak's hair, but ended up spluttering and coughing her way to the kitchen for water. 'I'll bring food to your room, nah?' She managed to call back to him. 'Don't get used to this, but for now it's more comfortable up there, until the kitchen is prepared.'

'Would you like me to sit with you?' Shalini asked as she brought in a tray with one of her sambal coconut curries and a plate of sliced fruit.

Zak shook his head.

'OK, but Lucas will be Skyping soon.' Shalini patted Zak on the shoulder. 'You understand I *had* to tell him, don't you?'

Zak nodded. It wasn't her fault. Mostly he felt sorry for Shalini, especially when she'd just Skyped Anil. She always put on a brave face, but afterwards Zak often picked up signs that she'd been crying. *Sometimes the world feels so mixed up, with my mum and dad so far away, and Shalini here leaving her son to look after me.* His own mum always said that Skyping made her feel closer to him, like she wasn't missing out but there had been no Skypes on this trip. Why? He loved to see her face as she was talking, to see into her world and for her to see into his. But afterwards it was almost worse than never having spoken. *What gets me is the way I'm lulled into feeling that we're in the same room. But then there's always a moment when it hits me that there's a screen and a whole world of distance between us.*

A memory of the homeless woman, Elder, holding on to Zak's hand in the wood flashed through his mind. Now he understood her look at the welcome surprise of human contact. *That's all that I want to be able to do – to reach out and hug my mum or dad. It's not asking that much, is it?* But these were not things that he could tell anyone without sounding like a wimp. At least he knew that his dad was safe. But he needed to speak to his mum right now, to call out, 'Mum,' and for her to appear at his door, but that was as likely to

49

happen as magic. Zak picked up his fork and mushed the curry around his plate. The hunger he'd felt earlier had vanished, replaced by a vague scent of sickness, and his throat felt dry, as if the dust in the house was settling on his insides.

Shalini tapped gently on the door.

'It's your father calling.' She carried in the laptop and turned the screen around so that his dad's unsmiling face came into view. Shalini picked up the tray of food, tutted at how little he'd eaten and quietly closed the door behind her.

'Well, son? What are you playing at?'

'*Well*, Lucas, I'm not playing at anything!' Zak knew how much his dad hated it when he called him by his first name.

'Don't you use that tone with me.'

Zak stayed silent while he watched his dad's mouth rant on and on about how if he earned himself a bad reputation among his teachers it would be 'near impossible to shake off'. One of the things that annoyed Zak most about his dad these days was how he kept repeating the same thing over and over, as if using slightly different words was a way of hammering some sense into him. Finally he changed tack slightly. 'You make sure you go and see that Mr Slater tomorrow morning and offer him a sincere apology. Have you any idea how embarrassing it is for me to hear from your history teacher that you said those words?' Zak noticed that even in the few weeks he'd been working in New York his dad's accent had grown stronger and just that seemed to accentuate the distance between them. His dad hadn't been able to stand the uncertainty of his mum being away for long stretches either, so he'd got out for good, moved to another city, another continent even! *He* was free to move out, to take on whatever accent he felt like. *So why am I the only one who doesn't get to choose?* Zak wanted to scream as his father droned on.

'I'm not in one of your lectures!' Zak interrupted.

Lucas leaned closer to the screen and for the first time in his life Zak registered something like dislike in his father's eyes.

'Do you know how hard your mum and I . . .' Lucas stumbled over these familiar words, as if he doubted that he had the right to talk about the two of them as if they were still a neat little family unit. They both kept reassuring him that the divorce did not mean anything would change between them as parents, but as his dad revised his sentence, Zak knew that Lucas didn't believe it himself. 'We've worked so hard to send you to a great school?'

'I didn't ask to go there,' Zak spat back.

His dad sighed deeply. 'Do you have to be so *obvious*? You're doing this to humiliate me. Isn't that right? Well, I have news for you – you're kicking out at the wrong person–'

51

That was it. Zak exploded, just as he had at Spite's insult that morning, but this time not with his fists. Instead, he aimed his sharpened words back at his dad, like poisoned arrows.

'Who else am I supposed to kick out at? Mum? She's not even contactable. And Lyndon never answers my calls. Maybe you'd prefer it if I took it out on Shalini or one of the builders?' He grabbed hold of the laptop and stomped down the stairs with it. 'Want to have a little tour around my lovely new home?' Zak scanned the screen across the room for his dad's benefit. 'I'm living on a building site, get it?'

A look of pain lodged in his dad's eyes. It felt good to lash out at him – why shouldn't he taste a bit of the fallout for himself?

'OK, son. I know this has all been difficult for you—'

'*Really?* You think so?' Zak said with a sneer, then pressed the red button to make his dad go away.

Shalini stood by the stairs shaking her head. 'This is not respectful Zak. Your father loves you. Please call him back,' she urged.

Zak marched past her up the stairs, his footsteps echoing on the bare floorboards.

'If he calls, I'm not here,' he shouted, slamming his bedroom door behind him. Shalini followed him up and stood outside his room for a moment then quietly opened his door, slid the lap-top inside and retreated.

Zak grabbed his gloves and started pummelling away at his punchbag till he'd worked up such a sweat that he collapsed on his bed, exhausted.

By the time Shalini came in to say goodnight Zak had already showered and was lying in bed staring up at the ceiling, listening to the news. Sometimes just the sound of his mum's distinctive Scottish accent was enough to soothe him. It didn't matter what horrendous disaster she was reporting on, all he could focus on was the fact that she was still breathing. The best was when she was 'live', because 'live' meant that she was *alive* at that second, no matter how crackly and jumpy the satellite connection, and as he listened to her talk he felt as if *he* could breathe again.

Shalini came in quietly, picked up the lap-top, carried it over to Zak's desk and sat on the bed by his side.

'*Thousands of children are on the move, some of them wounded, all of them hungry. The trauma they've suffered is plain to see in their eyes, but the will to survive is strong and so they make their way to the overcrowded refugee camps in the hope that tomorrow might bring them some semblance of safety. The scale of this humanitarian disaster is unprecedented. The question on everyone's lips here is what is the answer to such suffering and what more can and should the international community be doing? This is Jessica Johnson, reporting from . . .*

The newsreader's voice jumped in to fill the silence. 'Apologies, we seem to have lost the satellite connection there . . .'

The damned-up tears that contained all the tension of the day overflowed and trickled down the side of Zak's face and into his ears and hair. He made no attempt to wipe them away. Shalini's eyes clouded over too. She could never see him upset without feeling a swell of emotion in her own chest. She held out her arms and hugged him to her.

'I'm sure she'll be home soon,' she whispered as she patted Zak on the shoulder, switched off the radio and headed towards the door. 'She may call you in the morning, if they've got that satellite signal back up.'

'She might and she might not!'

Shalini paused at the door. 'You understand why your ma *has* to go away. It's important work she's doing. You should be proud of her.'

'What about you then? Why are you so far away from Anil? Looking after me . . . you don't *have* to be here!'

Zak registered the look of hurt in Shalini's eyes, and immediately regretted his sharp tone.

'I'm sorry . . .' *Now I'm doing what I told Dad I would never do . . . lashing out at Shalini just because she's here. Why can't I just keep my mouth shut?*

'You should understand, Zak, our situations are

not equal.' Shalini's voice had become harsh and formal, as if he was a stranger to her. 'This is a fact of life. I am sending money to educate Anil, to change things for him, for us. What can I say?' She shrugged. 'We all do the best with what we are born into. Your mother is rich enough to sit at home doing beauty treatments, but instead she is trying to make the world a better place.'

'I just don't get it. Why does there have to be all this fighting?' Zak sighed.

Shalini shook her head. 'In my country too, there is always unrest. As if nature didn't cause enough havoc. Everywhere in the world fighting is for the same reasons. Politics, land, power mostly, greed, using religion as excuse many times.'

'That's why I hate religion.' Zak clenched his fists.

'No. It is not gods who cause war. Without my religion, my life would be less. Always, the way I see it, ordinary people, no matter what belief, just want to live in peace.' Shalini shook the ends of her sari, sending up a cloud of fine powder and the image of the blue-scarfed Aisha crept once more into Zak's mind. He supposed that she covered her hair for religious reasons, like the Sikh man, Mr Kalsi, from the shop. Just as he thought this, Shalini came over to him and smoothed her hand over his hair.

'I don't know! You're starting to look like a wild

boy with this long hair!' She laughed, cupping his chin in her hands.

Zak attempted to smile back.

'Acha! That's better! I will do puja for you. Anyway, it's nearly Diwali. Fireworks always cheer us up! Tomorrow will be a better day.'

Chapter Eight

Thousands of children are on the move, some of them wounded, all of them hungry . . . Thousands of children are on the move, some of them wounded, all of them hungry . . .

Zak counted the herds, not of sheep, but of marching children. This is what happened when he listened to his mum's news reports at night. He found himself taking the little that she said and filling in the rest with his imagination. Now he scanned the faces he'd conjured from her words: a boy carried his baby sister, a pregnant woman hauled a woven blanket bag on her back and a toddler on her swollen belly. A skeleton-thin woman, placing one foot in front of the other like a robot, trailed three small children, all wide-eyed with hunger. Then through the dust haze he spotted a familiar face.

Aisha turned to him in her blue scarf and smiled as she walked onward, head held high. The woman holding the toddler stumbled. Aisha bent down, picked the child up and carried her on her hip. Zak followed Aisha's path through the endless stream of children. A bright red flash moved among them and he heard a girl calling out. She turned and her dreadlocks spun and coiled around his neck. Her cat-like grey eyes glinted in the sunshine. 'I'm hungry too,' she whispered as her braids tightened around his neck. Zak looked down and saw his own dusty Converse. He grasped at his neck, pulling and pulling until he was finally free of the girl's matted hair.

'That's right. You run away,' the snake-coil girl called after him. He watched his feet move over the rough terrain, picking a way between the dry rubble that littered the earth, his breath laboured, sweat coating his forehead. Now a voice somewhere nearby bleated, 'Mum, Mum, Mum.' He swung round to see who was calling out, but the procession of children were all silent now. Then the crowd stepped aside and pointed to a woman wearing khaki shorts and a white T-shirt. 'Mum, Mum, Mum!' His own voice sounded distant to him. The woman turned and stared. Her face was ancient, cracked and wizened. It was the old homeless woman who offered him her hand . . .

Zak felt a thud and a dull ache spread across the back of his skull, then hands underneath his body, gathering him up, lifting him.

'Shh, shh, just a dream,' Shalini whispered, lifting his head on to her knee. They were sitting by a pile of rubble in what had been, until yesterday, the kitchen. Shalini struggled to pull Zak to standing, then walked him slowly back up the stairs. 'You were sleepwalking again, calling out for your ma.'

'It wasn't Mum . . . it was that homeless woman,' Zak mumbled through his sleep-haze, allowing Shalini to guide him to his room and his bed.

'What homeless woman?'

'I was just dreaming, like you said.' Zak pinched his own arm. *Get a hold of yourself. The last thing you need right now is a lecture about walking through the woods.* He scrambled back through his mind, desperately trying to remember the dream. *How did I get myself down stairs without falling? What was I doing sitting among that rubble?* Every time that he sleepwalked it left him feeling as if he was standing on a cliff edge.

'Why don't we unpack some of your things tomorrow?' Shalini suggested through a weary yawn as she followed his gaze around the room. 'Try to sleep now.' She turned in the doorway and looked at Zak as he settled himself under his duvet.

'You know, there's nothing to be ashamed of, missing the people you love. I still long to see my family, even after all these years of working away from home.'

She turned the handle of the door quietly behind her. 'Now sleep well, my boy,' she whispered. Zak couldn't help but wonder if she really meant those words for him.

Chapter Nine

Aisha stared at herself in the mirror and brushed her wavy black hair until it shone. She swished it this way and that. Only a few days ago, picnicking in the wood, she'd wanted to dance to the sway of the branches. Not anymore. She felt like a sapling tree that had been uprooted from its soil and replanted in a very different climate. It had struggled at first, but then it had taken off, growing courageously. Now, just as it was starting to thrive, Liliana of all people had come along and cut it down.

The memory of the day that she had arrived in this country returned to Aisha like a slap in the face. Back then the whole world had seemed to tower above her like a giant shadow. She looked around the little bedroom that Liliana had decorated so beautifully for her. She would never forget the sweet smell of that welcoming vase of lilies her foster-mother had placed on the table. In those first traumatic days something about the flower scent wafting around the room had comforted her. Since her friend Muna had given her a copy of the Quran and a prayer mat, this room had become a constant comfort to her. Until Liliana had spoken of the possibility of this adopted family she'd felt as if she had everything she needed here in this room, except for her abo. Liliana had even installed a corner sink so that she could wash before praying. Aisha removed her precious prayer beads, turned on the tap and let the water stream over her hands. When she had completed her cleansing ritual she covered her head, knelt on her mat and began to pray, placing her forehead on the ground.

Afterwards she replaced her necklace and took comfort in the warmth of the beads against her skin. This was the only precious thing that she had brought from Somalia: the prayer amulet made of jet that had belonged to the mother she had never known. The central bead was the largest, made of engraved silver containing a miniature scroll of the Quran. Her abo had given them to her before they'd said their last goodbyes. Since the day she left Somalia she had never taken these beads off, except to wash and bathe.

'You know, this jet was alive once too, made of ancient trees from the forests,' her abo had told her as he'd placed them around her neck. The thought of her hoyo wearing these same beads against her skin made Aisha feel closer to the mother, who, in giving birth to her, had lost her own life. She could picture her father

61

now, proud and tall, with his white cap covering the crown of his head, his warm, bearded face looking at her with patient dark eyes, full of love. He had always made her feel as if he could put things right. She felt so close to him that as she summoned up his memory she almost believed that they were together again – that she could reach out and touch him.

'Wearing these will always connect you to what has gone before,' her abo told her as he placed the prayer beads over her head.

'Why do you want me to have them? Didn't you hate me when I was born? Every time you look at me or hear my name, you must think of my hoyo.'

The expression in her abo's eyes was one of pain.

'*Hate* you? Why do you think I called you Aisha? "Full of life and joy . . . alive and well." I was so grateful, bismillah, that you could be saved.'

'But I took her life.'

'She *gave* you life.' Her abo held her in his arms and cried. She had never seen him weep before.

'When I think of the day that you were born, it only makes my heart ache with love for all that I have and all I have lost,' he told her as he buried his face in her hair.

Aisha wiped away her tears and tried to bring herself back into the present. She walked over to her window and stared out through the darkness. Liliana's garden always helped. She had often thought that it was a kind of portrait of Liliana: small, loud and plump, full of surprising clashing colours that worked well together. Her garden was unlike any of the others on the street. Liliana and the old man who lived in the flat next door had knocked down the fence between them to form a communal courtyard garden, and their landlords had not complained because she had transformed two concrete yards into beautiful natural habitats full of wildlife and birdsong. Liliana's garden never seemed dull or empty – she managed to keep flowers blooming all the way through the year – but Aisha's favourites would always be the lilies.

There's no point even going to the meeting with this family. If they force me, I'll run away and then maybe Liliana will see how much I love her, how I need to stay here.

There was a gentle knock on her bedroom door. 'Your social worker understands that you need time to get used to the idea, so they've moved the meeting to next Thursday. Just give this family a chance, Aisha, and we can go from there. No one's going to force you into anything,' Liliana pleaded from the other side of the door and listened intently for any small response. None came. 'Goodnight, Aisha!'

She was met by a wall of silence.

Chapter Ten

Zak lay in bed, eyes open, not daring to sleep again. There was no way he could risk getting stuck inside another nightmare. It had left him with a feeling that he was going to have to *do* something instead of sitting victim-like waiting for things to change: for his mum to call, for his dad to Skype or for Lyndon to leave a message. He scanned his bare, clinical room. He supposed he could start to unpack the boxes, but if he did that, it would be like accepting that he was here to stay, that his dad was never coming back to live with them, that their old house, their old life, was gone forever.

Zak waited to hear Shalini's familiar sleep-wheeze through the bedroom wall, then he laced up his Converse and headed back down the stairs. The house felt different at night, lit only by the dim glow of the street lights. The dust had settled and the empty rooms were still and peaceful with the builders gone. Zak wandered around, trying to imagine what the place would be like once they'd unpacked, but he found it impossible to see beyond the piles of rubble swept into every corner. He stepped into what would one day be the living room, but he couldn't imagine a time when he would ever lounge in here with Lyndon and their mum and dad, eating a pizza on a Friday night like they'd used to.

Who did his parents think they were kidding when they said they saw no reason why their divorce shouldn't be 'amicable'? Even the word made you stumble and falter – it felt like it had nothing to do with friendship and even less to do with love. Zak kicked at a pile of rubble angrily, and as he did so, something caught his eye. He bent down and found it was just an old piece of plasterwork and was about to throw it back on the pile when he realized that this fragment was unbroken. He turned it over and was able to decipher faint lettering that he ran his fingers over: 'Albert Bainbridge, 1903'. There was something slightly unsettling about touching something this old. He smiled to himself . . . here was a piece of history in the 'pile of crap' that he'd been mouthing off about. If he was to tell Shalini about it she would say that this was 'karma' – that the house was trying to teach him a lesson. But he didn't believe in any of that stuff. Zak wrapped the plasterwork in a tea towel and walked over to the last remaining wall separating the kitchen and the living room. An enormous white cross had been marked on it. Zak reached out and touched it, letting his hand rest there. The strangest sensation came over him as underneath the skin of plaster he felt a faint pulse beating steadily. He pulled his hand away. *I must still be half asleep.* But as he looked at the wall the thought occurred to him that *if* history was so important to everyone around here, *how come they're so busy blasting away all traces of it?*

Zak carried the piece of plaster up to his room, placed it on his desk, unwrapped it and switched on his laptop. It took him a few attempts but finally he found a 'house history' site and began his search for 48 Linden Road. A photo of the house came up with some dull estate agent's details about how much it had been sold for at different times. Zak was surprised to find that it had belonged to only five owners since 1903. That didn't seem to be many, but none of the names listed was Albert Bainbridge. He typed in the name and the date and was amazed to see a black-and-white photo appear of an old man wearing a tweed hat, baggy cotton shirt and waistcoat, a bulging leather toolkit rested by his feet. He was pointing to a stained-glass window, a look of pride on his face. There were no bright greens and blues, or deep reds shining out of this black-and-white picture but the pattern looked identical to the stained glass in the front door of this house. Underneath the photo was written: 'Albert Bainbridge, master builder and craftsman'. Zak felt charged with a need to find out more. He glanced around his room. What had changed? Nothing, but it didn't feel quite as empty as it had, now that he could picture the man who had played a part in building this house and, from what he was reading, most of the other houses on Linden Road too. Then another photo caught his eye. Here was the same man with his arm around the shoulder of a boy of maybe fifteen or sixteen years old. The label read 'Albert and Edwin Bainbridge (Carpenter and Son–Apprentice). They were both smiling at the camera. There was something familiar about the pose. All his own photos were still packed away, but it reminded Zak of one of him and his dad standing outside the old house. That image of his dad with his arm slung over Zak's shoulder captured a time when Zak had believed that the two of them were as sturdy and unshakeable as one of the giant oaks in the wood. Zak placed some photo paper in his printer, and watched as the postcard-sized image of the old man and his boy slowly processed. Whirr by whirr, father and son emerged. Zak caught them before the paper fell to the ground and held them in his hands until the ink dried. As he studied the image it felt curiously like he was bringing them back to life. Albert Bainbridge and his son Edwin wore that same expression of solidarity that he and his dad had once worn. A lump of emotion formed in Zak's throat. Maybe there *was* something in Shalini's karma theory after all; perhaps finding this name in the plasterwork was meant to lead him to an understanding – but he had no idea of what? Zak placed the photo on his desk and shut the site down. *What am I doing? It's not as if any of this can make a difference to how I feel about living here.* He wrapped the plasterwork back in the tea towel, the photograph too, and placed the bundle under his bed. He checked the time; already three in the morning. No wonder he felt sick with tiredness. He lay down and closed his eyes but his mind hovered over all the happenings of the day, until it began to settle on the white cross painted on the wall of the living room below.

Zak got back up, switched on his lamp, felt under his bed and once again unwrapped the piece of plasterwork and the photograph. Albert and Edwin. Lucas and Zak. *Surely not everything from the past has to be thrown out as if it's worthless.* Maybe if he could find a way to bring his mum and dad back together they might be able to mend things piece by piece, like renovating an old house that was on the verge of collapsing. In the watery world of early morning, where ideas float like great beasts in the deep blue ocean, an idea formed in Zak's mind as the rest of Linden Road slept. An idea that seemed to Zak in his sleep-deprived state to be entirely logical. If he could persuade his mum to leave intact the wall where he'd found Albert's name, then maybe things would be set right again. If only he could speak to her. He checked his watch. His dad would be awake. *Maybe this wall is the way to get Mum and Dad to start talking to each other again!* For the first time in ages Zak felt the stirrings of hope. He clicked on Skype and dialled. After a few moments Lucas's face appeared on the screen.

'What are you doing up?' His dad's forehead creased with concern.

'Can't sleep.'

'Well then, good morning to you, son!' Lucas smiled at Zak and yawned. He rarely held a grudge. 'I tried you a few times before your bed time, but there was no answer. Guess you were all wiped out.'

'Sorry!' Zak muttered under his breath.

'No, *I'm* sorry.' Lucas smiled warmly. Zak got the impression that he meant that he was sorry for everything, not just last night's argument. Here was his moment to ask.

'Dad, if someone was about fifteen in 1903, what sort of things would have happened to them in their life?'

Lucas's faint smile grew to its widest straight-toothed grin.

'What's brought this on? Is this some project for school?'

'Kind of,' Zak lied.

'What sort of someone are you thinking of?'

'A builder's son.'

'Curiouser and curiouser! Well, World War One, trenches maybe. If he was very lucky he would have made it to the Second. Then who knows? Odds weren't exactly stacked in his favour.'

'That's grim!'

'Yeah! Listen, son, if this is your way of saying sorry—'

'It's not . . . Dad, there's this wall in the kitchen downstairs and I found a name in the plasterwork. I looked it up and got an old picture of the builder of this house and his son . . .'

Lucas peered closer into the screen as if trying to analyse Zak.

'The thing is, the builders have put a cross on the wall where I found the name and that means they're going to knock it down, and I've just got this feeling that they shouldn't.' Zak paused and stared down at his hands. As he spoke the words aloud the logic of his plan began to sound shaky even to himself. He swallowed hard as he picked up the black-and-white picture of Albert and Edwin. That was how it was supposed to be – father and son, working together, building dens, playing cricket, it didn't matter what, just together in the same place, in the same country. Now he and his dad couldn't even be in a room together to share things like this discovery any more. *I wish I was Edwin*, Zak thought to himself. *At least it looks as if his dad really loved him.*

On the other side of the Atlantic Ocean Lucas sighed deeply and tried to work out what Zak was really saying. He opened his mouth a few times to interject but then thought better of it.

'Go on, son . . .'

'I just don't want them to knock the wall down, that's all. Please tell Mum not to . . .' As Zak spoke he realized how odd this must sound and he found himself speaking words that he had never planned to. 'Just come back, Dad . . .'

Lucas placed his hand against the screen, as if that could somehow comfort his son.

'I'm sorry, Zak, it's not going to work. I'm sure you'll hear from your mum soon though, and it won't be long till you come visit me.'

'You've heard from her then?' Zak asked.

'No! But I'm sure she's all right. Jessica can look after herself.'

'You always used to call her Jess.'

Lucas nodded.

Even the way he said her name these days had a coldness about it. Like she was someone he had known in another life. Zak's mind was thick with a fog of sadness as he watched Lucas mouth words about them all having to come to terms with change, words that were meant to soothe. He couldn't even remember saying goodbye to his dad or walking back over to his bed, lying down and finally drifting off to sleep.

Zak was woken by a great crash. It felt as if the earth was shifting under him. He hurled himself down the stairs and into the room he'd been standing in just a few hours before. The entrance to the living room had been cordoned off and a large dust sheet hung in the doorway. Zak pulled it back and stared at the place where the solid wall with the painted white cross had stood just hours before. The builders were now covered in a thick layer of dust.

Shalini called down to him. 'Zak! You're not supposed to be in there. We're going out for breakfast this morning.'

'Why did they have to knock the wall down?' Zak whispered to himself, as the masked builders ushered him out of the room. 'It is not safe,' they told him. Shalini came downstairs, stared into the kitchen and held her hand over her mouth. She placed an arm around his shoulder, but Zak shrugged it off. As he walked away he turned and stared at Shalini and the ghostly silhouettes of the builders shrouded in dust. At that moment his iPhone buzzed.

Sorry I can't speak but, all being well, will be home by Monday, Love you my Zak, Mum X

And there it was – that warm wave that always washed over him as soon as he heard the news that she was coming home. Shalini placed a hand on Zak's shoulder as she read it too. A sparkling morning light streaked through the door as Shalini opened it. Zak looked back into the building to find the sun-bathed builders waving to them through the dust. He felt like laughing with joy as he read over his mum's text again and again just to make sure he had not imagined it. *This'll teach me not to fill my head with all this bad omen, karma nonsense!* Zak waved back to the men and stepped into a pool of sunshine.

Chapter Eleven

It was supposed to be silent reading time in the library, but every few minutes Muna would look up from her book and fire another question at Aisha. She was bubbling over with excitement at just the idea of this adoption.

'I don't understand why you're so upset. *You* were the one going on about how she won't let you fast at Ramadan,' Muna whispered.

From time to time Miss Sealy, the librarian, looked up from under her glasses and hushed the girls, but it was only a few moments until Muna started with her musings again.

'I mean, Liliana and her family are kind and everything, but if you had a sister of your own, how good would that be? As long as they live around here though. They're not going to take you away from us, are they?'

Aisha felt a chill weight grip her stomach – the thought hadn't even occurred to her that she might have to move area; that she might have to face leaving Liliana, her friends *and* changing school. How could Liliana even think of putting her through that?

Aisha shook her head. 'I don't know where this family live or anything about them.' She wished now that she had kept the whole thing to herself. Muna was probably her best friend in the group of girls that she hung out with at school. She was the one who had come over to ask her to sit with them in the canteen on the day that she'd worn her hijab for the first time. Aisha still remembered how happy she had felt at the invitation, as if she'd found a place in school where she truly fitted. Being with these girls stopped her feeling that her memory of home was fading. It was partly the trauma of leaving that had made her forget so much about life in Somalia, and blocking out the horror made the good memories fade too, as time passed and Aisha was afraid that who she had been before she came to this country might just slip away. Muna and her family had done so much for her. Just speaking Somali with them all was a comfort. Her mum having her over for traditional Somali meals, even sharing recipes with Liliana, giving her a Quran, taking her to the mosque and teaching her how to make wudu – to cleanse and pray at the different times of the day.

These things were part of her, and without Muna and the others it was true that she would have had no guides to show her the way. When she was with Muna's family she felt closer to her father, or 'Abo' as she still thought of him. But now she felt that she had also kept something back from her friends; she had failed to convey how important Liliana was to her. She'd often complained to them that Liliana didn't understand why she wanted to fast, or why she had decided to wear the hijab. These things she had confided in them, but what she hadn't chosen to express were all the things that Liliana *did* mean to her.

'You wouldn't need to have your head in that Quran Explorer App all the time if you were in a Somali family! It would be like everything you learn when you come to my house would just come natural. You wouldn't have to explain yourself and you could speak the language all the time, not just with us. But the sister thing's way the best. You're always going on about how lucky I am to have sisters and brothers. Better watch out though! They're bound to be stricter than Liliana.'

Everything that Muna says is kind of true, so why do I feel as if someone has reached inside me and pulled away my anchor? Aisha only half listened to Muna now.

'Yeah, didn't you say she even tried to persuade you not to wear the hijab? She shouldn't try to influence you. That's just wrong!'

How can Muna, surrounded by all her family understand?

Liliana has made me feel safe. She's given me a home and love and kindness, and I've put all my trust in her. It isn't about meeting the other family. How could Liliana even think of letting me go?

'I always thought that I was more than just another foster child to her,' Aisha confided in Muna.

'I know I joke about how lucky you are, not having all the rules, but when it comes down to it, no matter how nice she is, no outsider's ever gonna understand our culture and religion, innit?' Muna was saying as Miss Sealy peered at them over her glasses.

'What have you two been whispering about?' The librarian smiled warmly as they passed her desk on their way out.

'Nothing, miss!' Muna laughed breezily. 'Just talking about culture 'n' stuff!'

Chapter Twelve

Zak read down the long list of names on the war memorial outside his school and sighed with relief that the name Edwin Bainbridge was not carved into the stone.

He bumped into Mr Slater in the corridor coming out of registration. There would be no point in trying to explain to his tutor why he was late *again*. The teacher looked as if his patience was about to snap until Zak showed him the piece of plasterwork, and the photo he'd found of Edwin and Albert. By the time Zak finished telling him how he had come across the name, Mr Slater seemed to have lost track of time himself and launched into a passionate eulogy about his favourite subject.

'*Now* you're on to something! No use fighting the historian in you. You never know how it all connects up – that's what I meant when I told you that making sense of history's like following a trail through the

woods. Glad to see you seem in better spirits today.'
Mr Slater smiled and patted Zak on the shoulder.
'Find a path that grabs your interest, and then you're
away! I just wish I could get all my students to
understand. He was pointing at Zak now. 'That boy
who helped to build your house could have been part
of everything we've been learning about, and as you're
living within those walls you're connected to that time
too. See! That's the thing about history – once you
realize that no one lives outside of it, you're hooked!'

In break, Zak texted his dad.

All OK in NYC? All OK in London. Mum coming
home. Love you Dad, Zak X

After break, in 'project time', Mr Slater let Zak go to
the library. In the Local History section Zak scrolled
through pages and pages of things that probably had
nothing to do with Edwin and Albert, but he found
himself drawn to them anyway because this was the
time that they had lived in and the more he found out
about it, the more it shed light on who these two men
were. He followed the pathways of his own mind,
allowing himself to explore anything that interested
him. He picked out a book with a map of the old water
courses and was surprised to find streams and rivers
running all over the area, even through the woods
where he'd walked that morning. He Googled 'First

World War' plus his postcode, and a whole list of memorials came up. Apparently there was one in Home Wood. Now he was googling anything to do with the local area and the First and Second World Wars because, as his dad had suggested, this Edwin could have fought in both. There was a website that showed where each bomb had hit. He couldn't believe that they had landed in so many nearby streets. Zak picked up the photo of Albert and Edwin again and admired the look of solidarity, as if nothing and no one could shake them apart. The more he read, the greater the connection he felt to these two strangers who had lived a century ago.

There was no doubt about it. It was kind of addictive, this tracing of people in history. He'd watched a programme on TV where families went hunting through their ancestry. He'd seen the look of satisfaction and sometimes overwhelming emotion on their faces when they found the names of people in their family from generations before stamped and written on documents, certificates and gravestones . . . Now, leafing through a book in the reference section, he found another mention of a memorial somewhere in Home Wood. It looked as if it was in the opposite, wilder side, which seemed all closed off. According to the information, it was this part of the wood that had once been a burial ground for plague victims. *Yes, I read that on the sign.* Maybe this was the reason why people didn't walk there so often? He looked closer at the map and spotted something else too – an air-raid shelter. *That makes sense if the roads around the wood were being bombed.* He wasn't allowed to take this heavy tome of a book out of the library, but for the first time in ages he felt a bubbling up of interest in something. Maybe Mr Slater was right – he *was* following trails that seemed to be leading him back into the woods. Zak cast around to check that no one was watching and carefully tore out the map and stowed it away.

As he walked out the librarian nodded and smiled at him. 'Got what you came for?'

Zak felt the map burning a hole in his blazer pocket as he ran along the road and back into school.

'Find anything interesting?' Mr Slater asked in form time.

'Not really,' Zak mumbled.

'Never mind. Research can be a lengthy process. It's part of the joy of it . . . the hunt . . . the unexpected discovery . . .' Mr Slater's voice faded in to the background. At the weekend Zak had already decided that he would head off into the woods and see what he could discover. *If nothing else it'll help to kill time until mum comes home.*

Chapter Thirteen

A text jumped into Zak's inbox.

All OK in NYC. Happy all OK in London too
and Mum on way back. Love you son. It will get
easier. Promise. Speak later, Dad x

Zak smiled. It felt good not to be at war with his dad
anymore.

Walking home along the woodland path Zak
glanced up at a wanted poster with a hand-drawn
sketch of a dog. It looked like the copper coloured
one he'd seen with the homeless girl the day
before, the one she'd drawn on the pavement outside
the shop. Underneath the poster she had written a
note:

*Red is missing. If you find her, bring her back
to Kalsis Woodland Store. Reward offered.*

As soon as he emerged from the wood he saw the girl slumped on a chair strumming a few idle chords on her beaten-up guitar. Zak noticed that her eyes were red and sore.

'You haven't seen my dog, have you?'

Zak shook his head.

'Her name's—'

'Red. I know,' Zak interrupted.

'Sometimes I wish *I* was that dog! Everyone seems to know *her*. Well, you'll look out for her, won't you?'

'You're Iona?'

'How do you know my name?' she asked.

'I saw your signature on the drawing there.' Zak nodded at the faint smudge where her name had been. 'It's really good.'

'Thanks!' Iona whispered, looking down. 'It's faded now though.'

Zak heard her voice break and tears rolled down the girl's cheeks. He was shocked to see how young she looked when her face relaxed. Her grey eyes were wide and full of sadness, making her look like a very small lost child.

He found himself rummaging in his blazer pocket and passing her a tissue.

'Thanks!' Iona gave a great trumpet-blow of her nose. 'That's what she does, my Red, just ups and leaves me all on my own. Once a stray, always a stray, they say. But it's only usually for a couple of hours.

She's never wandered off for this long before.'

The tough edge had gone from Iona's voice, replaced by a desperation that was much harder to ignore.

'Without her I hardly make a penny in sales.' Iona indicated the pile of unsold magazines on the table next to her. 'I swear people care more about her than me!'

Zak felt in his pocket, found a pound coin and attempted to hand it to Iona.

She clenched her fist tight so that he couldn't place the money in her palm. 'I'm no beggar,' she said, pushing his hand away. 'But you'll tell me if you come across her, won't you?'

Zak nodded.

'You see, that dog's all I've got.'

Chapter Fourteen

Dear Liliana,
I thought you knew how alone I used to feel. I can't
understand how you could even think I can move
away now. My friends don't get it either, they think
the adoption is a good idea. Maybe if it had happened
at the beginning, it would have been better for me.
Now I know that the only person in the world who
can help me is my abo. I thought you would keep me
safe until he comes. I can't start all over again.
I love you and I thought you loved me,
Aisha

She swallowed back the tears, folded the paper in half
and wrote Liliana's name on the front. There was not
much to take with her. She remembered now how
little she had carried on to the plane to London, just
one small cloth bag. *Will I ever have anything much to
carry with me through my life?* she wondered as she
packed the small prayer mat that Muna had given her

as a gift along with her poetry book from Liliana. She wished she could have taken her beautiful Quran too, but there was no way that she would be able to keep it clean and dry. Instead she placed it carefully on top of her wardrobe.

Aisha felt around her neck and ran her fingers over her smooth jet. *At least I have my prayer beads.* 'For all that I have, and all I have lost . . .' her abo's words echoed through Aisha's mind as she placed her final belongings in her rucksack. She'd packed all her clothes and her big winter puffa coat, a sleeping bag, some food she'd collected over the last few days from the kitchen, camping equipment, some matches and a powerful torch. She'd squirrelled it all away in her room little by little so that Liliana would not become suspicious. She knew it was time when Liliana had knocked on her bedroom door to say that they needed to pop up the road for an hour to look after her grandchildren. The scene of her lie kept replaying in her mind.

'I'll stay here.' Aisha smiled and Liliana took the little encouragement offered as a sign that she was beginning to forgive her. She walked over to Aisha and wrapped her arms around her.

'I know you want to be more independent, but I can't leave you here on your own . . .' As the words came out of Liliana's mouth she noticed a look of scorn cross Aisha's face.

'You don't want to leave me for an hour to go up the road, but you're happy to let me go to a family you've never even met.'

Liliana sighed. 'You know that's not the same thing.'

'You go, I'm OK,' Aisha lied. 'I think I can survive for one hour on my own.'

'Well, if you're sure love. If you need me I'm on my mobile.'

Aisha took a final look around her bedroom, zipped up the rucksack and tested its weight. It was much heavier than she'd expected with all the tins of food she'd taken. Why did the image of herself arriving at Heathrow Airport with her flimsy cloth bag keep returning to her? She had tried so hard to block out that time of terror, and yet here she was choosing to step out of Liliana's safe haven . . . and she hadn't even thought about where she would go. It had been enough to decide to leave.

Aisha walked into the kitchen, opened her life story book and lay her note to Liliana on the first blank page. She had to stop herself from looking at the pictures of the picnic. That sunny day was a world away now. Everything had seemed perfect then, but now Liliana had spoiled it all. Aisha went out into the hallway, hoisted her rucksack higher on her back and headed quickly out of the door.

Linden Road was a well-lit street and so it was not until she reached the end of it that she realized quite how dark it was by the side of the woods. Here she was again for the first time in years walking without a purpose, without a destination. Her stomach lurched and rumbled with hunger. What was the matter with her? She'd eaten only a couple of hours before, but it was as if her body anticipated that she might need to ration out her food supply and was protesting. Perhaps her belly remembered the feeling of hunger that her mind had allowed her to forget. With every step she took she felt her rucksack growing heavier along with the memory of another weight that had once lodged permanently in her stomach; the cold stone of grief and loneliness. She turned left at the end of the road and followed the railings that bordered the woodland. She had never before felt afraid here at this time of night, but as a scruffy-looking girl with matted hair walked past, Aisha veered to the side. The girl looked insulted.

'Who you staring at? Where you off to anyway, veil-head? Going back to Africa? That's a fair way to walk.'

Aisha quickened her pace. She'd suffered this sort of abuse before and had learned to never look it in the eye.

The girl called after her again, but Aisha couldn't tell what she was saying. Probably some racist jibe.

When she was at a safe distance, Aisha turned back. The girl had slumped on the pavement outside Kalsis Woodland Store. Aisha watched as Mrs Kalsi waddled out and started chatting to the girl. She took her arm and seemed to be trying to pull her up and invite her into the shop, but the girl resisted and Mrs Kalsi seemed to give up and went back inside. *I wonder if Mrs Kalsi would be so nice to her if she'd heard what she just called me.*

The words stung but Aisha had experienced worse since she'd started wearing her hijab. It was why Liliana kept asking if it was worth it. Maybe it did make her a target, but she would not be bullied by ignorant people into removing it. She would never think of calling that girl names because of the piercings all over her ears and mouth. But she had to admit to herself that what *had* been going through her mind as she looked at the girl was this: *Is that what I'll become, a homeless beggar girl, filthy and smelling and reduced to sleeping on the streets like a dog?* Perhaps she had felt Aisha's disgust.

A police car crawled up the street and came to a halt. Aisha strode a little further along the road and sheltered under the shadows of the oak trees. She huddled down and watched. She had not hidden away in fear like this since . . . She closed her eyes and made her mind go blank. She would not think about that day. It was always easier to focus on something

89

else, someone else. As Aisha opened her eyes a woman officer got out of her car and stood on the pavement talking to the homeless girl. *Why would someone want to live on the street?* she asked herself, then remembered that *she* had left the only place in this country she had ever called 'home'. Soon Liliana would be back. She would go to the table and find Aisha's note and then she'd be calling around Muna, Mariam, Somaya and anyone else she could think of, checking to see if Aisha was with them. She would find her abandoned mobile phone on the bed, and her wardrobe emptied. It would only be a matter of time before she'd call the social worker and the police. But Aisha couldn't bear to think about Liliana's panic. She shrank further into the shadows as the policewoman climbed into her patrol car and slammed the door behind her.

Aisha clasped her prayer beads.

'You know this jet was alive once too, as trees from the ancient forests . . .' Her abo's words echoed through her head. Perhaps her hoyo and abo were leading her to safety here. *Should I hide in the wood instead of heading into town?* On the opposite side of the road was the part of Home Wood where she and Liliana had picnicked so often, but the wood that ran alongside this pavement was unknown to her. Aisha peered between the metal railings of the entrance into the dense, dark woodland. 'Keep out, this is *our* territory,' the trees seemed to whisper. Through the gloom the branches of a fallen tree extended towards her like the beckoning arms of a skeleton. Aisha shivered and waited for the police car to pass. She had already changed her mind about staying in the wood and was about to step away from the entrance when two men wearing high visibility jackets appeared and walked up a narrow mud path towards the metal railings. Aisha ducked behind a tree, just inside the wood's boundary.

'Sure you've checked the place over? No vagrants hanging about in there?' One man lifted and pulled a heavy gate to as his colleague took the other side and together they heaved closed the rusting metal that had been folded against the railings.

'Better off shutting up the place for good, I say. Who walks in here anyway? You'd have to be out of your mind to stick around here at night.' The taller man shivered.

'True! But if they don't fix these gates soon, we'll have no choice but to keep it closed; they could do someone an injury. Anyway, looks like the conservation people have got their way. It's got to be locked up for Halloween and Fireworks Night after all that bother last year . . . kids building fires. Lucky the whole thing didn't go up!'

Aisha held her breath as she heard the padlock being rattled.

'All secure!'

She stood stock still until the men's voices and footsteps finally receded into silence. She thought of the homeless girl lying on the pavement by the shop. Maybe Aisha would be safer in the shelter of these ancient trees than roaming the streets, at least for tonight and maybe for longer if the wood was going to be closed off for a while.

She took her first steps deeper inside and pulled out her torch. It was as if someone had turned up the volume on the woodland. Perhaps she was disturbing the sleeping creatures with the glare of her light because she heard life all around her: scurrying through the undergrowth, rustling leaves, bats diving, and now she thought she heard someone singing or something like a woman crying. She had not felt this kind of fear since the day she'd been forced to let go of her abo's hand and he'd handed her over to her guide; that had been the first time she'd understood how it felt to no longer be under the protection of someone who loved you.

Chapter Fifteen

Aisha walked further into the wood, away from the hum of the road. She followed a rough path cautiously until the scattering of light from the street lamps was completely swallowed by the thick leaf canopy. When she shone her torch into the darkness the fiery red leaves of autumn shone back at her, the wood ablaze for a second with colour. For the first time in ages the vision of her village burning to the ground came back to her . . . Aisha covered her eyes. She took a deep breath as she'd been taught to when the memories threatened to overwhelm her. But the sights and sounds would not leave and the image of her friends and family tearing out of their houses with fire eating at their skin was searing into her again.

The stench of charred flesh filled her nostrils. Lalu, her aunt was somewhere inside one of those burning houses. Aisha hid, playing dead, watching it all happen and desperately trying to block her ears from the yelps and screams of pain and the men with guns who came to destroy. She lay on her belly, in the sure knowledge that if they found her she too would be taken by the men and shot, she did not dare to breathe. A young boy stood in front of the marauders with flames licking his hair pleading for water, for mercy, and she could do nothing but sit by and watch in horror as his captors laughed and spat in his face.

Aisha tried desperately to tune in to the sounds of the wood, to bring herself back. As she returned to the present she realized that she was lying face down in the earth and that the light of her torch had died. *Why didn't I check the batteries?* Frantically Aisha clicked the switch off and on again. Nothing. Her heart sank at the thought of having to lie in that position until dawn. She felt in her rucksack for her sleeping bag. At least the weather hadn't yet turned cold and the earth she was lying on was soft and dry.

Once she was snuggled inside the sleeping bag, Aisha opened her eyes wide – maybe her vision would sharpen as it adjusted to the darkness. Gradually, gradually, she seemed to focus, picking out the tiniest contrasts of dim light between the branches. A shadow dipped and fell towards her, accompanied by a swooshing sound. Bats. They were flying around the wood now as if they owned the place, diving at her head, sensing her there. She covered her scarf with her coat and began to pray. But through her prayer came the sound of an animal, as it drew closer it felt about the size of a fox. Now it was walking over her legs it seemed even larger. She held her breath and did exactly as she had when she'd hidden outside her village. She did not move a muscle, but the animal seemed to sense her fear and climbed on to her stomach. It was kneading her with its paws trying to pierce the thick down of the sleeping bag. Now it was panting and sniffing around her. She could hold her breath no longer and a sob escaped from her mouth. She expected the beast to sink its teeth into her skin at any moment. She prepared herself and was grateful that she could not see it. Then a soft whimper came from the animal as it pawed at her chest as if trying to stir her, but she would not move, could not move. The animal whimpered again, backed away and lay on the ground beside her. Then came another sensation of something scurrying over her body, a long, thin tail trailing. She heard the squeal as the larger animal swiped it away and then positioned itself close by her side, close enough for her to feel its breath. She made a pact with herself. If, Insha'Allah, she was still alive in the morning, she would fast as she had wanted to do at Ramadan. But for now, all she could do was attempt to control her breathing.

She searched and searched her mind for something that would bring her comfort, and it was Liliana's voice that came to her, reading *Hansel and Gretel* . . . It seemed as if she was hearing the story for the first time. She had often felt embarrassed about wanting those stories, because she supposed that they were meant for young children, but she had always sensed that there was something beneath the surface that had to do with the kind of wounds that she had suffered . . . now listening to Lilana's voice in the dark she grasped exactly what that was . . .

The stepmother had left the children in the wood because they did not have enough food. Aisha could believe that. She had seen what the swell of an empty belly could do to people. And as for the witch, she'd been hungry and maybe lonely too, and she'd lured the children to her house of sweets but then the children had managed to outwit her and escape, so the children had won over hunger, the children were survivors. Two small people are taken into a wood and abandoned. *It's how I feel right now. It's happened to me once before. How am I supposed to feel when the person I trust most except for my abo is willing to let me go?* Now, as she felt the animal stir by her side, Aisha understood that the story was really about the terror of being left alone in the world, of being eaten up by your worst fears, by the wild animal sitting by your side waiting to attack.

Chapter Sixteen

Zak woke to the sound of a heavy engine labouring in the street outside his window. Lorries had started arriving with new furniture. By the time his mum returned the house would seem sorted compared to how it had been. Zak hated all this new stuff. It felt like living in a hotel. Why couldn't they bring the old table with them, the one they'd all sat around together for so many years? He peered out of his bedroom window to see two police cars parked outside a house further up the road. The woman he'd seen having a picnic in the woods – *Liliana, was that her name?* – was standing in a doorway, crying. A police officer was attempting to calm her. Zak got up, put on his school uniform and attempted to slip out past Shalini.

'Breakfast!' she called through to him.

'No time!'

Shalini hurried out and thrust a croissant and a carton of orange juice into his hand. 'Eat on your way to school then. I will pour water on your head tomorrow if you don't wake up in time!' she joked, ruffling Zak's hair affectionately 'Your Ma will be telling me off for spoiling you when she gets back!' She laughed and pushed him out of the door. *Shalini always seems as relieved as me when she knows Mum's coming home.* Zak was still smiling as he jogged down the street, only slowing as he passed Liliana's doorway.

'No, no, I think she's run away, because of the note I showed you,' Liliana was saying.

'At least that's better than someone taking her,' the police officer attempted to reassure Liliana.

'You don't understand! The child's had enough trauma in her life as it is. You've got to send more people to look for her. If only I'd insisted on her coming with me. I was just an hour or so up the road with my grandchildren. It was the first time I've ever left her in the flat. I wish I'd never brought up the adoption thing. She was happy with me before . . .' Liliana broke off, sobbing.

'Nobody's blaming you for anything, and we're doing all we can,' the police officer comforted.

Zak tried to walk past unnoticed but he caught Liliana's eye.

'Wait. Wait up!' she called after him. 'Can I give you some leaflets to hand out?'

The policewoman peered at Zak. 'Are you a friend of Aisha's? Have you any idea where she might be?'

'Sorry, I don't really know her,' Zak mumbled.

'You're that boy who wanted us to feed the homeless woman, aren't you?'

Zak nodded and took the flyers from Liliana's shaking hand.

'Her friend Muna made these last night, brought them round first thing. Said she couldn't sleep worrying about her. Maybe I should ask old Elder if she's seen her too. The more people looking out for my Aisha the better. The Somali families are searching . . . and the school teachers. They've even put a message out in the newsletter.' Liliana was burbling now. 'May God help me if anything's happened to that child. She put her trust in me, you know.'

She clung on to Zak's blazer. 'You will keep a look out for her, won't you? Pass those around for me, pin them on trees, in shop windows, school noticeboards. Please, please, just ask everyone,' she pleaded.

'I will but I've just moved in. I don't really know anyone,' Zak explained. He felt in shock too.

'I'd go myself but right now I'm not feeling too bright. Ask around won't you, love?' All the blood had drained from Liliana's face and she seemed to collapse into the policewoman, who placed a comforting arm around her shoulder.

'You're best off staying here in case she comes back. They often do of their own accord. We'll be pasting posters everywhere ourselves. But you know, we have a lot of success through social media these days, Twitter, Facebook . . . we'll get the word out,' the police officer assured Liliana as she led her inside.

Zak looked down at the poster of Aisha. It must be a recent school photo. She was wearing her uniform with her familiar blue headscarf and smiling. The strange thing is that he'd walked through the wood every day since the picnic, hoping he might see her again, and never even caught another glimpse, and now it turned out that they'd been neighbours all along.

Zak walked to the main road and down the hill past Kalsis Woodland Store. He was relieved to see that Iona was not sitting outside today. He'd only been into the shop a few times for bread and milk, but Shalini had already made friends with the couple who owned it.

Mr Kalsi stood at the counter.

'Excuse me. Would you mind putting up this poster?'

Mr Kalsi took it from Zak, studied it, then called out to someone in the back room. Mrs Kalsi appeared from behind a stack of boxes, puffing and panting and pushing her glasses up on to her nose.

'Oh! Oh! Not Liliana's girl?' she groaned, tapping the flyer.

Zak nodded.

'This is too worrying. You are one of her friends?' Mr Kalsi asked kindly.

Zak didn't know how to describe what this girl was to him. This complete stranger, whom he'd seen in the wood only a couple of times but whose face he'd found himself sketching, whose name he had memorized and who now turned out to have lived just up the road from him . . . How could he explain that? So he simply nodded.

'Good boy, good friend!' Mrs Kalsi squeezed his arm as he left the shop.

'You keep looking for her. City is a dangerous place for young girl on her own. We will ask everyone we know and pray for her. Must look after our community, nah?' Mr Kalsi said as he stuck the image of Aisha up in his shop window. Then he followed Zak outside and pinned another one on the noticeboard that opened with a key. He took down an old advert for a fundraising event that had long past and replaced it with Aisha's picture. When he had lowered the Perspex screen and locked it up, he placed the box of drawing pins in Zak's hand. 'Here, take these with you!'

Zak thanked Mr Kalsi, but as he walked away he heard raised voices between husband and wife.

'What do you mean, CCTV not switched on?' Mrs Kalsi shouted.

Mr Kalsi mumbled something about 'not enough hours in the day to do what he needed . . .' but his wife's voice came booming back at him.

'You think of drawing pins, but you can't remember important business? We could have seen the girl on camera, which direction she is going in.'

'Maybe, and maybe not!' Mr Kalsi replied.

'Well, we won't know now, will we? What is point of installing it in first place? You want to have another break-in? Not one time when we have needed it has this useless camera been switched on.'

Chapter Seventeen

The morning sun filtered through the trees just as it had on the day when Zak had first passed Aisha walking along this very same path. He stopped at a tree parallel to where he'd seen her and pinned up a poster. *Why would she run away?* Zak supposed you could never tell what was going on inside someone else's mind.

Zak bent down to pick up the pile of posters and felt someone approach and stand behind him reading out the message . . .

"'Missing, Aisha Eshun, aged twelve.'"

Now he knew where the snake coil girl had come from in his dream. Iona read on and then whistled in surprise. 'Twelve? Is that all? She looks older than that! She your girlfriend? What have you done – frightened her off?'

Her voice was back to how it had been before – all twisted and sharp.

'You won't find her round here anyway. I saw her

last night heading towards the city! Good luck to her I say. You don't want to know what a girl that age could get caught up in. Looking all innocent and everything with her veil too. She'll need all the protection she can get.'

'What do you mean?'

Iona scowled and looked Zak up and down as if he knew nothing at all about life. 'Trust me, I know what I'm talking about. Been on the streets since I was fifteen myself.'

'How old are you now then?' he found himself asking.

'Seventeen. You?'

'Nearly thirteen.'

'Thought so.' Iona sneered and stared at the image of Aisha. '*She* could be taken for my age, but you're both just babes in the wood! Ha! Literally!' Iona laughed and then her expression changed. 'Don't tell anyone, will you? I always say I'm older. It gets them off my case . . . Anyway, you seen my dog?'

'Sorry.' He shook his head. 'I'm Zak, by the way.'

'I know your name. Elder's been chanting on about you and this Aisha girl with the blue scarf for days now! You'd better watch out . . . Once you get inside her head you never know where it'll end!' She patted Zak on the cheek and he flinched and pulled away. 'Don't look so scared! She's harmless enough unless she's off on one. I'm only joking!' Iona laughed again, a deep warm laugh that seemed to belong to someone else.

'You think she might know where Aisha is?' Zak asked.

'Unlikely! You're probably just names wafting through her head!' But I'll do you a deal. If I look out for your girl – even ask Elder, if you like – then you'll keep an eye out for my Red?' Her mouth trembled as she spoke the dog's name.

Zak nodded and watched Iona trail away into the trees.

What was going on? It was as if he was becoming entangled in the branches of all of the stories that were taking place in this wood . . . He felt in his pocket for the old map he'd taken from the library. Finding Albert's name in the plasterwork seemed to have loosened more than dust. Zak looked up through the splayed branches and half expected to find Elder sitting in watch.

'I hope they find her,' Iona called.

Despite her sharp manner, Zak felt sorry for Iona as she walked away, shoulders slumped, dreadlocks swinging, calling out for her missing dog. *Everyone must need someone or something to love*, he thought as Iona's voice drifted off into the distance.

'Red, Red! Come back, girl.'

Chapter Eighteen

The road from school was busier than usual and a police van was now stationed outside the Kalsis' store. The woman officer Zak had seen in the morning with Liliana stopped and questioned people as they passed. She held a poster of Aisha in her hand.

'Any news?' she opened her notebook hopefully.

'I saw that homeless girl Iona on my way into school. She said she'd seen Aisha last night, heading for the city.'

The officer closed her notebook. Clearly she'd logged this information already, but thanked Zak anyway.

She pointed at the sky above their heads where a helicopter hovered. 'Well, we're covering all bases anyway,' the officer explained as she stepped into her car.

Zak felt slightly sick as he walked home; the intrusive drone bombarded his mind as the helicopter circled the same patch of ground like a persistent bluebottle. *Please don't let anything have happened to her*, Zak repeated over and over in his head as the blades whirred.

Shalini was waiting on the doorstep. She held out her arms to give him a hug. Zak read the tense expression on her face and turned cold inside.

'What's wrong?' he asked, shrugging her off.

Shalini's hand gestured softly on the air as if conducting an orchestra to play more smoothly, quietly. She only made this odd little movement when she was trying to calm *herself* down.

'Come inside.'

'Is it Mum? Tell me,' Zak demanded.

Shalini took hold of his arm and led him into the hallway.

'They called from the news team and yes, there has been some kind of disturbance. A number of journalists were missing when the flights took off. They are trying their best to find . . .'

Zak threw off Shalini's hands, sprinted up the stairs to his room and switched on his laptop for a full update of the news. He watched the images of children being shot and gassed, terror in their eyes. If his mum was caught up in all this . . .

Zak ran to the bathroom just in time to empty the contents of his churning stomach. He washed his face and drank some water, but the vile acid taste lingered. He stared at himself in the mirror. How could people do that to each other? What kind of god could look over a world like this? Zak heard Mr Slater's voice in his head reading the poem about the soldiers in the trenches. *I hate it all,* Zak spoke to his own washed-out face in the mirror. *If being a pacifist means refusing to have anything to do with killing, then that is what I am.*

He found himself replaying his mum's report of walking with the procession of children towards the refugee camps, reporting from the rubble. At least she had been safe then. She'd sounded calm and strong. As he listened to it over and over, his throat tensed again and he began to cough.

'Zak, are you OK? I'll bring you some sweet tea to settle your stomach. Your father will contact you any moment now.' Zak stood up and closed his bedroom door against Shalini's words of comfort. His computer buzzed. What was the point of talking to his dad if he couldn't even be here at a time like this? What was the point of him even being his dad? Zak clicked 'Decline'.

They had all been here once before. Waiting, waiting, waiting. After the agony of when she went missing last time his dad had tried to make his mum promise not to go off again. But she had and now Zak was the only one left waiting for her. That was all he seemed to do. It was the thing he hated most, the not knowing, being tied to every form of bulletin every second of the day, checking for news feeds, listening out for reports of her, about her, by her, and making a recording of each one in case it was her last. The computer buzzed with a repeat of his dad's Skype request. Zak grabbed his smartphone and smashed it hard into the screen of his laptop, cutting his knuckles in the process. He watched as dark red blood oozed from his skin. He walked into the bathroom and turned on the tap, letting the water run over it. 'Blood is thicker than water.' The saying kept repeating through his mind.

What does that even mean?

Chapter Nineteen

Sometime through the red terror of that long night Aisha's Aunt Lalu came to her with a familiar lullaby that ebbed and flowed over her like a gentle stream.

On waking, Aisha's mind was still clogged with a muffled sleep-haze. For a split second she didn't know where she lay or what fragment of her life she was caught up inside. Hiding in her village; being found by her abo and taken to Mogadishu; setting off for Kenya in the lorry; the thirst in her mouth, the hunger in her belly, crossing the road block and screaming for her abo to come back as the men on the road pushed a gun into his back and marched him away; her abo's hand being replaced by a stranger's. She remembered now being taken by the guide to Kenya and being put on the flight to Heathrow Airport; being interviewed; the bed at Monmouth House care home, the bed at Liliana's. Aisha had faced so many new walls that for the first year on Linden Road she had kept her eyes closed on waking, trawling her mind until she was sure that when she opened them again she would be safely in Liliana's room. Now she was back again in that twilight world of unknowing. She reached out and felt the cool earth beneath her fingers . . . and her mind tracked back to the wood that she had run into last night. Maybe she had dreamed up the beast that had sat next to her in the darkness? Aisha pushed the coat away from her face and felt the fresh morning air sting her skin. She turned her head to the side and slowly opened her eyes – to be met by those of an animal the colour of copper. She could smell its earthy breath on her face. It took a step towards her and she jumped back. It moaned and sat quietly down again. Not a fox, but a dog.

Aisha picked up a stick and flailed her arms around, shouting at it to leave her alone, but instead it sat patiently by her side. She stood up slowly and the dog stood too. She shoved her sleeping bag in her rucksack and headed deeper into the wood, making hissing noises at the dog to leave her alone, but it only hung back for a moment and then followed her. Every time she paused the dog did too, keeping a respectful distance. She hardly dared look the animal in the eye. She had always been afraid of dogs, and she was definitely not alone among her friends. Muna was the only person she knew who loved them and never gave up trying to persuade her parents to get one.

'The Quran says a dog is allowed if it's your

guardian, or looking after land. You said you sometimes don't feel safe in the flat at night, Mum . . .' Muna tried everything.

'I don't know about Aisha being the lawyer,' Muna's dad joked. 'Perhaps you two will be starting a practice together!'

If Muna was right this animal could have come to her as a kind of guardian, because, after all, it had sat by her side all night and kept her from harm. Aisha forced herself to look at it, taking a tentative step forward. The dog didn't move, but cocked its head on one side and she thought she read a kind expression in its gaze. It was as if the dog understood how much courage it was taking for her to approach. For years Liliana had tried to get Aisha to face her fear of dogs, and she'd hardly managed to even stroke one. As Aisha tiptoed closer, the dog lay flat and still on the ground and raised its eyes up towards her. Cautiously she reached out and touched the animal's head with her fingertips. Its coat was as soft as a wave of silk. Now the dog's tail started to wag gently. Although the animal was quite tall it was slender and delicate-looking, not like those squat, thickset dogs that terrified her in the park. It kept its head on the ground and its eyes raised towards her, almost pleading with her to be its friend. It was a strange thing, fear. Here she was, alone in a wood, tentatively stroking this dog without anyone but the animal coaxing her. She supposed that it was a question of need.

Above Aisha, the sky was lightening into a powdery-pink dawn. She checked her watch. Seven o'clock. The birds offered up a cheery morning call and Aisha could not believe how loud the wood had become, as if a parallel world existed here that she had been unaware of before. She walked on and the dog followed, keeping its distance a little way behind her.

They came to a fenced-off section of woodland and Aisha stopped to read a sign:

CONSERVATION ZONE. THIS AREA HAS BEEN CORDONED OFF FOR A TEN-YEAR PERIOD TO ALLOW FOR THE NATURAL REGENERATION OF THE FLORA AND FAUNA AND THE SPRING-WATER STREAM BED.

The overhang of foliage, brambles and undergrowth were thicker in this area. If she was to hide here it would be less likely that anyone would find her. With some difficulty she climbed over the fence, the dog took the more direct path and wriggled under it. *It's determined to stay with me*, thought Aisha as she carefully picked her way through a bramble thicket, following the dog as it sniffed its way further into the prohibited zone.

Aisha came to a steep muddy slope that was hard to climb with her heavy rucksack threatening to unbalance her. At least the ground was dry. She took two steps sideways and then switched direction to avoid a face-plant. The dog ran headlong from the top of the slope to the bottom and waited for her to pick her way down, its tail wagging in expectation. Despite herself, Aisha smiled at the animal's look of concern as it waited patiently for her. When she'd finally made it to the bottom, she'd found herself patting the dog's head to reassure it! She rummaged in her rucksack for a biscuit. The dog quietly sniffed at her offering as she placed it on the ground. At the sight of the food Aisha's own stomach complained loudly. If she was going to fast, as she'd promised that she would, then she had to get this hunger under control.

She shrugged her rucksack higher on to her back, grabbed a stick and beat her way through the undergrowth. After a while she came to a place where the earth rose up again in a steep mound and she had to climb and scramble over the clinging ivy to reach the upper level. She stopped and listened for a moment to the sound of running water. She climbed up over a flat ledge and meandered between some younger trees until she found the source. The stream was deep and narrow and cut its path in a zigzag pattern. The steep banks were lined with ferns, and great mollusc-like toadstools grew from cracks in the bank. On the far side the woodland seemed to have a life all of its own. Aisha had the feeling that nothing had changed here for centuries. Above her the sound of an aeroplane cutting through the clouds startled her out of the wood's cocoon. She watched as it made its way across the sky, lights flashing. Aisha could never look at a plane without wondering if there was someone else like her up there, flying into the unknown. She closed her eyes and listened carefully. If it wasn't for the distant hum of traffic and intermittent sirens faintly crying in a faraway place, she could have really believed that she had crossed a border into a wilderness.

A fallen tree lay over the stream, as if somebody had felled it to use as a crossing point. Aisha bent down and placed her hands in the flowing stream. If this was spring water as the sign said, when her bottles ran out she would be able to drink it. She leaned down, dipped her fingers in and tasted. It was slightly earthy and sweet. The stream was deep enough to immerse her body in, and the bank narrow enough for her to construct some kind of screen around herself to cleanse before praying. She had made her promise to fast and she would stick to it. Today she had missed rising at dawn, to pray and break her fast as she would have done if it really was Ramadan. *I'll have to wait to eat till the sun disappears from the sky.* She was determined not to let her stomach dictate to her.

Aisha washed her hands clean, then her face, nose and mouth. Then she bathed her feet, feeling the water gurgle between her toes. She took a jumper from her rucksack and dried herself. *Why didn't I think to bring a towel?* Afterwards she carefully cleared an area of ground and placed her prayer mat on it, knelt down and began to pray. She had tried to explain to Liliana that praying made her feel stronger and closer to her abo, to her aunt, cousins and home. Here in the wood it was possible to believe that no time at all had passed from the day she'd left Somalia. Aisha opened her eyes, scanning up through the diffused light, and felt for a moment at perfect peace. It was broken by the vision of an ancient figure standing motionless on the other side of the stream.

The old woman with the bright red hair was holding a stick and pointing to a leaf that appeared to be spinning on air. As it rotated faster and faster it caught the sunlight and turned to pure gold.

For a moment Aisha was transfixed too. How could the leaf be flying around and around on the same spot, held by nothing, like a woodland spirit caught in a vortex?

'Walk around the leaf-spirit, Elder, walk around, nature's threads should never be broken.' The old woman veered off to one side and ducked under the leaf. From here Aisha could see that it was hanging on a fine, gossamer thread that glistened in the sun.

Now that she was no longer caught in the leaf-spell, Aisha realized that the woman was heading in her direction. She held her breath, her spine stiffened and she found herself crouching to avoid her eye line. She backed away from the stream on her haunches and she noticed that the dog's ears pricked at the sight of the woman. Aisha couldn't stop the animal as it trotted over the fallen log and crossed the stream. *That must be a good sign*, Aisha told herself, attempting to bring her breath back to something like normal. *Aren't dogs supposed to have an instinct for people? Surely if it had reason to be afraid, she would be barking or growling.* Either way, Aisha couldn't be sure, and she had no wish to talk to the woman, here in the middle of the wood on her own. 'Over here!' Aisha whispered to the dog, and it paused, sniffed the air and returned to her. Aisha slipped on her trainers, picked up her prayer mat and quietly walked away from the stream, hoping that the woman had not seen or heard them.

The dog began scratching and burrowing at some ivy, exposing a large concrete slab. It seemed as if it was searching for something. *Did it know this place?* Then, without warning it disappeared underground.

Aisha eased herself over the concrete ledge and crouched down on her hands and knees to see where the dog had gone. She pulled back some brambles and was surprised to find an opening and steps leading down into a dark room. She could just make out the dog's bright eyes shining through the gloom and was taken aback at how relieved she felt that the animal seemed unharmed. She crouched low to avoid knocking herself out on the ceiling. The fine mesh of a spider's web clung to her face. She ducked under one cobweb and then another and another until she finally entered a kind of basement room. Two stone benches ran along the sides. At the end was a bunk bed with blankets folded on an old mattress. She felt like an intruder into a place that had been undisturbed for years. The dog leaned into Aisha, feeling her discomfort, and she found herself placing her arms around it and drawing it close. Above her head she could still hear the old woman ranting on. Whether or not she had reason to be afraid of her, it was a relief to be hidden away.

Aisha stroked the dog. She noticed that as she rhythmically touched its silken coat her own breathing settled and calmed. The dog looked up at Aisha and the strangest thought came to her. *It's as if Allah has sent this red dog to protect me. Like Muna said. It's my Guardian.*

To Aisha's relief the old woman's voice eventually faded and merged into the constant flow of the stream.

Chapter Twenty

Over dinner Shalini tiptoed her way around the conversation, gently reminding Zak every so often to contact his dad. As she spoke Shalini looked at him cautiously as if half expecting an explosion. He refused to meet her eyes.

As soon as he heard Shalini's bedroom door close Zak began to pack as he had watched his mum do so many times. Now it was his turn. It wasn't easy to find what he needed because everything was still in crates, but after rummaging around he managed to locate his wind-up torch and some warm clothes. Then he walked over to his desk and picked up the plasterwork and the little photo of Albert and Edwin. He felt in his pocket for the old map of the wood. If the air-raid shelter that he'd read about in the library was still in the wild bit of Home Wood, he intended to find it. It would be a good place to hide out for a while, to cut himself off from everything. *If anything has happened to*

Mum, I can't stand to see it on the news, or hear it on the radio, or have someone arrive at the door and tell me that she's just another casualty of war. Zak scowled – the irony had not escaped him. *I'm running away to find an air-raid shelter from an old war to escape from a new one.*

He walked down the stairs, searched through some boxes in the hallway and found a sleeping bag. From the kitchen he took a small pan, a bag of apples, bananas, some tins, bread and a bottle of water and shoved them into a carrier in the top of his bag. He checked his wallet. He had a twenty pound note and some change. It would have to do. He closed the door quietly behind him and stepped out into the gentle autumn breeze. He noticed that the lights were still on in Liliana's flat as he passed her door. He felt a pang of guilt, imagining Shalini finding him gone in the morning and having to break the news to his dad. Maybe he *should* have left a note, but what would he have said? That he couldn't stand the waiting and not knowing again? That he was terrified that his mum might not come back. That he just needed to get away from this fake home. That he had to shut himself off from the news of a world that he could do nothing to change.

A police van was parked on the corner of Home Wood, the doors flung open. Two large Alsatians lay panting in the back. Zak retreated into the shadows of the trees on the opposite side of the road. From here he was able to watch without being seen.

'And you've searched the other side too? The helicopter picked up something in there.'

'These two only sniffed out Elder, ranting on as usual.'

'Poor old girl. As long as you're sure the place has been scoured. I'd hate to think there'd been any wrongdoing and the child had ended up in there.'

'Don't worry. If she was, these two would have sniffed her out! Mind you –' the police officer pointed to one of the panting dogs – 'when Tyson saw Elder he rolled over belly up like a pup!'

'Probably felt sorry for her. I know I do, but there's no helping some people. Anyway, according to that homeless kid, Iona, the girl headed straight off into town.'

'Well, that'll be it then. We'd better send the message out to step up trawling the streets. I think we're done here.' The policeman patted both dogs on the head, fastened the bolts on their cage and slammed the van doors closed.

Chapter Twenty-One

Aisha's headscarf and face were now covered in a layer of cobwebs. She coughed and cleared her lips and mouth of the fine threads. Now that the old woman had gone she felt as if she could breathe again. She stood up and walked over to the bunk beds and was relieved to find no cans or bottles; no evidence that anyone had been here in years. It was dry and a place to shelter, and if she cleaned it out it would be somewhere to stay where no one would think of finding her. She had read about places like this where families had hidden underground when a city had been bombed. If only there had been a safe place for her aunt and cousins to run to when the attackers had come to her village.

The dog followed her back outside. She looked around tentatively and headed towards the thick woodland to the right of the shelter where great arcs of bracken grew. She ripped off some fronds and dragged them back inside. As she entered she gently wafted them through the air to sweep away the remaining cobwebs. She remembered how carefully the old woman had manoeuvred her way around the fine web that the golden leaf had hung on to avoid breaking it. Aisha gently swished the giant arms of fern over the floor like a broom. A live carpet of insects scuttled about as she swept and cleared. The far end of the shelter was almost as dark as night, but near the entrance the light streamed in. As she swept, her eye was caught by writing on the walls. There were names, and next to some of the names were simple children's drawings that had faded to grey but were still clearly visible. Each name was written in distinct handwriting like a signature, as if the people who had been here had been marking out their territory, making it their own.

There was swirly adult writing as well as crude lettering by young children.

Albert Bainbridge   *Peggy Lowie*

Eddie Lowie   Maisy Lowie

It was these names that Aisha felt drawn to. She could almost hear a pleading voice in the child's writing . . . 'My brave daddy, come home soon.'

The emotion rose up in Aisha's chest and she took a deep breath and slumped down on one of the benches.

The dog padded over and placed its head on her knee. How strange that she had found herself in a place where other children had wished and wished for their father to come home. It was the reason why she could never settle with the idea of being adopted by anyone, not even Liliana. If someone was missing, surely there was always a chance that they could be found. She had been to Heathrow Airport with Liliana once when they were going on holiday and had been mesmerized by the greetings between the waiting people and those arriving off long-haul flights. If you watched closely enough you could read their bodies like maps, in the expressions on their faces, their arms flung wide in abandon. You could tell how long they had been parted for and how much struggle had gone into finally being reunited. Aisha thought she could spot the ones who had really believed that they would never see each other again. She couldn't count the times since then that she had dreamed herself there, watching her abo walking through that barrier. Whenever she woke after that familiar dream she could always still feel her heart bursting with joy until slowly the happiness turned sour as she realized that she had to wake up.

Aisha was sitting on one of the cold benches where the children who had scribed these names must once have sat. Their words seemed like a gift across time, a sort of welcome, and she felt somehow comforted to be in a place where people would have understood something of what she'd come from. This term at school they'd all had to do a project on the First World War, and she'd researched and presented an essay on the Somali soldiers who had fought and died in that war. Even Miss Roberts hadn't known about that. Aisha had been quite fired up with this discovery but she could tell that some of the others in her class were not interested at all. They just seemed to think that everything was a game.

Sometimes she wished that she could make them understand what war did to you, how it tore your home apart, how one day it could drop a bomb into the middle of your world and explode everything, leaving a crater in your heart. On some days she felt like joining in with Miss Roberts and shouting at the kids who messed about. She'd rehearsed in her head plenty of times what she would like to say to them, but never would:

Do you know what it's like to leave your dad behind, knowing he's been taken as a prisoner; to have to say goodbye and have no idea when or if you'll ever see him again; to have to step off a plane into a cold new country, with no one to love you? That's not history. That's my life.

Aisha closed her eyes and wished that the children who had written this message on the wall so long ago had been granted the happy ending that they had longed for. *If they got their father back, and if I pray hard enough, then maybe I'll get to see my abo again too and there'll be no need for any more talk of adoption.*

Chapter Twenty-Two

'Uncover the ivy, unravel the vine, back through time to the years when the bombs fell and the children hid in their underground cell.'

The old woman's voice grew closer now. Aisha curled up in a foetal position towards the back of the lower bunk bed. Even if the woman came in, she might not find her there in the darkness hiding against the wall – as long as the dog kept quiet. For the moment, Red lay on the floor beside the bed.

'Uncover the ivy, unravel the vine, back through time . . .'

It sounded as if she was right outside the shelter. Aisha heard someone thrashing around at the entrance and now here she was peering in, her ancient face framed in the entrance. Aisha cowered away. It was one thing seeing the old woman at a distance, but having her this close made Aisha feel breathless. It was only the dog who stilled her fear as it got up, approached the woman and leaned against her. *So she did see us crawl inside the shelter after all. If the dog has no fear then maybe I have no reason to either. But what does this woman want with us?*

Aisha could just make out the doll strapped across the old woman's body and the frayed basket that she carried over her arm. She'd come right inside the shelter now and begun shuffling along the bench, unpacking a bag of golden-coloured apples which she laid out in a row as she rambled on, without meeting Aisha's eye.

'You'll be safe in here with the other children. Brought you some apples from my store. Always got more than enough. I bring what I can for my little war babies, my poor children.' She patted the dog's head as she spoke. 'Elder loves a cuddle,' she confided. 'But what are you doing here, you naughty girl? Have you run away too? Come to see old Elder, have you?'

The homeless woman looked up at Aisha for the first time.

'But I see fear in your eyes!' She shook her finger at Aisha and kissed her doll's head. 'Look, my Crystal – she's afraid of your mama. You tell her, baby. No poisoned apples here, no rotten ones either.'

Aisha was frozen to the spot. She stared at Elder, willing her to go away. From the corner of the shelter something scuttled and the dog ran over and chased it out.

'Rats and mice, mice and rats.' The woman pulled

the doll out of her sling and hugged her close as she peered around the shelter. 'It's dry all right, warmer than you'd think at night, but I never could settle here myself. Too much longing. Can't you feel it?'

There seemed no point in hiding away any more. Aisha eased herself off the bed, sat on the bench opposite Elder and edged along so that now she was closer to the entrance herself. From here she could smell the musty, rotting odour coming from the homeless woman, but at least she was out of her reach and if she needed to run, she could. Aisha's hands rose automatically to her prayer beads and the old woman leaned in to get a closer look. Her expression changed and she seemed suddenly excited. She reached under her own clothes to reveal a long leather lace with three large amber-coloured beads attached.

'You wear jet, I wear amber – woodland jewels.' She lifted the beads for Aisha to get a closer look. 'You and me, wearing wood-memories against our skin. See!'

Elder held her beads even closer to show Aisha, who recoiled once again from the old woman's smell.

'Look under the surface. In this one a tiny butterfly, in this a family of leaves and here's a ladybird, see! Maybe a million years old. Chant the old verse if she lands on you, and your wish will come true . . . How does it go? My mind's so slow.' She knocked her hand against her head as if to dislodge the rhyme. '"*Ladybird,*

ladybird, fly away home, your house is on fire; your children will roam". . . Know that one?'

Aisha nodded. Despite the old woman's potent smell and strange rhymes, she found herself mesmerized as she looked inside the enormous amber beads, the size of small hen's eggs.

'Wood memories to have and to hold. But these old eggs are keepers not hatchers. Suspended in the sap of ancient pine, they'll take you back and back in time.' Elder pointed to Aisha's prayer beads. 'Yours the fossil wood and mine the hardened resin. Never cold against your skin when you carry the heat of the past within. Did you know that?'

Aisha shook her head slowly, unsure of how to respond to this strange woman who seemed to suddenly break into riddles. It was true that her jet beads always stayed warm, even in the coldest weather, if that's what she meant.

'These belonged to my mother,' Aisha found herself saying.

'Mine too. Before the thread broke there were more, but only three of my treasures left now. My inheritance.' She clasped them close to her chest.

Aisha felt sorry for the woman. Now that she was actually listening, she made a little sense after all, and it seemed as if she was desperate to talk to Aisha. Perhaps she was just lonely.

The woman smiled as if she was grateful to Aisha

for listening. She lifted her hands to her hair and began twisting the tangled mass of leaves that she'd threaded into it. As she wound the red strands into an even greater mess a look of utter confusion fell across her face.

'Where are we? Who are we? I forget, small talk, any talk. What's your earthstar's name?'

'Sorry?' Aisha asked, confused.

'Your name? Your name?' the old woman insisted.

'Aisha.'

'Aisha,' she repeated in a whisper. 'Sounds like a prayer, like a promise on the breeze. I don't have another Aisha written on my leaves!'

She shuffled along the bench so that now they were sitting opposite each other. If she'd reached out to her now, she would be close enough to touch her. Aisha's heart was beating fast. She felt her body alert and ready to flee, and yet there was something about the woman that demanded that she stay.

She fixed Aisha with her intense gaze. 'Who else? Who else?'

'Who else what?' Aisha whispered, hardly able to make her voice produce a sound.

'In this place of longing. Who else are you missing?'

Was it that obvious? It was the most unsettling feeling, as if the old woman was drawing the responses from her, extracting the truth whether she wanted to tell it or not.

'My abo – my father,' Aisha mumbled.

'Yes, yes, I need mother's name and father's name.'

'Amina and Abdi Eshun.' Aisha's voice caught on the names that she had not spoken out loud since she'd first arrived in this country, when she'd been forced to answer all the official questions. Just saying her parents' names instantly brought tears to her eyes and she let them roll down her cheeks unchecked.

'You come from war?' The old woman reached out and patted Aisha on the knee, and this time she did not pull away or jump in fear. 'Seeking refuge? That's all right.' She beckoned to Aisha. 'Come and shelter in old Elder's wood. Aisha stay here with my wartime spirits.' She pointed up to the names that were written on the wall. 'People think time just runs straight, but –' she leaned forward as if she was letting Aisha in on a secret – 'sometimes shoots from the past push up and want to be seen again,' she whispered.

Aisha leaned back. What could she say in response to this?

'Your name's Elder?' Aisha asked, but the old woman ignored her. Now that she was this close, Aisha was horrified to see how cracked and ulcerated her skin was. It hung from her bones and in places had been rubbed red raw to the point of bleeding. Across one calf she had strapped leaves like a kind of poultice.

'I forget how scary Elder is. Sight for sore eyes these days. But I won't trouble you. Elder needs to know who's in her wood, but all is good, all is good. Let the spirits rest. I won't trouble you,' she mumbled as she shuffled out of the shelter carrying her doll over her shoulder, patting it on the back.

Aisha squatted at the door and watched Elder rummage around in a sack-like pouch attached to her waist. Once outside, the old woman began to scatter breadcrumbs. A cascade of crows and ravens swept in, their black wings hovering over her as she ambled away.

Aisha cast her eyes around the concrete walls and breathed a sigh of relief that Elder and her searchlight eyes were finally gone. At least, as she had observed, the place was dry. The dog paced back to Aisha's side and sat down next to her. Aisha picked up one of Elder's golden apples. She raised it to her nose and smelt the sweet, slightly spicy scent. Maybe she would eat one later. Her stomach was telling her to bite into it right now to still the hunger pangs that had gripped her almost as soon as she'd left Liliana's flat. As she gathered the fruit together in a pile Aisha surveyed the cold dusty walls and her attention was caught once more by the faded writing. She noticed now that to the side of the pictures was a score tally with dates written in children and adult writing. Was it recording some kind of game?

2/9/1940

Albert   Eddie
卌 卌   卌 ||||

4/9/1940

Albert   Eddie
卌 |||| 卌 卌

5/9/1940

Albert   Eddie
卌 ||| 卌 ||||

What had Elder been talking about? Hadn't she said
that Aisha should share these apples with *the others*?
Aisha scanned all the pictures and words that
decorated the walls and a high pitched child's voice
entered her mind. 'My brave Daddy, come home
soon.' Aisha shuddered. *Who else does Elder think
lives here?*

Chapter Twenty-Three

The road was quiet as Zak approached the wild side of Home Wood. He had not expected the gates to be locked. He walked along the perimeter, but the metal railings were secure, leaving him no choice but to climb. He threw his rucksack over first and counted one, two, three . . . to measure the drop. Then he climbed steadily up, feeling for footholds where he could. The tops of the railings were pointed and he paused for a moment, considering the best way to ease himself down. Then, from out of nowhere, thousands of diving shadows flew at him, a rush of wings bombarding his head. He lost his grip on the railings and fell head first towards the ground.

He was running faster than he'd run in his life, through thick mounds of earth stacked up on either side of him. His feet were frozen solid but still he ran. A voice rallying him on. 'We'll get through this,' and Zak looked down at his feet to see his own thin Converse trailing through the mud. His breath clenched inside him. There was a white silent flash and out of this light walked Edwin – the boy in the photo. He came and sat by Zak's side and propped him up. He felt inside his thick woollen jacket and pulled out a small black-and-white photo of himself with his father. 'If we get through this, I'm going to take over the family business. Do you know my father Albert?' Edwin asked.

Zak nodded.

'I'll be a carpenter too, that's the plan.' Edwin told Zak as they huddled in the filth of the trenches. 'Have you got someone back home?'

Zak felt in his pocket for a picture but found nothing. A rat scuttled across his palm and his hands started to shake uncontrollably.

'You'd better get used to the vermin in here!' Edwin warned.

Zak's head felt as if someone had taken a mallet to it. He winced as he opened his eyes on to a dimly lit den. The smell was overwhelming. Earth, damp stale air, bitter herbs, mouldy clothes, sweet ripe fruit, old washing powder. He groaned as he attempted to lift his leaden head, but it wouldn't move. His stomach contracted and he felt as if he was about to heave, yet there was nothing left in his gut to vomit up. How long had he been here?

'Red leaves for your sore head, rest now, here's a comfy bed. Gave me a shock, poor old crock, hurt your head, thought you were dead.'

Zak tried to speak, but his mouth was dry and cracked. Elder tilted his head gently forward and offered him sips of water out of a jam jar.

'Now, now, Crystal! Stop your grizzling. Green-eyed monster got you? Didn't I tell you? Earthstars are coming in to land now. This one fell straight out of the sky, didn't you? Half the night it took, to drag you back to Elder's. Look! Had to make a stretcher to pull you in. You're thin, but even so you're too big a load for me to carry!'

Zak moaned and turned his head to the other side, where the blank-eyed Crystal stared back at him.

Chapter Twenty-Four

Aisha was woken by a sharp pang of hunger. Last night after going up to the stream to cleanse and pray she'd been tempted to eat greedily from her store, but she'd forced herself to hold back, eating the cold beans and bread slowly, attempting to savour every mouthful. Afterwards she'd eaten one of Elder's apples. It had tasted sweet and sour at the same time. She'd placed some bread and beans on a dry leaf for the dog too. It had sniffed at the unfamiliar offering and eaten reluctantly. Gradually the warm feeling of food in her stomach had allowed Aisha to climb into her sleeping bag and drift off. But sometime during the night she'd woken again feeling ravenously hungry. As she stirred, the dog jumped on to the end of the bed. She was about to shoo it away but then she felt its comforting heart beat and sat up and stroked its soft head. A streak of light snaked its way across the floor. Perhaps dawn was already breaking. The dog looked up at Aisha and tilted its head to one side in a question.

'Thank you for staying with me,' she whispered. It was strange hearing her own voice after not speaking for so long. Her stomach rumbled noisily and the dog whined.

'You must be hungry too,' she said, easing herself out of the sleeping bag. She gasped as she felt a fine net against her face and an enormous spider scurry down her neck. How had it managed to spin a home for itself so quickly? *If only it was that easy for humans to start again.*

Cautiously Aisha stood up, her eyes adjusting to the dim light. She rummaged in her rucksack for her toilet bag, grabbed the blanket from the top bunk bed that would have to serve as her towel, pulled back the tangle of branches that covered the shelter entrance and stepped out. She had ventured so deep into the wood that she could not imagine that anyone would find their way to her, except for Elder. *I wonder where she lives.* Aisha surveyed the land that surrounded her hiding place and looked up through the trees to the brightening sky. She walked away from the shelter into the thick bracken and weed. Today she would have to sort something out, dig a hole and build some kind of screen around it so that she could not be seen by Elder when she needed to be private. Aisha collected some water in her bottle to wash the floor of the shelter with. She was determined to keep it as clean as she could, with the dog walking in and out.

When she had filled the bottle she took off her shoes and washed and dried her feet. There was a definite chill in the air this morning, but there had been no rain for weeks. She wondered how it would feel living out here in the wet and the cold. She reached up to her neck for her prayer beads and looked around to see if there was any sign of Elder. The woodland on the other side of the stream felt unnaturally still. There was a little flat square of bare earth on the bank that she had swept and cleared and made into her prayer area. She'd created a border of branches around the space like a little garden. She lay her mat down and began to pray, leaning forward and touching her head to the mat. The dog kept its distance as if it sensed that she should not be disturbed at this moment.

Afterwards she felt peaceful and strangely less hungry. She walked back to the shelter, took some bread, triangles of cheese and one of Elder's apples and scrambled to the top of the steep slope from where she could clearly see the sun begin to rise in a deep orange glow. The silver wings of an aeroplane glinted, reminding her that she was still part of the world outside. If she was going to hide away from that world for a while, she would have to ration her food. She supposed that once her supplies were gone, she would need to go back and face Liliana, Muna, Somaya, Mariam and her social worker. She could hear Muna's bright voice in her head and felt wracked with guilt, but she wasn't ready to go back yet. She had already worked out that if she ate only two meals a day, with the cans of soup and beans she'd stored, she would have enough to last her for a good while, especially if she rationed out the cans. She had seen how little food people survived on in Somalia. She could manage.

'Fasting can make you feel humble . . . appreciate every morsel that passes your lips . . . stops you becoming greedy.' Muna's mother had told her that, but during Ramadan Aisha had not had the chance to test it out. It was true that every piece of food that she now placed in her mouth she appreciated in a way she had never done before. She took a slice of bread, and dropped some on the ground for the dog. It sniffed at the morsel as if it wasn't sure, but as Aisha ate, it copied her. *What do dogs normally eat?* Meat, she supposed. It would probably go hunting for food if it was hungry. As she ate, Aisha watched the morning light ripple over the bark of trees, its intensity turning the trunk from the colour of golden sands, to desert orange, to copper red. Maybe fasting had sharpened her senses, but there was no doubt that this morning she felt a closeness to the earth of Somalia. Last night, for the very first time, she'd dreamed of moments in her past that had not been anything to do with war or fighting. Running through her village, splashing in the river, her aunt singing her lullabies, playing with her cousins and sharing a meal together. In her dream all these tiny normal moments had been bathed in the warm light of home, and when she'd woken she had felt a different kind of longing, to close her eyes and sleep again – to go back to that time before the fighting had scarred her memory of her homeland. She couldn't explain to herself exactly how it was, but she did feel closer, now that she was alone in this wood, to her abo and her aunt and to the spirit of her hoyo she had never known.

Chapter Twenty-Five

It was dead quiet inside . . . What was this place? The air was filled with a thick white mist. Zak stared up through the cloud to a ceiling that seemed almost entirely made of cobwebs. Thousands of specks of woodland had caught in the fine threads, as if the web was sieving the air, capturing the tiniest of nature's particles and insects. Zak watched the roof-web sway as an army of insects crawled across it. Through the web he could just make out that the roof beyond was made of slatted branches over which was lain something that looked like a green tarpaulin.

Zak let his head roll from one side to the other. If he didn't try to lift it, he could look around. The room was large enough to stand up in. Its sides were made of sticks and twigs that supported a tarpaulin layer just like the roof. The place was a cross between a yurt and an enormous ancient den. Toadstools, with their smooth white surfaces and dark textured underbellies, grew between the stick-slats meshed together by a layer of moss . . . resembling green velvet wallpaper. Against this surface a wall of sticks had been neatly stacked, reaching halfway up to the ceiling. The doorway was child height and seemed to be covered by a collection of evergreen pine branches, through which a fine mist was swirling its way inside. Zak felt underneath his body and found that he was lying on a thick bed of dry leaves. He scrunched a handful between his fingers and let them drop back to earth, wondering, as he became hypnotized by the floating journeys of tiny white feathers, if he was still dreaming.

He squinted around the rest of the den. To his right a long branch protruded from the side wall with piles of clothing draped over it. To his left there was an old-fashioned metal pram. Strewn around the mossy walls were jam jars, pans, an old kettle, bowls, cups, cartons and a stack of frayed wicker baskets. Zak's eyes were drawn towards a broken porcelain head, the kind that might have been moulded by a potter, broken in the heat of a kiln and rejected. Plants had begun to grow from every orifice of the smashed skull cavity. Zak felt a sharp, piercing pain shoot through his own head and turned away, placing his fingertips on his forehead to find a raw gash of flesh.

He closed his eyes and opened them again. Perhaps he'd had a fall and was just imagining this place. *Walk through what's happened in your mind. Try to remember how you got here.*

Running, I was running through the mud, and children were fleeing and I was following Edwin the soldier and a girl with a blue headscarf. Cat's eyes shining, something coiled around my neck, something tight . . .

There was no order to the thoughts and images that seeped through the fog of Zak's mind. He began to splutter and cough as the damp air settled in his lungs.

'Earthstars come shooting down, falling into Elder's nest. The children are hungry and hurt, must care for them. Warm red leaves for a bed, misty day for a misty head. A little elderberry tincture will make that cough better, clear the throat, and if it won't . . . you can sick it up,' The old woman droned on.

Now Zak had a vague memory of shaking hands with her, and of breadcrumbs dropping on his head. He must be imagining all of this. *Was she some kind of witch who had lured him into her lair?* As she approached him he turned away. The air was stale and thick with the musty stench of her, mixed with a sickening sweet smell of yeasty fruit and mulching plants.

'Now, Zak, take some of this, it'll make you well again. I made it myself.'

Zak? Is that my name? It sounded strange in his own ears. The old woman stood up and rummaged among the pots for a spoon. It was then that he noticed a rucksack leaning against the buckled wheel of a pram. *Is that my bag? It looks newer and cleaner than everything in here.* But he had no memory of it except a vague inkling that he had run away from something or someone. How long had he lain here unconscious? The woman mixed the thick black liquid in the jam jar she held and, painfully slowly, she knelt down and settled on the leaves. Zak's head throbbed worse when she attempted to raise it up. He was desperately trying to follow the dim paths of his own thoughts, when the woman thrust the spoon into his mouth. At first he resisted, pressing his lips closed, but she forced the spoon past them and tipped his chin backwards so that he had no choice but to either swallow the vile liquid or choke. At first he gagged at the bitter taste and then he submitted, helpless, as she ladled spoonful after spoonful into his mouth. *My name is Zak – that's what she called me. If this is poison, at least I know my own name before I die. My name is Zak, my name is Zak, my name is . . .*

She set the jar of liquid down and took a glass pot of something from her pocket and started to smear it across Zak's forehead. His mind grew heavy and he felt a bony arm wrap around his shoulder and ease him back on to the bed of leaves.

'Now, now, no need for you to worry. Seasons changing, heavy mists will settle so you think they'll never clear, but then, my dear, the sun will always find its way through the Elder thicket.'

Zak moaned as he listened to the old woman's ranting and felt her smoothing his tangle of hair with her hand. *I have to find a way out of here. But back to what?* He searched his mind for where he had come from, but the only image that surfaced was of rubble falling on his head. He had the feeling that he had been sitting in a trench with a soldier. *Have I been caught up in some kind of war?*

'Now, my Crystal, your turn to take some calming medicine. Lime leaves for you. One for you, one for me, one for you, one for me. Settle down, my darlings, and I'll tell you the tale of the ancients. Elder doesn't give up without a fight. Break my branches and they'll grow again; fell me and I'll chase the sun in another direction. Wild hair, wild branches, clawing their way towards the sun. No one listens to me, but if they did they would know that Elder was the best of earth-mothers, the luckiest of trees to seed as long as you don't mess with her, don't dig her up whatever you do.'

Zak followed a trail of tiny white feathers that drifted through his mind and felt himself wafting to the ground. Then a cloth was placed on his fore-head . . . *So cooling . . .*

'Elder for beginnings and Elder for endings. Elder is fire, Elder is passion. When the wild wind takes me across the threshold I can tell you all the tales that your mother and grandmother and old mother earth told. I can root things out, teach you what to keep and what to throw away, I can draw the spirits up through the earth. Don't you worry, Zak! I'll write your name and keep you close.'

The old woman took a pile of leaves and began to scatter them over Zak's body.

Chapter Twenty-Six

Aisha lay awake listening to the mice and rats scurry around the shelter collecting crumbs until the dog growled and barked sending them scampering away. Alert to the sound of the rodents returning, Aisha made a rule for herself that from now on she would only eat outside.

Although she hated the sound and sight of the rats, it was the huge spiders that really made her skin crawl; the scrabble of their stick legs set her heart beating in panic mode.

In the morning she found a tree stump close to the stream and made that into her table, to keep her food separate from the shelter and the little area she had marked out for prayer. She rationed her supplies carefully, sharing half with the dog. Some days the animal seemed hungry, on others it hardly ate at all. Perhaps it wasn't used to the kind of food on offer. Still, it looked healthy enough, Aisha thought, as she patted the animal's stomach, noticing for the first time that it was a 'she'.

As each day passed, Aisha dreaded the onset of darkness a little less. She lay on the lower rung of the bunk bed listening to the hollow night sounds of the wood and was amazed to find that they did not upset her as much as she'd imagined. She felt it was because the dog was by her side, acting as her eyes and her ears. The trust Aisha was beginning to place in the animal allowed her to block out the night-time sounds of the wood, close her eyes when darkness fell and drift into sleep.

The rummaging in the undergrowth, squirrels scrambling up trees, the haunting call of the owl that lived somewhere close by and the morning knocking of the woodpecker had become the rhythm of her night and morning.

Aisha's first few days had been completely taken up by caring for her most basic needs. She had made a ritual of sweeping and washing out the shelter, and she and the dog had come to an arrangement about what Aisha had termed 'our private business' – as if the dog could understand!

She had constructed a three-pronged tepee structure out of long branches secured at the top with stripped ivy vine. She'd pierced a hole in the middle of one of the scratchy moth-eaten blankets that had been left on the bunk beds in the shelter. Where the sticks met at the top she pulled the coarse woollen cloth over and tied it on with more vine. With the three pronged sticks splayed open the blanket stretched out and covered the length and width of the simple frame from top to bottom, providing a tent-like screen. When collapsed, Aisha could carry it around under one arm. She could go the toilet, bathe in the stream or wash her hair without feeling that the curious eyes of the animals were watching her – and if Elder should come back she would at least be covered and out of sight. It made Aisha smile that the dog always sat at a respectful distance, its back turned away from the tepee, as if, while guarding her, it did not want to invade Aisha's privacy. Once there had been a sudden scurrying noise nearby and the dog had set up a piercing insistent bark. Aisha had quickly hushed her, afraid that if the animal was heard then she too would be discovered.

Aisha thought back to her first night when she'd been frozen with fear. She had surprised herself that she could manage so well on her own. Strangely, the fasting seemed to have put paid to her constant feeling of hunger. It was as if her mind had taken over and showed her stomach how strong she was. Aisha's hand rested on her waist. Unlike the dog, she had definitely lost weight. She bent down to pat the animal and as she did her head spun slightly and she lurched forward as the wood reeled in a red rush around her. The dog leaned into her side and whined, sensing that she felt unwell.

'It's OK. I'll be OK in a minute,' Aisha reassured her.

After a while of sitting still, Aisha's light-headedness began to pass. *I'm going to have to stop fasting and eat,* she told herself, *or I'll risk passing out on my own in the middle of this wood.*

Chapter Twenty-Seven

'Zak Johnson, the twelve-year-old son of an eminent historian father and a war-correspondent mother, went missing from his home in London three days ago. Police are making extensive investigations into the reasons behind this disappearance. Members of the public are requested to report any sightings of the boy . . .' A photograph of Zak popped up on the screen.

Liliana jumped up off the sofa and leaned in closer to the TV. This was the boy she had seen just a few days ago, the one she'd given the leaflets to . . . the one who lived up the road. *What* was going on? She watched the interviewer talk to Zak's father, who was appealing for his son's safety. How was it that two children could go missing from the same street and one of them attracted national news coverage while the search for the other seemed already to have spluttered to a standstill? Liliana stared at the TV screen. Now the news switched to images of children caught in the Syrian conflict. She held her hand over her mouth as the camera panned over a sea of orphaned children. How could this one boy's life be so important and yet all these children's lives be worth so little?

It was not in Liliana's nature to be bitter, but at this moment she felt that she, like these children, was powerless. She switched off the TV, made herself a cup of tea and sat down at her table where Aisha's story book still lay open. The blank pages stared at her accusingly. Her hands began to shake as she touched the paper. Would Aisha's accusatory letter be the last entry?

In the week since Aisha had been missing, time seemed to have slowed for Liliana, however much her own children rallied around her she could not take her mind off her missing foster daughter. She picked up the local paper. On the front page was a photo of the homeless girl she'd seen sitting outside Kalsis Woodland Store. The girl was holding up a sketch of a dog.

Red dog missing. *Big Issue* seller broken-hearted. Reward offered by Mr and Mrs Kalsi

the headline read. Tears rolled down Liliana's face as she hunted around for the previous week's paper and the photo of Aisha they had featured on page thirteen,

Liliana's least favourite number. She had tried not to let such superstitious notions enter her head, but still there was no news. She'd phoned the paper every day, struggling to persuade them to update the story, to keep the search for Aisha alive, but this was the best that they had offered. Now seeing this photo of a missing dog pasted over the front page made Liliana's blood boil. She wiped away her tears roughly and felt the outrage burn her insides.

Come on, Liliana. Where's that fight of yours? She spurred herself on. She had fought hard as a single mother, and as a foster-carer for children who had nothing. She had always done what she could for those who came into her orbit. Perhaps she could do nothing for those orphan children on the news, but she would fight for her Aisha. *I will not stop until Aisha's face is on the television screen next to that boy's. What makes them so different? She's as wanted as him. We are neighbours after all.*

154

Chapter Twenty-Eight

It was on the third day that Aisha had first spotted the pair of tiny birds climbing up and down the pine tree opposite the shelter. What had caught her eye was the streak of blue that spanned their heads and neck.

She'd watched them for hours as they searched for insects in the tree hollows. They were such pretty, plump little birds. It looked as if their eyes were edged with a long sweep of black liner. For the first time this morning they had not flown away when she came out of the shelter and Aisha had watched them hopping down the pine's trunk head first like tiny blue-backed acrobats, calling out to each other in their high-pitched little voices. She knew it was ridiculous, but the birds seemed so comfortable in her presence now that it felt as if they had befriended her along with the dog.

Aisha picked up the pile of conkers that she'd taken to collecting – one for each day she'd been in the wood. She shined them up, and counted them out again. Was it really possible that she had been here for seven nights already? Now that she had got to grips with the routine of living here, the tiny blue-backed birds, the rich colours of autumn and the companionship of the dog were starting to make her feel protected by the wood.

These animals had come to her side and seemed to want to stay. She felt around the dog's neck, but there was no collar. It seemed right, now that they had befriended each other, to give it a name.

'You're the same colour as this, so I'll call you "Conker",' Aisha announced, throwing one up the hill for the dog to retrieve. It returned and dropped it at her feet. Aisha had come to love the way the red dog leaned into her. She bent down and smoothed her hand over its dome-shaped head and her silken floppy ears. She was surprised to discover that the salmon-pink insides were as soft as velvet.

Aisha found herself hugging the dog, its tail batting hard against the earth as she did so. *This is a very simple relationship: I trust you, you trust me. I love you, you love me. I lean on you, you lean on me.* How clear did it sound? But she had trusted and loved her foster-mother, and yet Liliana had been willing to let her go. She had trusted her abo too, when he'd told her that one day they would be reunited, and still, after all this time, he had not come to find her.

Aisha placed her head next to Conker's, and whispered into the dog's ear. *I lean on you, you lean on me.*

Chapter Twenty-Nine

Liliana took a deep breath and prepared herself to meet Zak's mother and father. It had only taken the few steps up the road for her to lose the resentment she'd felt towards the boy and his family when she'd watched the news. As she walked along Linden Road she remembered Zak's gentle face, his concern over the homeless woman in the wood, and how he'd handed out leaflets of Aisha which she'd seen posted up at the Kalsis' and all over the area. *This isn't about how influential his parents are compared to me, or politics or power for goodness sake. It's about two vulnerable young people missing from the same street.* She knew only too well that Zak's parents, like her, would be in hell every second of the day and night that their child was not at home. So Liliana took a deep breath, steadied herself, rang the bell and then stepped back as she heard someone running headlong towards the door.

'Zak! Zak, is that you?' The silhouette of a small figure appeared through the intricate stained-glass panelling. Even though Liliana could see the woman, she got the feeling that she was being monitored through the screen of the state of the art intercom. She wasn't at all sure how something like this worked.

'No, sorry, my name's Liliana. I live up the road. I came about Zak. I've met him once or twice . . .'

The door was flung open by a woman in a pale green sari who now grabbed hold of Liliana's arm with surprising force.

'Where? Where did you see him? What day was this?'

It took Liliana a long time to get the woman to understand her reason for calling round. When she finally managed to explain why she'd come, she grew calmer.

'So you are a carer too. My name is Shalini. Sorry to meet in these circumstances. But how can this happen?' she cried, wringing her hands so tightly that Liliana found herself reaching out and touching her arm to comfort her.

'I have my own son back home. Now I feel as if I have failed everyone. You know, I love Zak like he was my own boy.'

Liliana *did* know. She nodded slowly as the deep well of her own sadness threatened to overwhelm her again.

'And have you heard, his mother's missing too?' Shalini placed her hand on her head as if she could not take in the words that she herself was speaking. 'The only good is that she knows nothing about this.' Shalini shook her head sadly and bit her bottom lip. 'I think that was the final straw for him. The poor boy was so desperate to see her, and then at the last minute she was caught up in some trouble – we don't really know.'

'Sorry, I don't understand . . .' Liliana interrupted.

'No, no, *I* am sorry. I am not making any sense!' Shalini took a deep breath. 'Zak's mother is Jessica Johnson – maybe you have seen her on the news? Reporting from war zones mostly . . . She's in Syria right now.'

Liliana thought that she might recognize the name. An image of a thin, strained-looking woman with cropped hair and a soft Scottish accent came to mind.

'I can't believe this – mother and son missing at the same time. Lucas, Zak's father, has come back to UK. He's talking to press about Zak and waiting for news of Jessica at the same time. Poor man.'

'Doesn't he live here?' Liliana asked.

'New York. They're divorcing,' Shalini explained.

Liliana nodded. It was hard to take it all in. *How could people's lives have got so complicated?* But then her own marriage had not worked out either. She sighed as she remembered those faraway turbulent times. She longed for the peace and simplicity of her flat, sitting at her little table with Aisha and sticking photos in her story book. Seeing Shalini so upset made her falter – but she knew she must persevere to see if this family could bring their influence to bear in the search for Aisha. Perhaps *they* could do what she had failed to and make the media cover this simple human story of two missing children from the same street.

It was after midnight when Liliana finally left, with Shalini's assurance that she would tell Lucas about Aisha and try to get a journalist to pay her a visit.

The two women hugged on the doorstep, holding each other tightly, as if they both feared falling if one of them let go.

Chapter Thirty

Aisha tried to give Conker the 'wait', 'come here', and 'sit' orders in Somali and English. When she spoke to the dog in Somali it tilted its head from one side to the other as if desperately trying to work out what was being demanded of it. Aisha supposed that Conker might feel like *she* did when she'd first started learning English and people would fire streams of words at her that she couldn't decipher. It had sometimes taken her ages to pick out enough to piece together what was being said. She remembered feeling as confused in those moments as Conker looked now. But the animal that had once made Aisha shrink away in fear now made her laugh, and the sound of her own laughter eased her sense of being alone.

I'll stay here until the food runs out, and if they find me before that, I'll go back to Liliana. By then maybe she'll understand how much I need her. Aisha stroked Conker's head as the dog burrowed her soft pointy nose under her arm. *I swear this dog understands just how I feel. If*

Liliana appeared right at this moment, Aisha would run and burrow into her too. *How can I love anyone new the way I love Liliana?* Aisha spoke her question out loud. Conker lifted her head and stared up at her. Was she trying to tell her something? She knew it was possible to go from fear to trusting and eventually to love, as she had with Liliana but she had no energy left to do that all over again. For the first time the thought came to Aisha how hard it must have been for Liliana to suggest the adoption.

She climbed on to the roof of the air-raid shelter, walked up the small slope to the stream and studied her shifting reflection in the flowing water.

Chapter Thirty-One

Zak opened his eyes and stared around the den. It was quiet and peaceful here now. He felt as if someone had removed a great burden from him. He shook his head again in an attempt to assemble his thoughts into some kind of order. Now he could piece it all together more clearly – he had run away into the wood and somehow got hurt. That homeless woman – Elder – must have found him and brought him here. But where was she now? He sat up warily and was relieved to find that his head no longer ached. He held his hand up to his forehead. When had she put the bandage on? Some details were beginning to come back to him now. Had she been here last night, or maybe this morning, or one or two days ago . . . ? Time had concertinaed confusingly. His last memory was of her forcing him to drink a bitter-tasting medicine. He remembered what had passed through his head as she'd ladled it into his mouth. *I may never wake up again.* He scanned the den, looking past a washing line of pegged-out doll's clothes. *She must be crazy.* Then, under the washing line, he recognized his rucksack. How weird that he knew that this bag was his even though he still couldn't manage to connect his own name to himself. The old woman had told him that he was called Zak, and yet the name seemed to float somewhere out of reach refusing to belong. *Whoever I am, and whoever she is, I have to get out of here, before she comes back.*

Chapter Thirty-Two

Liliana peered at the photos on the noticeboard. Mrs Kalsi had cut out the article about Zak from the national paper and pasted it up next to the piece on Aisha and the one about the homeless girl's missing dog.

Mrs Kalsi joined Liliana and placed a comforting arm around her shoulders. 'What a business. Two lost children, and the dog too. I was saying to Ashok only yesterday, this whole thing–' Mrs Kalsi pointed to the posters – 'it has unsettled us all, you know?'

Liliana nodded, but continued to stare at the image of Aisha as if concentrating on her picture could bring her back.

'But what am I thinking? You look so pale. Come, Liliana, why don't you sit for a moment and take some tea?' Mrs Kalsi indicated the little metal table and two chairs on the pavement. The ones she'd bought so that Iona wouldn't have to sit on the ground to sell her magazines. But Mr Kalsi joked that his wife spent so much time sitting and nattering with her friends that they should just open a cafe and be done with it! Mrs Kalsi still remembered the day she had set out the table and chairs and invited Iona to make this her pitch.

'I don't need all this! I'm happy to sit on the floor,' Iona said.

'But you need to look professional; you are doing business and this is your place of work,' Mrs Kalsi insisted. Iona surprised her by jumping up and placing a kiss on her cheek.

Mrs Kalsi had never spoken of it to anyone, but that was the first time she had felt a motherly affection for the girl begin to grow inside her. So what if it was because she had never been blessed with children of her own? What did it matter *why* she felt this warmth towards this awkward, lost girl? On that day of setting out the table and chairs she had decided that no matter how difficult Iona was, she would try to help her whenever she could.

'I thought I would go for a walk in the woods and see if I can find that old homeless woman.' Liliana sighed. 'You never know – she might have seen Aisha.'

'Elder? It's possible. She'll be coming to see me soon to pick up her poppies. Always does at this time of year. Poppies, pins and gold pens. Don't ask me why – never tells me what they're for no matter how many times I ask – but always she has to have the same metallic gold ones, medium tips. Very particular about everything!' Mrs Kalsi laughed and made a precise little gesture joining her thumb and first finger together as she twisted her hand this way and that. 'Same with poppies. She says no red poppies for her, only white will do. Usually we get just a few for Elder and the traditional red to sell at the till, but actually Ashok is stocking a box of both this year. He likes to debate the difference in meaning of the white and red poppies with customers. The other day I came in and he was telling how his Sikh 'brothers' fought in both world wars! I said, "Ashok, they only come to buy milk and bread!" "That is where you are wrong," he tells me. "Man cannot live on bread and milk alone!" "Well," I say, "if you would stop talking, they might buy something else too!" Only thing he could think to answer was "That is rich coming from you, my dear!"'

Liliana smiled. It always made her feel a little better, coming to talk to the Kalsis.

'I'm the one who hennas Elder's hair for her, you know. She's been coming for my hairdressing services since the 1970s!'

'You're joking!'

'No joke. She won't stay in the homeless shelter. Says she cannot stand to be inside concrete walls, so I do what I can for her, you know? I found out years ago she liked my henna treatment, so when she comes I clear the creepy-crawly lice and sometimes she even lets me near her feet if I use the special elder balm she brings me. Surprisingly good for hard old feet like mine.'

'Don't! You're making me itch with your talk of lice!' Liliana groaned and began to scratch her own head. 'But you're a saint, Mrs Kalsi! I could do with some of that henna and foot balm myself . . .' Liliana sighed, running her hands through her own wiry hair.

'No! No! No saint!' Mrs Kalsi protested, biting into a slice of flapjack. 'Only simple woman with sweet tooth, who likes to help a little – that's me!' She grabbed hold of one of several rolls of fat around her stomach and laughed.

Liliana joined in, though it was obvious that Mrs Kalsi was only trying to distract her from her misery.

'Don't you worry. I'll ask Elder if she's seen your Aisha. I'm telling you, I have a positive feeling. How do these New Age people say? Good vibes, isn't it.'

Liliana squeezed Mrs Kalsi's hand. 'It makes me feel ashamed – a woman of Elder's age without a roof over her head.'

Mrs Kalsi rested her head slowly from one side to the other in a gesture that seemed to say that she didn't quite agree. 'What is Elder's age? I don't know. She is offered shelter, but she says she cannot live inside. What to do? And how do you know she doesn't have somewhere she calls home?' Liliana smiled. Mrs Kalsi's best stories always started with questions. 'Elder was the first person through our door the day we opened. I remember it like yesterday. She came into the shop and asked for "green tarpaulin". Ashok only had blue in the back room. He said, "I'll give it you for nothing," but she insisted only green would do!' Mrs Kalsi knocked her hand against her head in mock-frustration. 'We were crazy busy setting up the shop so I told Ashok to tell her this is not a hardware store, beggars can't be choosers, nah? But he got it into his head that if he did as she wished, then our business would be blessed. How could I argue with that?'

'With difficulty!' Liliana laughed.

'Exactly, so off Ashok went to buy green tarpaulin, and next time Elder came in he gave it to her. She was *so* happy! We asked her where she was taking it, but she started chanting and didn't say. We think she's got a home somewhere around here. Maybe in the woods.'

Liliana also remembered when Mr and Mrs Kalsi had opened their store. She was already bringing up her own girls alone by then and the couple had been so kind. Later they had taken the time to get to know every one of Liliana's foster-children, and once Mrs Kalsi had even asked Liliana how she might go about fostering herself. The couple were so much part of this community now, she couldn't imagine the area without them.

'I'll ask Iona. That girl's out all day and night roaming the streets, looking for her dog. You never know – she might come across her.' Mrs Kalsi pointed to the faded chalk drawing of Red. 'It's worth a try – though this girl can be a little rude, you know. But how do you say – her bark is worse than her bite.' She laughed but Liliana's heart felt too heavy to rally.

Mrs Kalsi went on. 'I've sent the picture she drew of her dog for the missing poster into the Royal Academy exhibition. Little naughty of me, I know, but how can she understand how a life can turn around if she won't accept any help?' She placed a finger to her lips. 'But don't say a thing to her – she has no confidence in herself.' She nodded to Iona, who was straggling along the pavement towards them smoking a cigarette.

'No luck finding Red?' Mrs Kalsi called out to her.

Iona shook her head dejectedly and drew deep on her cigarette.

'Why are you spoiling young lungs with this poison?' Mrs Kalsi tutted.

'*You* sell them!'

'Not to you, and *never* to children!' Mrs Kalsi looked outraged at the suggestion.

'Well, I'm not a child, am I?'

'You're not an adult either,' Mrs Kalsi told her.

'I'm nineteen!' Iona replied, sticking out her pierced tongue.

'Hah! So you say! You know I don't believe this – you are making up as you go . . .' Mrs Kalsi shook her head. 'How old are you actually?'

Iona shrugged. 'What does it matter?'

'It matters OK. Why don't you tell the police you are just a child? Then they will make sure you are looked after.'

'I don't *need* to be looked after! Get off my case, will you?' Iona ground the butt into the pavement.

Mrs Kalsi walked inside the shop, muttering. 'I know *I* need to be looked after. Mr Kalsi too – isn't that so, Ashok?'

'Whatever you say, Mala!' Mr Kalsi's laughter reached them outside the shop before his wife reappeared with a dustpan and brush, a sandwich and a carton of juice.

'What makes you so different?' she asked.

Iona didn't answer but reached for the sandwich. Mrs Kalsi indicated the cigarette stub and handed her the dustpan and brush instead. Iona sighed and swept the little bit of pavement.

'Now go wash your hands,' Mrs Kalsi ordered. Iona raised her eyes to the sky and disappeared into the shop, grumbling under her breath and almost colliding with Mr Kalsi as he came out and placed an extra chair at the table. When Iona returned, she grabbed her sandwich and drink and sat cross-legged on the pavement, leaving the chair empty. As she ate, she traced her fingers over what was left of her chalk drawing.

'Sorry about your dog going missing,' Liliana said quietly.

The girl looked up at Liliana and sneered. 'What do you care?'

Mrs Kalsi tapped Iona on the shoulder. 'Don't you speak to my friend like that, madam! You're not the only one with troubles.' Mrs Kalsi pointed to the picture of Aisha in the window. 'Her child is missing.'

'Not much like you, is she?' Iona laughed. Liliana flinched at the harshness of the girl. She had never seen so many piercings in one ear, but it was the ones through the tongue and lips that made her feel queasy. *Still,* Liliana thought, *the pain of getting those done was probably child's play compared to what she's suffered.*

'I'm her foster-mother,' Liliana explained.

'So you don't *have* to care then,' Iona snapped back.

'I don't *have* to, but I do. Just like Mrs Kalsi here looks out for you.' Liliana watched the expression on Iona's face soften.

'Fair play. I'll keep an eye out.'

'And for the boy too,' Mrs Kalsi asked, pointing to Zak's picture.

Iona stared at the photograph of Zak and frowned.

'What am I now – Kiddie's Neighbourhood Watch?' Iona finished her sandwich, jumped up and headed off down the road without so much as a goodbye or backward glance.

'Not selling your magazine today?' Mrs Kalsi called after her. 'Customers will fall off, find another seller maybe . . .'

'No one's interested in buying anyway, not without Red by my side!

Chapter Thirty-Three

A siren sounded and blared on and on. People were running through the woods and a little boy stumbled down the steps of the shelter, followed by an older girl. 'Come on, Grandad,' she called, and a woman guided an elderly man inside on shaky legs. The little boy sat on a bench, swinging his legs.

'Can we play a game, Grandad?'

As the old man struggled to get his breath, he took a small pouch from his pocket and tipped out a ball and some little metal things with prongs. He scattered them in front of him and bounced the ball then gathered up as many of the silver prongs as he could before catching the ball in the same hand. 'Beat that!' he challenged the boy.

He got up, walked over to the wall and drew a line down it. He wrote the name 'Eddie' on one side and 'Albert' on the other, and the date:

4/9/1940

Albert   Eddie

'If you have to play, give our Eddie a fighting chance!' the woman laughed, and the old man seemed to grow sad.

'Sorry, Daddy, didn't mean to upset . . .'

The old man shook his head and wiped his eye.

'Up to ten?' He asked the boy who nodded enthusiastically.

'I'm going to win you Grandad!'

This time the boy threw the ball again, scooping up all ten of the scattered metal objects and catching the ball. He handed the pen to the little boy, who proudly scored his point on the wall.

Albert   Eddie
  | |

'I told you I'd win you!'

'Beat you!' the woman corrected. 'You can play some more after your teas.' She began unwrapping a cloth containing sandwiches and passed them to the girl, who took one and handed them along the line. Eddie grabbed his and began to eat greedily.

'Who's that foreign girl?' Eddie asked, nodding in Aisha's direction. He stared at Aisha and carried on eating.

'Eddie, don't be so rude. Offer one to her. After all, she's gone to the bother of coming in and making the place nice.'

'But she's sleeping in my bed,' the little boy complained.

'Don't you be so selfish Edwin Lowie. You've had good use of it. She needs it now! Don't you worry, my love, you're not on your own. We're here to look out for you. I'm Peggy.

The woman smiled at Aisha and handed her a sandwich. 'Hungry?' Aisha nodded and began to eat.

'What's your name then?' the girl asked.

'Aisha.'

'I'm Maisy.' The girl smiled sweetly. 'I'll not mind if you sit with me!'

'Aisha,' the mother repeated. 'Unusual one that. Never heard of it before have you, Albert? Pretty enough sounding though, isn't it?'

At the sound of Conker's growl, Aisha woke from her dream with a start. The dog was pacing up and down, sniffing along the benches. Aisha stroked her head and hunkered down further inside her sleeping bag. Conker jumped on to the bed and Aisha shifted over holding the dog close until both of their heartbeats returned to normal.

'Did you see those people too?' Aisha asked. As if in reply, Conker buried her head in Aisha's jumper sleeve and whined.

The light was breaking through the evergreen branches that Aisha had placed over the entrance way. She'd heard the cries of foxes the night before and held her hands over her ears to block out the piercing noise that sounded like a woman screaming. She'd become worried that a fox would stroll in as she slept.

Aisha unzipped her sleeping bag, got up and pushed the branches aside. They had served their purpose, keeping out not only the foxes but a swirling mist that now crept freely into the shelter. Aisha peered at the score tally between Eddie and Albert again. *It's as simple as this, I read the writing on this wall, and then started picturing the people behind the names. I made those people up. Conker could have been disturbed by anything – maybe a rat or a mouse scurrying across the floor. That's all. Nothing here's changed* – so why did it feel as if that family really *had* been inside the shelter looking after her, keeping her company as she slept?

Aisha shivered with cold and her stomach rumbled. She threw on her coat and trainers and climbed up the steps sending her line-up of conkers that she'd used to count the days she'd been here flying into the fog. The mist curled around her head enveloping her in a heavy shroud. Conker sniffed at the entrance and whined. Aisha scanned the trunk of the tall pine tree that had begun to drop its pointed cones. No sign of the little blue-backed birds today and none of their cheerful song either.

'Come on, Conker. It's only fog.' Aisha attempted to coax the dog further outside, but the animal refused to move from the entrance as she peered out at the mist-shrunken world. Above Aisha's head dark branches protruded like crooked limbs. It seemed to have come out of nowhere, this damp mist that tasted slightly metallic, like the polluted fumes of the city. Aisha started to clamber up on top of the air-raid shelter to get to the stream, but she couldn't even see her own hand in front of her. Conker nuzzled against her side as she eased herself back into the entrance. The dog's head appeared to be floating on a cloud as it tilted its face this way and that. Aisha went back inside the shelter and brought out some matches. She gathered some leaves and twigs and attempted to light a fire just outside, but the damp had seeped into everything and time after time the flames spluttered out.

'Conker! We'll eat in here today,' Aisha called out to the dog, but Conker hovered in the entrance and whined. Had the dog also felt the presence of the wartime family?

Eventually, painfully slowly, Aisha managed to coax the dog back inside the shelter. She sat down and felt faint with hunger. She opened a can of custard and began to pour it into her mouth. She placed some on a shiny leaf for Conker, but the dog sniffed around, rejected it and lay down. It was a gloomy grey light inside and the damp had penetrated every surface. Aisha climbed back into her sleeping bag and Conker lay down next to her. It felt as if it was dusk, not dawn. Aisha longed to be back in school chatting with Muna, or lying in her bedroom at Liliana's. *It's just your imagination getting the better of you*, she told herself, as memories of her dream bombarded her, along with Elder's words: 'You can share these with the others.'

Don't start letting your imagination take over, Aisha warned herself. *You're in a wood, there's a homeless woman, there are no 'others' and there is nothing wrong with these apples.*

Aisha picked one up, bit a large chunk out of it and turned to Conker.

'Now what are we going to do all day, me and you?'

Conker nuzzled at her side as she lay back down on the bed. Aisha's stomach lurched and she felt as if she might be sick. She closed her eyes and listened for what she had come to think of as the woodland orchestra, but the birds were quiet today. Once, in the distance, she thought she heard someone calling out, and Conker pricked her ears and sat up. But the mist had managed to muffle everything, creating an eerie silence that Aisha now felt trapped inside.

Chapter Thirty-Four

Mrs Kalsi and Elder were crammed into the back room of the shop, surrounded by stacks of stock. In the corner there was a sink. In front of it was a chair on which Elder sat as Mrs Kalsi smeared henna mix over her wet hair. She finished by wrapping a plastic bag over the old woman's head.

'Bag lady!' Elder laughed loudly at her own joke, and Mrs Kalsi patted her on the shoulders and smiled. It was always like this when Elder turned up. Her visits were erratic. For a period she would appear every week, and then with no rhyme or reason they would not see her again for a month or so. Because she never knew exactly when Elder would be back, Mrs Kalsi always wanted to make the most of it and do as much as possible for her. So, as she waited for the henna to take hold, she soaked Elder's hands, massaged them with Elder's homemade balm, and cut her horn-like nails, all the while chatting as she worked. Elder was in a talkative mood today.

'Locked me into my own wood. "Come to the shelter, come to the shelter," they say. "It's nice and warm, we'll give you food and a bed and safety, treat your skin. You're getting too thin, old Elder." Full of advice, very nice, but Elder knows they just want to lock you in. Concrete walls are no good for a Gypsy soul . . . Can't cage me in their shelter so now they're trying to lock me out of my wood, or into it. Lights out, curfew, what a cheek!'

'It's not the way you're thinking, Elder. The police lady told me they've closed the wood for Halloween and fireworks. Only so no young ones go making mischief,' Mrs Kalsi explained as she washed the henna from Elder's hair. 'You haven't seen any children in the wood, have you? The ones I showed you – those pictures in the window? They're still missing, you know?'

Elder shook her head. 'How much is that doggy in the window? The one with the waggly tail . . .' She sang as Mrs Kalsi combed and searched through every strand of her hair.

'Anyway, if the gate to the wood is locked, how did you get out?' Mrs Kalsi asked.

'Elder's no fool! By the Gypsy gate. Found a hole in the fence big enough for little Elder to squeeze through. Had to strip a few layers off. Shrink myself.'

'I was thinking you are looking thin when you walked from that mist,' Mrs Kalsi said as she parted

Elder's long straggly hair, examined the comb and grimaced at the bug that crawled over her thumbnail. She clicked it and sighed with satisfaction.

'True! There's not much of me left under all my rags!' Elder agreed.

'Sure you don't want to take a bath now, put on new clothes?'

Elder shook her head. 'I go down to the stream. Best water, fresh water, shocks the heart, keeps it going, stops it slowing.'

Mrs Kalsi nodded, walked over to a cupboard, took out a clean white towel and handed it to Elder. 'Promise me to come back next week so I can comb it through once more?'

'A promise is a promise is a promise!' Elder nodded sniffing the clean towel as if it smelt of the most delicious perfume, then she hugged it into her stomach and tilted her head backwards into the sink.

After she had rinsed Elder's hair out, Mrs Kalsi picked up a plastic bowl and filled it with warm water, then added a few drops of liquid antiseptic. The storeroom began to smell like a hospital. She took one of Elder's feet and placed it in the bowl, then the other. Elder leaned her head back and winced in pain but she kept them soaking in the water. Mrs Kalsi gently ran her hands over Elder's cut, cracked soles and the old woman's features began to relax.

'Temperature OK? Not too hot?' Mrs Kalsi asked.

'I'm in heaven, just in heaven!' Elder sang without opening her eyes.

Mrs Kalsi smiled, walked through to the front of the shop and returned with a pair of socks.

'Wool for this cold weather!' she said as she carefully dried between each flaking toe and eased the socks on to Elder's feet. 'I bought wellington boots too. Dry feet must make you feel little better, nah?'

Elder nodded gravely. 'Wet and cold creep into your soul.' At the thought of it, she shivered, only relaxing again when she felt the heat of the hairdryer on her scalp.

Drying Elder's hair was always Mrs Kalsi's favourite part. Afterwards Elder seemed to spring to life again. Mrs Kalsi had discovered that if she played old-fashioned music like Vera Lynn and Frank Sinatra, then Elder would sing along and sometimes even twirl slowly around the shop, as she was doing now with her clean, dry, bright-red hair and new green wellies.

'How's baby Crystal?' Mrs Kalsi asked as Elder sang along to 'We'll meet again, don't know where, don't know when—'

Elder stopped dead in her tracks and scowled. 'Wouldn't leave a real baby in the wood on her own. What do you think of me?'

Mrs Kalsi had become used to these mood switches so she followed Elder's cue and changed the subject. 'Cup of tea and samosa?' she asked, and led Elder by the arm through to the front of the shop. In all the years that Elder had been coming to her, she had never managed to find out the old woman's story.

'Oh–hoh!' Mr Kalsi clapped his hands at the sight of the coiffed Elder. 'She's looking like L'Oreal girl from TV advertisement!'

Elder laughed at the compliment and flicked her wild Pre-Raphaelite hair over her shoulder and for a brief moment you could trace in this proud gesture what she might have looked like when she was young.

'Not going to eat?' Mr Kalsi nodded towards the samosa.

'Appetite like my little sparrows!' she admitted.

On her way out, she paused and peered up at the noticeboard.

'You'll tell me if you see these children, won't you, Elder?' Mrs Kalsi reminded her.

Elder stared at the posters for a moment and slowly nodded. She was still nodding her head as she walked further up the road, opened the overstuffed metal drawer of the Oxfam clothes bank and pulled out some random bags. She sorted through them, stuffed a few items of clothing into her own bag and disappeared into the heavy mist of the road.

Then there was a screech of brakes and a man's voice shouting, 'Watch where you're going, you silly old cow!'

Mr Kalsi hurried out of the shop and stood with

his wife peering into the mist. They both sighed with relief when they heard Elder's chanting start up again.

'What does Elder know? Too slow. Elder hasn't seen any children, only Crystal. Silly old cow, grown too thin, lock her in, lock her in.'

Back on the other side of the road Elder bent down, eased a broken railing aside and crawled through on her hands and knees.

'Crawling to standing, standing to crawling, up-up, Elder.' She wobbled as she attempted to uncurl her creaking spine and stumbled awkwardly on to her feet. She seemed to be struggling to get her balance as she walked. 'One, two, one, two, come on. Elder, soldier on.'

Chapter Thirty-Five

Zak stood up a little too quickly, making his head reel and his stomach lurch with hunger. He grabbed his rucksack, pulled the drawstring tight and hoisted it on to his back, then stepped out of the den into the mist. Above the low-branch doorway was pinned an enormous wreath made of hundreds of red leaves sparkling with golden handwriting. The very outside layer bore a leaf with the name 'Zak' carefully written in metallic gold ink. He reached out and touched the letters and something inside him settled. *That's my name.* 'Zak,' he whispered. Now he looked closely, he could see that every leaf had a name written on it. It was as if Elder was marking people out, collecting them. The golden writing was freshest on the outside of the wreath, on the leaves that looked like they had most recently been pinned there. Some of the names he vaguely recognized. 'Aisha.' He whispered the name and a vision of a girl standing in a shaft of sunlight appeared in his mind. Zak followed the swirling leaf layers into the centre of the wreath, where the golden names were burnished and fading. Out of the hundreds of leaves, the name Edwin sprang out at him. *But why? What were wreaths for anyway? To put on your door at Christmas . . . and for funerals.* Zak's spine tingled.

'Elder takes the storm away. Never fear, Elder's here!'

At the sound of her approach, Zak stepped out into the fog and found himself sprinting away from the direction of her voice. Trees loomed out at him like giants. Several times a branch caught him and he stumbled and fell before clambering up again. He paused and hunted in his rucksack for a torch. Had he packed one? Or had he imagined that too? As he ran on he felt as if he might have been here before, following someone through the wood, tumbling over branches and tree stumps. Now he froze as he spotted a man ahead of him in a khaki uniform wading through a deep trench, turning from time to time to call to Zak.

'It's me – Edwin! Don't be afraid. Stay with me now . . .' The young man beckoned to Zak as if he was part of his battalion and it was his responsibility to rally him on. 'Edwin.' Zak whispered the name – that too was one of the names Elder had written on her leaf wreath.

Zak careered head first over a low fence and face-planted in a tangle of brambles, the thorns piercing his skin. Struggling to his feet, he tugged his clothes free, stamping on the sharp clingers till he made his way to a small clearing where he collapsed exhausted. He opened the bag and rummaged for something to eat, found a banana and ate it ravenously. After a few moments his head settled. He closed his eyes and the image of a woman with a gaunt face, short brown hair and pale blue eyes filled his mind. She lay her hand on his head and stroked his hair and the word 'Mum' emerged involuntarily from his lips.

'Come home, Zak. Come home safe,' she whispered over and over again as he pulled his sleeping bag from his rucksack and climbed inside. The wood grew deathly still as if the birds and the animals could sense danger approaching and had gone to ground. There was a low, angry rumble of thunder and then the sky darkened, heaved and released the full force of a torrential rainstorm. Within seconds everything was soaked through. The scent of the earth, parched for so long, rose up to Zak's nostrils. Zak's chest strained and he began to cough, and the cough turned into a hoarse bark that made his chest burn.

'Come on old boy, don't give up now. Not far to go,' the soldier encouraged, pulling him up. Edwin unzipped the sodden sleeping bag, thrust it back into Zak's rucksack and began to scramble his way through the undergrowth. He felt in his pocket for a map that he thought he'd placed there but found nothing. *What use would a map be anyway, if I have no idea who I am, where I am, or what I'm looking for?* His memory was returning in confusing snippets that were hard to piece together, and even then he wasn't sure if what he was beginning to remember was real or belonged to a dream. When he'd packed, had there been a wallet and something wrapped in a towel . . . ? And a photograph. A black-and-white one, he could see it now, of a father and son. But who were those people in the photo? His own dad and him? The rain dripped off his hair as this bizarre collection of – what were they? – memories, dreams or hallucinations began to surface . . . Zak looked ahead at the soldier – Edwin, who was beckoning him forward again. *What do you want from me? Why do I have to follow you?* Zak longed to ask him but stayed silent.

'Keep moving. We'll get through this, if we stick together,' the soldier encouraged him.

Zak felt as if he was about to step off the edge of the world. He winced in pain. *What has that woman done to my head?*

Chapter Thirty-Six

'What's the matter with you, my friend?' Aisha asked Conker as the dog trembled by her side.

Conker nudged Aisha back, raised her head and sniffed the air. Aisha felt a blast of cold sweep in. Overhead the sky growled and a roll of thunder echoed through the wood then out of nowhere the rain began to fall making a deafening din as it drummed on the roof of the shelter.

Aisha closed her eyes and tried to think of happy, secure memories, of her abo carrying her on his shoulders when she was a little girl, of drinking hot chocolate with Liliana and of singing with Muna and her other friends. Aisha hummed quietly at first and then her voice grew in force as she sang the lullaby that her Aunt Lalu had always sung to her when she'd felt troubled. Conker lifted her head and listened intently. When Aisha stopped singing, Conker nudged her again, as if to urge her on. There was comfort in hearing her own voice reach above the din of the rain. As she sang she stroked Conker's back and eventually the dog fell silent and both of them drifted in and out of sleep.

Aisha sat on Lalu's lap as she sang her favourite lullaby. Lalu's voice was deep and gravelly with a break in it.

'Now you sing it to me, baby,' Lalu was saying.

Aisha's soft voice soared with the words and Lalu clasped her hands together. 'You can sing just like my dear sister Amina. Shame I didn't inherit your hoyo's voice, but what a gift she has granted you.'

Chapter Thirty-Seven

Zak's body shook with cold. His head was a tight knot of pain and, despite the young soldier's encouragement, he knew he could not go on for much longer. But now a soothing song rose up from somewhere deep underground. Zak tried to decipher the words, but it was being sung in a language he could not understand. Wherever the sweet sound was coming from, he was sure it could not have emerged from Elder's rattling lungs. Zak turned this way and that, following the song to its source. He had the feeling he had heard this voice before. As he ploughed on through the rain, the voice drew louder and closer. It seemed to carry him forward, and even though he stumbled and fell often, he felt as if he was moving towards safety.

Aisha kept her eyes closed longing to sink deeper into her lullaby sleep but something was pawing at her arm insistently, pulling her away. She opened her eyes and gasped at the sight of a dog peering into her face. As she sat up and let go of her dream reality came rushing back in. The dog pushed its nose into her side as if to nudge her fully awake.

'Conker, my friend,' she whispered as she rubbed her eyes. 'Why won't you let me sleep?'

She yawned and the earth-mulched scent of the wood brought her back to her senses. Conker whined and the hair on the back of the dog's neck bristled as it continued to paw at Aisha. She reached out and stroked her head to calm her, but Conker only whined louder.

'What's the matter with you?' Aisha asked, following the dog outside.

The ground fell away under Zak. He attempted to find a foothold, but failed and began to slide on his back, water rushing down a steep mud slope either side of him. He tumbled over and over through the rivulets of rain, clawing at the earth. Instinctively he curled in on himself shielding his face with his arms, letting the momentum take him, his head crashing with a pounding pain against the ground until he finally came to a standstill. An image of a doll's head coming away from its body entered Zak's mind. He wiped his face as if to clear away the picture as well as the thick layer of clay mud that now coated his skin. He opened his eyes to find a dog staring at him, panting in his face. Beyond it stood a girl with a blue headscarf and the face of an angel. A name surfaced from somewhere deep inside him.

'Aisha,' he whispered.

Chapter Thirty-Eight

'Ungrateful boy. Why didn't you keep him here, Crystal? Now don't you start your yelling. Sorry, quite right. Not your fault.' Elder picked the doll up and cradled her close. 'I know, my baby. Always by my side. You'll never leave me, will you, my sweet?'

Elder sat in the doorway of her den. 'We'll wait here until the rain stops, drop, drop, non-stop sky-crying.' She lifted her feet off the ground and admired her new wellington boots. 'No more plastic bags for these old feet. People think Elder's an old nutter, lives in the gutter, but Elder sees the earthstars landing. You're the first, my Crystal, then the girl with the blue scarf and the red dog – that's three. Now the boy Zak comes falling into my nest.' She stood up, walked over to the pram, unwrapped something from a towel and inspected the piece of plasterwork, the black-and-white photo of Edwin and Albert, and a torn map. 'That's four lost souls, but the Elder branch bears five leaves, sometimes more. Five little leaves gathering in

Elder's wood and if they stay they'll flower in May and we'll gather their starry heads . . . When the rain has stopped we'll go, you and me, my Crystal and find the last lost earthstar roaming alone, calling for her dog, poor child. Nearly there now . . . just one more leaf to go.'

Elder threw the recycled bags on to the floor and placed Crystal in the pram. Then she manoeuvred it backwards out of her den and on to the rough path. The rickety wheels splashed mud over her clothes and into her face.

'Need a mudguard. Mrs Kalsi made me look pretty, and now I'm all filthied-up, but you've got to get out, not lay about, feeling sorry for yourself.' Elder leaned heavily on the pram for support as she walked.

'Ooh, look at that now! There's my breath-mist, warm breath, cold air, dragon breath, dragon hair!' She pulled her fingers through her long strands and got stuck halfway. 'Elder's leaf crown's all of a mangle tangle again, wrung through the weather-mill.' She pushed the pram up the path leading to the high metal fence that bordered the wood.

'Too bumpy? I'll carry you from here,' she told Crystal, lifting the doll into her arms and scanning the fence for the place by the Gypsy gate where she'd managed to crawl through the last time. The ground was sodden and the wet soaked through all her cloth layers and seeped into her bones. Her head emerged first. She held Crystal out in front of her for safe-keeping as she eased her way out on to the pavement.

'What the hell!' Iona stumbled backwards. 'Sorry, Elder!' she mumbled as she realized who it was emerging from the wood. Elder slumped down on the pavement, puffing and panting.

'The apple doesn't fall far from the tree.' Elder smiled at Iona. 'I've come looking for you!'

It had been a while since Iona had got a close-up look at Elder and she had definitely aged. Every time she saw her and smelt her rank stench, Iona had an urge to run away. If she stayed on the street all her life, refusing help in all seasons, would *she* end up as mad and sad as Elder?

'Take Crystal for me?' Elder asked. Iona did as she was told, sat down next to the woman and listened to her wheezy breath. Iona stared at Elder's skin; it seemed to have sagged away from her cheek bones, as if there was no longer enough substance inside her to fill it up. *How has she survived all these years with just her baby doll for company? Now Red's gone I feel as lonely as the day I stepped off the ferry-boat from Iona.* What had the ferryman said as she had emptied the contents of her stomach into the sea? That it had been the roughest crossing in years. It had been rough all right, and it had lasted much longer than the crossing. That was the day that she'd left behind everything and everyone who had been her world, even shedding her real name

197

and adopting the name of her island.

'Weather's changed,' Iona muttered, looking up at the brooding sky.

Elder nodded and took Crystal off Iona's lap. 'Watch how you hold her head! Need to cup it. Don't you know anything about babies?'

'Not much!' Iona admitted.

The two of them sat in silence for a while, staring at the road. *I must be desperate because it feels better to be sitting here with Elder than on my own*, Iona thought. A tall man wearing a waxed jacket and buckled green wellingtons walked towards them, his golden retriever wore a coat smarter than anything Iona had ever owned herself. She made her usual assessment. What was the betting that he was going to find something in the middle distance so interesting that they would become invisible? If that had been his plan it was foiled by his dog, which sniffed around Iona as she fussed over it.

'Look at you in your designer coat!' Iona laughed as she patted the dog, but she was looking up at the man as she spoke.

'Are you the girl who's lost her dog?' the man asked. Iona nodded. 'I read about it in the paper,' he explained and took a ten-pound note from his pocket.

'I don't take charity,' Iona said, rummaged in her bag. 'Here – buy a copy of the *Big Issue*.'

'Keep it!' the man said, offering the cash to Iona again.

She clenched her fist and refused to take it. With the other hand she thrust the magazine towards him once more. 'Take it!' she ordered.

'I don't want it!' he said, still holding out the ten-pound note.

'Why not? You might learn something!' Iona sneered.

'Suit yourself!' The man shrugged and went to put the money back in his pocket, but before he could, Elder reached up and grabbed it.

'Get a warm meal inside you both,' waxed-jacket man mumbled, and for a brief second he let his eyes rest on Elder and her doll. A look of pity swept over his face. *Perhaps I was wrong about you after all*, Iona thought as she took in the expression of genuine compassion. 'It's turning nippy now,' he said, and off he walked.

'As if *we* don't know how cold it is! Hurry along now. You go back to your comfy house and sit by your fire!' Iona shouted after him, and the man's pace quickened as he walked up the hill. Elder chuckled, turned the ten pounds over in her hands in disbelief and started to crawl back through the fence.

'Where you going with that?' Iona asked Elder's backside as she started to ease herself through the railings. 'That's half mine!'

199

'Woof! Woof! Woof! Woof!' Elder barked, wiggling her bottom and squeezing her way through the hole in the fence.

'What are you doing that for, you mad old bat?'

'Mad old bat? This mad old bat knows where your dog's at!'

'What?! You know where Red is? You've seen Red?' Iona squeezed through the fence after Elder. 'Have the money. What do I care?'

'Come on, Crystal, don't you cry, someone singing an old lullaby.' Elder had reached the pram. She placed the doll in it and began to wheel her slowly back through the wood. It seemed to Iona to take hours as she followed Elder along her bumpy paths listening to her chunter on and on. The old woman seemed frailer than Iona had seen her before. 'Hear that? Haven't I had enough of tears?' Elder paused and pointed between the trees. 'There goes old Hannah, never stops her weeping and wailing like a banshee, tears enough to keep the spring water flowing. Hush now, Hannah, don't you cry, Elder will sing you a lullaby!' Iona peered in the direction in which the old woman was pointing but saw no one. Eventually they reached a sort of den and Elder turned to Iona, her face grey with exhaustion.

'She wears me out with her crying, that poor Hannah, but she knows what it is to die of a broken heart and young, too young. I feel them all you know, spirits past and spirits present. I'll lead you there in the morning. Now Elder needs to sleep.' She wheeled the pram inside the den and beckoned for Iona to follow. Then she lay down wearily. 'All my earthstars in formation now.' Elder spoke through a wide yawn that exposed her rotting teeth.

'What are earthstars?' Iona asked, but Elder, though awake, did not answer.

Chapter Thirty-Nine

'You've got to be joking. This is where you live?' Iona surveyed Elder's den.

'Where do *you* live?' Elder asked, patting the ground for Iona to sit down next to her. Iona had noticed this disconcerting habit of Elder's before; how she could move straight from a raging rant to a perfectly normal and searching question.

'I get by. Hostels for a while, squats, Mrs Kalsi's storeroom, on the street. I'm always moving on.'

Elder nodded, sat up and attempted to pull off her boots. 'Mrs Kalsi's present.' She smiled as she struggled to reach her feet. Iona helped her pull them off. 'Itchy feet, itchy feet.' Elder's voice rose in discomfort as she removed the woollen socks and scratched away at her toes.

'Chilblains.' Iona grimaced in sympathy at the sight of them.

'Bane of my life. I've had enough of walking on these old hoofs for one day,' Elder agreed.

'But you'll show me where Red is in the morning won't you Elder?' She got no reply. In a few minutes the old woman was snoring. *Please, please, please don't let her be making this up just to get me to stay with her for the night.* Iona understood more than anyone how it felt to be desperate enough for company that you'd invite anyone in just to see yourself reflected in someone else's eyes. Iona examined the cobwebby roof. Even with all the rain, this place was still dry. *Good on her. She must have added so many layers to it over the years that she's managed to make it watertight.*

Iona smiled as she spotted the ten-pound note strewn among the leaves of Elder's bed. She picked it up, walked over to the pram and placed it under the mattress. A family of woodlice scurried over her hand as she tucked the note away. She swiped them off. *If in the morning Elder leads me to Red, I'll tell her where the money is. After all, everything in life is a deal.* There had to be something in it for everybody, except maybe the likes of Mr and Mrs Kalsi, but they had their religious thing, and she couldn't be doing with it when they started going on about their everyday charitable acts, why they helped her and old Elder and anyone else who needed them. She could hear Mrs Kalsi now when she had first taken up the pitch outside their shop . . .

*

'So if you don't want my charity, you must *do* something for yourself.' Mrs Kalsi placed a copy of the *Big Issue* in front of Iona. 'You can sell it from outside my shop, if you want.'

To her surprise Iona had found that she actually liked selling the magazine. It seemed like a fair you-have-to-look-me-in-the-eye trade. It was the same when she busked. There was a trade-off that was not just about someone pitying you or salving their conscience.

As these thoughts flowed through Iona's mind she lay down next to Elder and peered into her ancient face. Strands of bright red hair were strewn over the leaves. With all the emotion drained from her features she looked like a mask of herself, as if the real Elder had seeped down into the earth, leaving just this shell of a body behind. Iona shivered. 'Don't you go dying on me,' she said out loud. Like Elder, she had taken to talking to herself. Being so close to this ancient homeless woman was like looking into the future and walking among the broken fragments of her own mind. At least Elder didn't ask too many questions. Iona preferred not to talk to the counsellors at the hostel about why she had taken to the streets. What business was it of anybody else's? She'd had her reasons. But as Elder slept, cradling her doll tightly in her arms, Iona wondered, not for the first time, what had brought the old woman to this sorry state. Iona looked down at Elder's feet and gently felt her toes. They were icy cold. She walked over to a pile of clothes and laid a jumper over Elder's legs and a moth-eaten sheepskin coat over her bird-like body.

Chapter Forty

Conker sniffed at the boy's blood-stained bandage as he lay on the ground outside the entrance to the shelter.

Aisha was sure that he had whispered her name, but he was so mud-smeared that she could hardly make out his features. The dog tugged at the sleeve of his coat and Aisha stared as Conker licked the boy's face clean. Now she knew him. This was the boy who had been in the wood when Elder had scattered breadcrumbs over them, the one who had talked to Liliana at the picnic. Had he come to find her? Aisha bent down and touched his head and the boy opened his eyes. He was shaking with cold and his head felt feverish. Aisha pulled the sodden rucksack off his back. Then she took hold of his arms and dragged him inside with some difficulty, being careful not to knock his wounded head as she lowered him down the steps. She was not strong enough to lift his dead weight so she grabbed the mattress from the lower bunk, lay it on the floor and rolled him on to it. She went out again, lugged his rucksack in and opened it, but everything was sodden. Aisha took her own sleeping bag, unzipped it, placed it over him and watched as the boy's eyes grew heavy. Conker lay over his stomach as if to add an extra layer of warmth. Aisha stared down at him as she unwound the filthy bandage that covered his forehead. The cut was deep and probably should have been stitched, but it seemed to have begun to scab over and was surrounded by a raised purple bruise. She took a plastic bottle of water, knelt down next to him and gently cleaned the wound. The boy stirred and his dark eyes opened for a second, but they seemed to hold no expression at all. Aisha was grateful when he settled into a deep sleep.

How can everything change so quickly? Aisha felt in shock. As the boy slept she began to pray, and after some time when she opened her eyes again she found that he was staring back at her.

'What happened to your head?' Aisha asked gently.

Zak didn't reply, but traced his hand along the gash on his forehead and winced as he felt the wound. He had a vague memory of the old woman smearing something bitter and foul-smelling into it. What had happened to him since he'd come into this wood? He didn't even know how long he'd been here. He felt as if he had been mugged and left blindfolded.

'I'm Zak,' he said, the name still a question in his

mind. But this girl 'Aisha' he knew. As he stared into her eyes memories came flooding back: her look as they had stood together in the wood bathed in sunshine, with friends eating a picnic, her honey voice, his own hands sketching her and . . . pinning a wanted poster to a tree . . .

'People are looking for you.' Zak struggled to piece the fragments of his memory into some kind of order. 'I've seen this dog before too.'

An image of a frightening-looking girl with snake-coiled hair bombarded Zak's mind. 'It's not your dog, is it?'

Aisha shook her head. 'She just turned up.'

'Like me!' Zak smiled at her, but she didn't smile back.

'Are you going to tell them where I am?' Aisha asked, holding the dog close to her.

'Who would I tell?

Zak stared at Aisha and then looked around at the stark concrete walls of . . . *What was this place? An air raid shelter? Had he been looking for this?* The sound of the soldier's voice spurring him on through the driving rain returned to him. The only thing he knew for sure was that he had left his old life behind him. The debris of memories that now floated through his mind consisted of: a familiar staircase, a wall falling, a woman trailing a silk sari through piles of dust, someone walking in a procession with children, a

208

news report, a shouting man on the other side of a screen, a black-and-white photograph of someone in a tweed cap with his arm wrapped around his son . . . Zak shook his head. Maybe if he could sleep for just a little longer his mind would clear.

'I'm not going to tell anyone anything. I think I might've run away myself,' Zak told Aisha.

Chapter Forty-One

'Patience is a virtue, virtue is a grace, Gracie was a little girl who wouldn't wash her face!' Elder laughed. 'Silly old rhymes stay in your head. That one's better off dead.'

'But you promised you would take me to find Red this morning, Elder. You're not making this up, are you?'

Elder ignored Iona as she continued to mix a dark liquid in a jam jar and afterwards pour it into a plastic bottle.

Iona stood by the entrance and read the names on a wreath of leaves.

'Why have you got all these names up here?' Iona stared at the golden writing and started to read out some names: '"Amina, Abdi . . . Aisha, Zak" . . . Those two are the kids who've gone missing, aren't they?'

Elder did not answer.

'Who *are* all these other people, anyway?' Iona turned around and waited for a response as Elder mixed her foul smelling liquid.

'All my earthstars at one time or another! The ones I look out for.' Elder pointed to a leaf and Iona traced her fingers over the letters of her own name. She turned over the leaf next to it and found 'Red'. Her cheeks warmed as she flushed with hope and happiness.

'So here we are!' Iona laughed. 'Some good it's done us!'

'Give it time. Now, this should do the trick . . .' Elder said, screwing a lid on the bottle.

'Is Red ill?' Iona's voice was full of concern.

'Don't you worry. Red's in fine health.' Elder smiled at Iona and took a glug of the liquid herself. She shook her head and pulled a face as she swallowed.

'Bitter, bitter brew!' She shuddered and then coughed to clear her throat.

As they walked through the wood Elder seemed to retreat into her own world, singing and chanting as she went. Occasionally she would rummage in her pouch, scatter breadcrumbs to the winds and laugh as the birds flew down and greeted her in a noisy welcome.

'The rain has gone, my lovelies, and we're all more chirpy now!' Elder chatted on as two little blue-backed birds settled right next to her. They seemed almost tame.

'There you are, my nuthatches. Been keeping one

of my earthstars company? Little blue veils for your heads too. Treasures, aren't they? Never lose their balance, not like old Elder, always toppling over these days!'

It was enough to drive Iona mad. The more Elder trailed around, delaying the moment when she could be reunited with Red, the more full of rage Iona grew. Part of her felt sorry for the woman and the other half wanted to lash out, to shake her and shout at her. Iona hated it when this vile anger rose up inside her because she knew exactly where it came from. Her elbow ached dully. *Is there such a thing as body memory?* she wondered as she cradled her arm where the last fracture had been. The break that had finally made her decide to leave. *Don't, don't, just don't become like him!* Iona willed herself and desperately tried to scour her stepfather's snarl of hatred from her mind. The snarl of rage that always came before a heavy blow.

Elder sat down on a tree stump and caught her breath. She patted the wood for Iona to join her and then looked straight into the girl's eyes.

'That's right. You come and sit with old Elder for a while. We could both do with catching our breath. Now, I have something to tell you!' Elder turned Iona's shoulders towards her so that she had no choice but to meet her eyes. 'Don't be trailing on forever like old Elder. Take your dog and find a home.'

Iona watched Elder's chest heave up and down and felt her armour beginning to crack. *What is the matter with me?* she wanted to scream. Up until now she had made sure that no one would ever get to that hurt place again and here was Elder showing her a crumb of kindness and breaking through her guard. At least when Iona was angry she felt strong, but Elder's kindness made something crumple inside her, and she was afraid that if she started to cry that she might never stop. Instead of allowing the tears, she spoke a name she had not heard herself speak for many years.

'You wrote the name Iona on your leaf, but my real name's Lucy.' Her voice faltered as she uttered the name, as if saying it yanked her back to a past that she had worked so hard to break away from.

'Lucy.' Elder repeated as if she was trying to get used to the idea. 'Tell me, who is this lost Lucy?'

'Just someone I used to know.' Iona sighed.

'Lucy Locket lost her pocket, don't know where to find it . . .' Elder sang, slipping away again out of reach into another world. Now the old woman was struggling to lift her layers of petticoats over a piece of low fencing that led further into a wilderness of brambles.

'You sure we're going the right way? I can't hear anything,' Iona asked doubtfully.

Elder turned, looked up at the trees as if she was

taking direction from them and nodded.

Iona drew up close to her side and took Elder's arm to support her.

She turned to Iona and smiled warmly. 'You think that man with the posh dog thought that we're family? You and me . . . and Crystal?' Elder nodded. The idea seemed to please her.

There would be no better time for the question Iona had always longed to ask Elder.

'What happened to Crystal?'

'Crystal's a doll!' Elder snapped.

'I know that. But the real Crystal?' Iona asked gently.

Elder paused and placed her hand on Iona's hair. 'If I was your mother I would brush your lovely locks, and find pretty clothes for you and feed you up and spoil you rotten. You're too skinny.'

Iona nodded and held on to Elder's arm a little tighter. Here was the irony. She had longed for her mum to fight for her, to take her side, but her mother had chosen the Ogre over her . . . Elder would never have done that. All she seemed to want was a family of her own to look after.

She was off now on one of her nature rants, going on about woodlice and some kind of mushroom she was calling a 'deathcap'. Once or twice she waved to the invisible woman called Hannah she seemed convinced was roaming the woods looking for her children. At one point she bent down and pointed out a strange star-shaped toadstool that grew from the hollowed-out base of a tree.

'Deathcap and earthstar together. Mark my words – from this tree the spirits will fly. So Lucy Locket, this is where I leave you.'

'So where's Red?' Iona asked, but before Elder could answer the dog was bounding up the hill towards her, barking in delight and knocking her over, tail beating so hard that it turned the earth into a drum.

'My Red! My Red!' The dog was licking her face all over, whining and nuzzling into her. Then without warning it turned and ran back down the hill. Iona heard someone shouting and caught sight of the missing girl she'd passed on the street. She was about to call to her when she remembered her promise to Elder.

'Elder's not a silly old cow, Elder knows, Elder knows what Elder grows,' the old woman was chanting as she walked away.

'Elder! Your ten-pound note's in the pram, under Crystal's mattress.'

The woman paused for a minute and nodded. 'You know, Lucy Locket, they didn't even give me ten pounds for my Crystal. Just came one day and took her away. Said I wasn't right in the head. It's made me heart-sore sad all my life.' Elder sighed as she wandered away singing 'Lucy Locket lost her poppet, don't know where to find her . . .'

Iona was so stunned by Elder's revelation that for a moment she couldn't say a word. Then she called out to her, 'Thank you!' Elder paused for a moment but didn't turn back.

Chapter Forty-Two

Three women sat at the table outside Kalsis Woodland Store and watched Elder's painfully slow progress up the street.

'She's definitely slowing down. I'm not sure she'll survive another winter,' Mrs Kalsi observed with a sigh.

'I can pay, I can pay. I can pay my way!' Elder grinned, brandishing a twenty pound note in one hand and ten pound in the other.

Mrs Kalsi pushed her chair away from the table. 'Well, she seems fired up today! Excuse me, ladies. I have a customer to serve.'

Elder seemed to grow in stature. She nodded to Liliana and Shalini, held her head high and walked into the shop.

'Oh-hoh! Won the lottery then, Elder?' Mr Kalsi asked as she laid the money on the counter. Elder ignored him.

'I'll carry the basket and you can choose, tell

me all you need,' Mrs Kalsi said.

Outside, Shalini and Liliana smiled at each other as they listened to Mrs Kalsi chatter on: 'Good to see you've got your appetite back . . . now, let me see nutritional content . . . Apricots – full of iron, you know – and nuts . . .'

'Plenty of nuts in the wood, apples, plums, blood red berries, Elder's harvest.'

'OK, OK, cans then, with pull-off rings so you won't need an opener. Spaghetti . . . you still got those old pans I gave you? Matches? Candles?'

'More matches.' Elder demanded.

'Soap and shampoo? No, no – beauty treatments are my gift.' Mrs Kalsi insisted and placed them in the basket, along with a box of plasters and some antiseptic cream.

'I know you make your own ointments, but in case you don't have time. Now bread is good, bagels, waffles, yes, very tasty.'

At the counter Elder took a few white poppies from Mr Kalsi's box by the till, then seemed to rethink and grabbed a whole handful.

'Sure you have enough?' Mr Kalsi laughed. 'Oh! I almost forgot – I found you this wind-up torch. We don't need it any more. It might come in useful.'

'Now Elder, are you ready for final comb through?' Mrs Kalsi asked as she reached out and touched Elder's hair that was already matted.

Elder swatted her hand away. 'Not today.'

'But, Elder—' Mrs Kalsi began.

'Listen to what Elder says.' The old woman was shouting now.

Mrs Kalsi had long ago learned not to argue with her.

By the time Elder emerged from the store she was carrying two hessian bags crammed full of shopping.

'Stocking up for the cold weather?' Liliana asked.

She nodded and looked down at the newspapers that were laid out on the table. A photograph of Zak and the girl Aisha caught her eye. Underneath the picture was another photo, of a woman. The caption read: 'Family in Crisis.'

Mrs Kalsi followed Elder's gaze.

'Still missing?' Elder asked.

The three women nodded.

'Elder's eyes are open wide,' she said, rummaging in the top of her bag, bringing out three white poppies and handing them to the women.

'Flowers for remembrance – wear them.' It was more an order than a request.

'Thank you. Do you need a hand with those bags?' Shalini asked, and stood up to help her.

The old woman shook her head. 'Elder can look after herself,' she said proudly, but every few paces she had to set the bags down to rest.

The three women sat in silence as they watched

219

Elder cross the road and turn the corner. Silently, one by one, they pinned the poppies to their clothes.

'Where does she go to find shelter in this bad weather?' Shalini asked.

'Won't tell me. Says she has her places,' Mrs Kalsi replied.

'She had a lot of shopping there!'

'Bargain shop . . . only ten pounds!'

Shalini patted Mrs Kalsi on the arm. 'It must have cost a lot more than that! You are very kind, Mrs Kalsi.'

'No, no, just doing my duty, nah?'

Shalini nodded.

Mrs Kalsi clapped her hands together as if to lighten the mood. 'But this is good news, now that both children have come to attention of national papers. It will be turning point, surely.'

'You will thank Zak's father, won't you, for organizing this?' Liliana tapped the photo of Aisha.

Shalini nodded. 'Poor man – gone grey overnight. I thought that happened only in books, but he really has. His wife and son missing at the same time. Can you imagine?'

'But I thought you told me they are divorcing?' Mrs Kalsi asked.

'Yes! But you know, they are still caring people. If only Zak could understand that.' Shalini sighed. 'My problem is, now he is gone I have nothing to do here.'

Shalini wrung her hands together. 'Nothing but wait at home for news, and take the phone calls from his brother. Lyndon's calling every few hours, poor boy. Feeling guilty for not returning Zak's calls.'

Most days Mrs Kalsi was able to find a way of getting them to forget their worries just for a moment, but today they were both well and truly lost in their own suffering and now she was also beginning to worry about Iona. It was unlike her to go wandering off for so long these days and without her guitar too. Every time Mrs Kalsi passed its battered frame leaning up against her store room wall it made her fret. *That girl's never gone off before without her music.*

'You know the old man who lives next door to me?' Liliana asked.

Mrs Kalsi nodded. 'I haven't seen him for a while.'

'That's because he's been taken into hospital. He hadn't been in the garden, so I knocked and there was no answer. He'd taken a fall. I feel terrible I didn't check on him before, but I've been so caught up with Aisha going missing . . . I went to visit him today . . . but I don't think he's got long . . .' Liliana placed her hands over her mouth and attempted to compose herself.

Tears pricked Shalini's eyes as she stood up and sighed. 'Every year we go to Diwali fireworks together, Zak and me. I am hoping that maybe he'll come back when he sees the sky full of lights . . .'

Liliana and Mrs Kalsi hugged Shalini and she walked away, her shoulders slumped.

Mrs Kalsi clasped Liliana's hands in hers as they watched the younger woman go. 'There is always light in the tunnel. Don't ever give up hope for your Aisha, my friend,' Liliana shook her head and kept her gaze on the pavement. Mrs Kalsi took her by the chin and raised it so that Liliana was forced to look her in the eye. 'Think of old Elder. Whatever torment she has in her mind, whatever discomfort she suffers, there must always be a small seed of hope in her heart, or how would she carry on? You must too, for your Aisha.' Mrs Kalsi reached over and patted the poppy pinned on her friend's coat, bringing a faint smile to Liliana's face.

'Thank you,' she whispered, clasping both hands over the flower she wore next to her heart.

Chapter Forty-Three

Aisha and Zak held each other's gaze. It had been seriously awkward between the two of them, sharing the confined space of the air-raid shelter and trying to make conversation. At first Aisha hadn't hesitated to help. How could she leave him injured and at the mercy of the elements? But then, when Zak started showing signs of recovery, it dawned on her that they would be staying inside the shelter together, and that made her feel as if the little private world that she'd created for herself had been invaded.

Even through his concussed memory haze, the boy seemed to feel her discomfort. 'I won't stay,' he'd mumbled. 'Just need to get my head straight.'

Last night she had taken the tepee construction and pushed it tightly up to the bottom bunk so that it acted like a screen between them. As well as the blankets she'd hung all of her clothes over it so that the two of them were no longer visible to each other. It made Aisha feel more secure having this boundary between them, even though Zak seemed only half aware of what was going on and incapable of standing up on his own. He now slept on a mattress on one of the benches. Conker sat by her feet, occasionally padding over towards Zak as he stirred in his sleep. *I have nothing to fear from him*, Aisha reassured herself.

Even so she had lain awake most of the night, thoughts whirring around her mind. She remembered how happy she had felt that day she'd seen this boy, as she and her friends had shared a picnic in the woods with Liliana. She remembered too passing him on the path when Elder had started dropping breadcrumbs on their heads. All that seemed a lifetime away now. *Is the old homeless woman more than she seems?* Aisha shivered. *Try to think clearly. You can't sleep because of the cold and because this stranger has appeared and shaken everything up. Don't go reading too much into things.*

She felt chilled to the bone because she had given Zak her sleeping bag and even though she'd put on just about every piece of clothing she'd bought with her and covered herself in the spare blanket the damp still seeped into her bones. *The reason I'm feeling troubled tonight is because I've been living in my own world and now I have to find a way of sharing it.* Even the sound of Zak's breathing changed the atmosphere of the place. But she *did* feel sorry for him. It seemed as if he'd been through some kind of battle with himself.

*

In the bright clear morning Aisha had to creep past Zak with her tepee screen and the blanket she'd taken to using as a towel, so as not to wake him. Conker had stayed by Zak's side. The ground was still sodden and slippery from all the rain, and little puddles of water had collected everywhere. Later, as Aisha sat on the tree-stump table eating stale biscuits, she watched Zak emerge from the shelter and stretch as if waking from the deepest of sleeps. He peered around, looking for her, calling out her name but he could not see where she sat. She watched him slip and stumble up the steep mud slope to the rough tangle of woodland. Red followed him as if she was more worried for his safety now than Aisha's. *That is such a sweet natured dog*, Aisha thought as she watched her struggle up the slope to stay close to the boy's side. At that moment she had thought about picking up her bag, walking out of the wood and returning to Liliana and her friends, but she didn't see why she should be forced out by him. Anyway, a part of her was curious to know why he was here.

All he'd managed to say so far was that he had been looking for an air-raid shelter. He'd mumbled something about a soldier he was following and that he'd stuck posters of her face on trees for a woman with grey hair. He couldn't remember her name, but Aisha knew he meant Liliana. In the distance she heard the soaring siren of a police car or ambulance and felt a stab of guilt. It was one thing hiding away in the wood, not knowing what was going on in the outside world, but she had tried not to think about what Liliana, Muna and her other friends must be going through and that the police might actually be looking for her. It was odd that the more she thought about that world outside the wood, the louder it seemed to become. Perhaps while she had been here on her own she had found a way of shutting it out. Maybe that was what she'd needed all along, to close off the rest of the world so that she could work out what was really going on inside her. Above them a helicopter hummed quietly now as it moved away and grew louder again as it returned.

When Zak came back to the shelter Aisha kept her distance from him, but as the day went on she became a little more at ease around him. She showed him: where the stream was, the place where she prayed and the tree stump she used as a table. She told him too about the privacy tent she'd managed to construct. But everything was different now. She didn't feel that she would be able to continue her prayer ritual as before. When he had taken all his clothes out of the rucksack and hung them on the trees Aisha understood that he meant to stay and that she would never be able to get back to the peaceful world that she had created here.

Zak must have read the look of dismay on her face.

'Do you mind if I stay till I get my things dried?' he asked her.

'I don't own the place.' Aisha shrugged.

'Do you have matches?'

Aisha nodded.

'I was thinking of trying to light a fire, just a small one. To dry out my sleeping bag and clothes,' Zak told her.

'OK. I don't think the smoke would be seen above all these trees,' Aisha said, looking up through the thick protective canopy.

They carried the sticks out together and piled them up. Zak took some dry leaves from inside the shelter and placed them between the slats of wood. He tried over and over again to get it lit but the damp seemed to have seeped into everything including the matches Aisha handed him, and the flame wouldn't take.

'It doesn't matter,' Aisha mumbled, and went back inside.

Zak felt that it *did* matter. If he could have just done this one thing he might at least feel as if he was contributing. He stood outside the shelter, not knowing whether he should follow Aisha.

'Mind if I come in?' he called to her.

'OK,' she called back.

Aisha had taken herself up to the top bunk and Zak sat down on the bench near the door. He was restless and stood up again and went over to the wall where his eye was caught by what looked like a score-tally. As Zak read the names Albert and Eddie his head swirled in confusion. These people seemed oddly familiar to him.

'Do you know anything about them?' Zak asked Aisha, looking up at her.

'I did have a strange dream . . .'

'I feel like *I'm* still in a dream.' Zak sighed heavily and his head spun with confusion as he pictured the golden names written on the leaves of Elder's wreath. *Who else had she written there?*

'Why don't you try to retrace your steps?' It was what the therapist had asked Aisha to try to do – unblock her memory.

Zak studied the names in front of him and found himself telling Aisha about his journey through the wood the night before, and being led by a boy called Edwin wearing a soldier's uniform. Zak touched the names on the wall and he had no idea why but he half expecting to feel a heartbeat. Eddie was the name written here but the soldier's name had been Edwin. The names were so close. *You're just grasping at straws to try to make sense of things*, Zak tried to put the names out of his mind. But a black-and-white image of a man and a boy kept stubbornly surfacing.

'I think I might have brought a photo with me,' Zak told Aisha as he rummaged in his rucksack, finding nothing. He caught the sceptical look on her face as he told her about the name he'd found in the plasterwork of his house. 'I think the father was called Albert.'

He was making no sense.

For his part Zak felt gormless and in the way but, looking at these names on the wall, and seeing Aisha again made him sure that he had been drawn to this place for a reason. *But why?*

'Are you hungry?' Aisha asked. She had read the same line of poetry over and over and was no closer to taking in its meaning.

> *'Time drops in decay,*
> *Like a candle burnt out'*

But at least burying her face in her book saved her from feeling self-conscious.

'No thanks. I still feel sick, but I've got food. I must have packed expecting to be away for a while.'

Aisha nodded and turned a page. It felt so odd to hear the boy's voice in here. Zak got up and started pacing around. He picked up the branch of thick pine that Aisha had used as a broom and started absent-mindedly sweeping a few leaves out from under one of the concrete benches. Then he caught sight of something in the far corner. He bent down and seemed to collapse flat on his stomach.

'Is this yours?' Zak asked Aisha, who was already

climbing down from the top bunk. She shook her head as he held a small green drawstring bag. He loosened the tie and took out a red rubber ball and a handful of dull silver objects with pointy ends and placed them on the bench. She sat down a little apart from Zak.

'Jacks!' Zak held the metal objects in his hand then let them fall. He bounced the ball and picked up two prongs that were close together then caught the ball in the same hand. He'd played it once on holiday with his dad and Lyndon.

Aisha examined the names written on the wall again.

'Want a go?' Zak asked, passing the jacks and the ball to Aisha. He noticed that her hands were shaking. 'Are you all right?'

'I have never heard of this game before, but I dreamed of an old man –' she looked up at the names on the wall – 'called Albert, and a boy . . . Eddie . . . playing it like you did just now, throwing the ball up and gathering the . . .'

'Jacks,' Zak tossed four in the air and caught them.

And that's how Aisha and Zak broke the tension between them and began to talk. Not about each other, or why they had run away and found themselves in this place. Instead they spoke of Aisha's dream about the wartime people whose names were written on the walls above their heads.

'It was the kind of dream that haunted me, even in the day. Have you had dreams like that?' Aisha asked.

'I think so.' A picture of himself sitting in a pile of rubble entered his mind. As Aisha spoke about her dream, gaps in Zak's mind began to reconnect. Now he remembered more details: the gargoyle above his school entrance, fighting with a boy, sitting in a library and finding an air-raid shelter on an old map. He saw his own fingers tearing the map from a book. Now his hands were wrapping a piece of plasterwork in a towel and placing a black-and-white photo of a boy and a man in a rucksack.

Zak's skull felt as if it was held in a vice. Aisha's dream and this game of jacks seemed somehow to connect them both to this place. But he was still not convinced that any of his thoughts were real. Was Aisha even here in the shelter with him? Or had he dreamed her up too? After all, when he'd seen her here he'd thought she was an angel.

Zak grimaced as he felt the bump on his head – it was tender and swollen to the touch. Had the old woman attacked him and knocked him out to keep him in her den? Aisha walked over to her rucksack, took out two of Elder's apples and offered one to Zak.

'Elder, brought these for me. Do you want one?'

'I'm not eating an apple off her.' Zak shuddered. 'She freaks me out. Do you know she's got your name and mine written on her wreath made of leaves? What does that mean?'

'I don't know,' Aisha replied.

'So she's been in here?' Aisha nodded. Zak pictured Aisha's name in golden letters. What could Elder want with their names?

'I don't think she means any harm, and she hasn't bothered me, but she did tell me the apples were to share with the family.' Aisha peered up at the names written on the concrete. 'I think she meant *them*!'

Chapter Forty-Four

As Aisha watched Zak sleep, she realized that if his drowsiness continued she might have to find a way to get him out of the wood so he could get help. But he had seemed to grow clearer in the head as the day had gone on so maybe, if she could make him eat when he woke up, he would recover fully.

Aisha climbed up to the top bunk, lay down and tried to read, glancing up to check on Zak every few minutes. He slept peacefully at first but soon began to toss and turn fitfully. Conker lifted her head and padded over to him. To Aisha's amazement Zak stood up with his eyes open, patted the dog on the head and walked out of the shelter in a daze. Aisha had never seen anyone sleepwalk before and there was something ghostly about it, as if a part of Zak had stepped out of his body and was roaming around without him. Conker looked at Aisha, as if to ask what was going on? Perhaps she sensed that the boy was still asleep, because the dog shadowed him as he climbed over the shelter and headed for the stream. The curious thing was that he was sure-footed, as if he knew exactly where he was going.

Aisha followed him but kept her distance. *Perhaps if I don't wake him, I'll find out what's going on in his head.* She listened as he called out repeatedly in his sleep. 'Come home, please, Mum, please come home.' He was close to the stream now and Aisha hurried to catch up in case he fell in, but before she could get to him he tripped and tumbled to the ground. Conker licked his face and Zak opened his eyes.

'Are you awake now?' Aisha asked gently, kneeling down by his side.

Zak nodded.

'You were talking in your sleep . . . about your mum. Has she gone somewhere?'

'She's on the move with children,' Zak replied, as if what he said made perfect sense.

'What children?' Aisha prodded. Perhaps in this place between sleeping and waking he might be less guarded with her.

Zak thought about it. 'Refugees.'

'Where *is* your mum?' Aisha asked.

He shrugged. She helped him up and they walked slowly back to the shelter and sat on the benches facing each other.

'Maybe you don't *want* to remember.' Aisha sighed. 'I felt like that for a long time.'

'Why?' Zak asked.

Perhaps it was because they were sitting in the middle of a wood held in the quiet trust of the ancient trees; perhaps it was Zak's blinkered vision of his own past, and the fact that he might not even be able to take in what she was saying, that made it easier for Aisha to speak to this boy who seemed hardly even to know himself or where he had come from. Aisha looked up at the names of the wartime family who had once sat on these benches, and she had the strangest sensation that she wasn't just telling Zak. The shelter felt crowded with people urging her to speak. 'I'll sit with you.' The girl's voice from her dream echoed back at her. As she told her story she felt as if arms were reaching through the walls to comfort her. She hardly looked at Zak as she began to voice what she had always kept bottled up inside. She found herself telling the details of the horror that she had fled from, how her Aunt Lalu and family had been butchered, and how she had last seen her abo being arrested at a checkpoint – a gun in his back. She had never even spoken to Liliana, her friends or the therapist of the acrid smell that still came to her of burning flesh, or the pure evil in the eyes of the men who had attacked her village like a pack of wild rampaging animals.

After she had finished speaking there was a heavy stillness in the shelter, as if it had become a court to hear and witness her account.

'I'm sorry,' Zak whispered, but he knew how inadequate those words were and he wished he could find others to express how his heart went out to her. His head swam with all the horrors of what she had been through. His mum's face entered his mind. He saw her, as if on a screen in front of him, and heard her voice: 'This is why I go away Zak. *Thousands of children are on the move, some of them wounded, all of them hungry . . .*'

'One day, I'm telling you, I'll defend people who suffer what I've suffered,' Aisha told Zak, clenching her jaw just as his mum did when she was determined to see something through; it was always a sign that there was no point in arguing. Zak believed Aisha. *There is nothing unreal about this girl*, he thought.

'You've made me remember what she does – my mum, she's a journalist,' Zak said. 'She reports on conflicts, in war zones, refugee camps. I think she's been to Somalia.'

'I would like to meet her.' There was a light of hope in Aisha's eyes. 'Maybe she could help me find my abo!'

'Maybe,' Zak looked doubtful.

Aisha waited for him to tell her more, and after a long pause he began to speak.

'She's missing too,' Zak whispered.

'Is that why you ran away?'

'I think so.' Zak still felt as if his own mind was cloaked in a fog that was only slowly clearing. Memories loomed out at him like stark branches piercing through the mist. *Nothing adds up.* I do have a memory of a girl in a blue headscarf dancing and happy and free, but that girl didn't seem to be connected to the story that Aisha had just told him. Maybe he had made that girl up because he'd felt so miserable. Zak picked up the bag of jacks, tipped them out, and gathered them in time to catch the ball. Perhaps he had been meant to find this girl here. To understand that nothing was as it seemed. Aisha was not the perfect angel of happiness dancing through the sun-bathed woods he had imagined her to be.

Suddenly Conker lifted her head and listened for a second, then yelped and tore out of the shelter.

Chapter Forty-Five

'Conker!' Aisha hollered after the dog who was barking wildly, her tail beating the ground. Aisha followed then ducked back into the entrance of the shelter but it was too late – the homeless girl had already seen her.

Iona stared down at Aisha and the two girls' eyes locked for a moment but then Iona looked away, distracted. She had stepped out of sight now, but not ear-shot. *Was she talking to someone?* Red began to trot back towards Aisha and she knelt down to stroke her.

'Red! Get back here!' the homeless girl ordered as she appeared again at the top of the slope but this time the dog did not move from Aisha's side.

'You stole my dog!' Iona shouted at Aisha between clenched teeth.

Aisha's heart was beating fast, but she stood firm and shook her head slowly. 'I didn't know she was yours.'

Iona looked as if she was ready to run at Aisha

and bash her fists into her face.

Zak stumbled out of the shelter, squinting into the light, taking in the girl with coiled hair. He placed his hands around his neck. Now he knew for sure where he'd seen that dog before.

'Well, well, well, if it's not Zak! What a cosy little scene! You look a bit worse for wear!' Iona heard the snarl in her own voice as she stumbled and slid down the slope towards them, her finger jabbing the air.

'He's hurt,' Aisha whispered, holding out her arm as a barrier, as if she thought Iona was about to attack them both.

'What do I care?' Iona hissed. 'Ever go near my dog again, either of you, and I'll kill you.'

Zak stepped forward, but before he could intervene the dog was baring its teeth at . . . how strange that he could recall this girl's name . . . Iona. She took a step backwards. She had never sensed a moment of aggression from Conker until now.

'Sorry, I shouldn't have . . . Red hates fighting. Me too. It's why I need her by my side. Keeps me in order.' Iona sobbed as she clung on to her elbow and crumpled to the ground, defeated. The dog came to her side, nuzzled into her and whined.

'Have you hurt yourself?' Aisha asked, noticing the girl's wince of pain as she clutched her arm.

Iona shook her head. 'Old wound,' she said,

239

turning away from Aisha, 'flares up from time to time. Well, my Red. I thought I'd never find you.' Iona sighed as she stroked the dog's coat. Then her expression changed. 'There are people looking for you two! All over the place. You're in the papers.' She pointed at Zak. 'Especially you! It was on the news and everything. They think you might have been kidnapped!' Iona looked him up and down sceptically. 'Maybe I should trade you in myself!' She laughed, rummaging in her bag and bringing out dog biscuits. She fed Conker from her hand and the dog ate greedily. 'Don't you pretend that they've starved you to death – you look healthy enough to me! Been spoiling you with treats, have they? Let's get out of here, Red! Leave these two babes in the wood to their little game of hide-and-seek!'

Zak felt himself able to breathe again as he watched Iona step away from them a few paces. But Red whined and circled Iona's legs for a moment and then ran back and forth across the short distance between the two girls.

'She had no name on her collar, so I called her Conker,' Aisha explained. The dog lifted its head as if it recognized its new name.

'She's called Red!' Iona yelled at her. At the sound of this name, the dog lifted its head again.

'Looks like she answers to both,' Zak intervened.

'What are you now, the United Nations?' Iona

snapped. 'She's my dog, and you can't take her away from me like this.'

Aisha stepped forward and placed a hand on Iona's arm but got a shove in the chest in return.

'Take your hands off of me, and keep away from my dog too.' Iona's finger was jabbing the air again as Aisha fell backwards.

Zak stepped forward to help, but the dog was already between the girls, viciously growling at Iona.

'Look what you've done! Turned her against me,' Iona said accusingly. Tears of anger stung her eyes as she slumped to the ground next to Aisha, defeated. Now the dog lay between the two girls and pawed Iona.

'OK, OK, I'll be gentle,' Iona promised the dog. Aisha held a hand out to stroke it and as she did drew slightly closer to Iona, as if approaching a wild animal that might spring into attack-mode at any moment.

'I didn't steal her. She found me and just stayed by my side,' Aisha whispered.

'Aha! Sounds about right,' Iona nodded. 'Got a heart of gold, this dog.' Iona pressed her face against the dog's head then wrapped her arms around its neck and it snuggled in close to her. 'Well, *I'll* be needing her back now . . . looks as if you two have got each other at least. Come on, Red, it's just you and me again, girl.'

Iona stood up and started to walk away, calling for

Red, but the dog whined in the entrance, refusing to follow.

Iona shrugged. 'Well, if you take on Red, you'll have to take me too.' And without waiting for an invitation she walked all the way to the bottom of the slope and followed her dog inside the shelter.

Chapter Forty-Six

Zak and Aisha hovered outside, wondering what to do about the homeless girl. Zak sat down while Aisha walked around aimlessly. Iona's anger was infectious, and Aisha felt the outrage rise up in her. *How dare she arrive like this and take over my shelter?* As soon as she'd thought it Aisha checked herself. Since when had it become hers? She was starting to sound like one of those people who went on about migrants invading – they always sounded so simple to Aisha, like toddlers saying, 'I was here first, it's mine, you can't come in.' When she heard people talking like this on the radio or TV, or even in earshot of her in the street, she wanted to scream at them, 'Do you think humans just leave their homes for no reason?' Now here she was starting to think just like them. She liked Zak, found him easy to talk to, so he was *allowed* in, but she didn't like the look of Iona so she wanted her out. *What does this make me?* Aisha asked herself. She supposed that the shelter didn't belong to anyone apart from the people who had once built it, and why had it been built anyway? Because the world had been at war. *It's a shelter*, Aisha told herself. *Surely nobody should be denied shelter.* Out of the corner of her eye she caught sight of one of the blue-backed birds walking head first and fearless down the trunk of the pine. Aisha took a deep breath and stood tall, preparing herself to face Iona. She didn't want a fight, but it didn't feel right that this girl should be able to stride in and take over either.

'Let's go in,' she said to Zak, bending her head to walk inside. Zak followed. The two of them sat down on the bench on one side, facing Iona, who stood up as they came in and remained standing. The dog lay on the floor between the three of them as if unwilling to take sides.

'Let the bombs rain down!' Iona said, twirling around to take in the surroundings of the air-raid shelter. Then she started rummaging in her backpack. She took out a pasty and began to eat it greedily. 'I'm starving!' she said.

Aisha was surprised at how invaded she felt. Zak's appearance in the shelter had been different because his confused state had meant that she'd been able to take charge. She understood how disorientated he was and had felt a sort of sisterly wish to protect him. And she knew what it was like for a parent to be missing too. Even though she guessed that they were about the same age, Zak seemed younger to her. But then she often felt this about her peers. Zak didn't feel like a threat to her at all. But this homeless girl was different.

Aisha glared at Iona as she stuffed in another mouthful of pasty, and felt her anger rise. 'You're not starving!' she said, surprised by the strength of her own conviction. 'You should see what starving *really* is. It makes you sick just to look at it: swollen empty bellies, hungry eyes, lips dry as the desert.' Aisha was determined to stand up to this girl – if there was one thing she knew how to do, it was face off a bully. The expression in Iona's eyes hardened.

'You don't know anything about me! I've been so hungry I've just wanted to curl up on the street and never wake up.'

'Well, you can't eat that food in here! It's haram and the rats will come,' Aisha warned.

'And how do you know *I'm* not a rat! A big sewer rat. I'll do whatever I want! What's haram when it's at home anyway? Does no one talk any sense in this wood? You sound just like Elder!' Iona shook her head and continued eating.

Zak wondered how Iona had become so hard and embittered.

'Where are you from then?' the girl asked Aisha.

'I don't see what business it is of yours,' Zak jumped in.

'You mean which country?' Aisha spoke directly to Iona, ignoring Zak's interruption. She had been interrogated many times and in many ways since she'd arrived.

'You have a voice of your own then,' Iona said, sneering at Aisha.

'Somalia.' Aisha spoke the word with dignity and pride, as if she was talking about a person that she loved.

'Refugee?' Iona asked.

Aisha nodded, closed her eyes and let her head rest back against the concrete wall. Conker jumped up beside her.

'Aye, well, I suppose we're all refugees here. Hey, Red!' Iona half laughed as she peered around the air-raid shelter again.

Zak watched as Aisha's breathing slowed. Was she praying? Or perhaps she just couldn't stand to talk to Iona for a second longer.

He turned his attention to the homeless girl. If it was possible, he would have liked to stare her right out of the shelter.

The girl grinned defiantly and stared back as if it was a game between them. Finally she broke the silence. 'What's up with her then?' She pointed to Aisha, who was so still she hardly seemed to be breathing at all.

'Why don't you just leave her alone,' Zak whispered.

'She's been through a lot.'

'Haven't we all! Join the club! I don't know what you two are playing at in here, but you should go back home. I've seen that Indian woman out looking for you.'

'Shalini.' Her name came to Zak from somewhere deep inside and with it came an enveloping warmth of protection and an image of her in a pale blue dust-covered sari, standing at a front door surrounded by scaffolding. Perhaps it was the scaffolding that closed the circuit in his mind, clicking every memory firmly into place. He saw it all now, played out scene by scene. School, the boy Spite and Mr Slater . . . his outburst . . . going back to the new house . . . seeing Aisha and her friends in the wood, the cinnamon smell of their picnic food, and hunger rumbling in his belly . . . finding the name in the plasterwork . . . the photo of Edwin and Albert . . . the map . . . arguing with his dad on Skype, the report from his mum . . . waiting and waiting for her to come, the wall falling down . . . and Shalini standing there on the doorstep, clasping her hands and telling him that his mum was missing.

'She's Sri Lankan,' Zak corrected Iona.

'Think I care where she's from?! All I know is that she's looking for you and as for her—'

'My name's Aisha.' She opened her eyes as she spoke, then turned to Zak and ignored Iona.

There was no sign of sleep in those eyes, but Zak was glad that Aisha looked calm and strong now. She would need to be to deal with Iona's barbed comments.

'Well, *Aisha*, that woman Liliana is walking around as if someone's pulled her heart out. You should think yourself lucky, both of you. At least you've got people out there who are searching for you, missing you, and never giving up. What have I got to keep me going? Except my temper and a dog that keeps leaving me.' Iona laughed at her own grim state, grabbed the dog close and held her tight.

'It's true what you said before. I don't know anything about you. But you don't know anything about *me* either!' Aisha replied calmly.

Iona nodded slowly, as if she accepted that what Aisha said was true. Zak didn't know why he was surprised to see Aisha fighting her own corner so capably. Perhaps it was the terrible story she had told him of her past that had made him feel that she would need protection. Now that he remembered his own reasons for running away, he began to feel that he should have been stronger. The day that he'd first seen Aisha in the woods returned to him clearly. *How could you have a past like Aisha's and still want to sing?*

Iona now turned her attention on Zak; her grey eyes like searchlights.

'What happened to you anyway?'

Zak did not reply but noticed the hardening lines

forming around the girl's mouth.

'Don't you look at me like that! I'd like to find you a mirror so you can see your own sorry face!'

Iona had a right to be angry about the dog, but there was something in the way she spoke and behaved that gave Zak the impression that she was enjoying the power she held over them both.

'No wonder that dog left you!' Zak spat back at her, as he gathered an armful of dry wood that Aisha had stacked inside the shelter. 'I'm going to try to light a fire again.'

'You do that!'

Zak grimaced. He hated the fact that Iona's accent reminded him so much of his mum's.

'Who d'you think you are – Tarzan? Man go make fire!' she called after him.

Chapter Forty-Seven

Zak breathed in a deep draught of cold air. Why did Iona have to turn up just as Aisha and he were getting to know each other? He felt grateful to Aisha for bringing him back to himself, and he wanted to talk more to her, find a way to help her in return, but there was no chance of that with this vicious girl around.

He had expected Aisha to follow him out of the shelter. He didn't like to leave her in there with Iona. Zak stood by the entrance and listened, but still not a word passed between the two girls. Perhaps Aisha was having her own protest, a kind of sit-in, refusing to be ousted by Iona. What could they be doing in there? Zak remembered how Aisha had closed her eyes when Iona had gone on the attack, as if she could turn her gaze in on herself. Maybe they had both fallen asleep. At least it was calm in there now. And the dog seemed settled enough.

Zak built the fire he and Aisha had started stick by

stick until it formed a pyramid, as his dad had taught him to once on a camping weekend. His memories poured out of him now, as if a floodgate had been opened: the look of pride on his dad's face as Zak built and lit his first fire. He must have mixed it all up in his mind, the present and the past, but something Mr Slater had written on the board at school kept returning to him . . . Zak repeated the phrase as if grappling with the words might help him understand: 'If the privilege of memory is pain, then the act of remembering is love.'

'You know, Iona means blessed!' He heard his mum's voice in his head. 'We could be in the Caribbean, not Scotland. How lucky are we to have weather like this every day for two weeks, I'd say *we have* been truly blessed!' she said as they'd stood on the ferry-boat watching the white sands recede across the sparkling sea. 'Sometimes I wonder whether I'll ever move back home I tell you, I never feel as at peace as when I'm here.'

'Do you really want to come back and live here?' his dad asked his mum, taking her hand as they stepped off the ferry-boat on to the mainland.

'Well! It's not practical, is it, but you know what I mean! Don't you sometimes feel that a tiny piece of your heart's still in New York?'

His dad nodded, held out his long arms and she

walked into them. They kissed, and Lyndon and he groaned at the gross-out sight of them being all 'lovey-dovey'.

It was true that remembering even the happiest times was painful now, but it was better than the blanket of fog that had invaded his mind before. He took a deep breath and walked back inside the shelter to search for the matches. Aisha was sitting exactly as she had been before, her hands on her necklace. This time she really did seem to have fallen asleep. Iona's bag was strewn open and chalks of every colour were laid out on the bench. Zak stared at what had once been a dull concrete wall. Iona was in the middle of creating the most amazing giant portrait of Elder with her wild, leaf-threaded crown of red hair.

Iona glanced down at Aisha.

'She nearly sent me to sleep too with her praying. There's something to be said for it though. Calmed me down.'

Zak looked closer at Iona's artwork. 'That's just like Elder!'

The girl had even managed to capture the texture of the ragged layers of the old woman's clothes.

She threw her arms in the air and released a ghoulish chant. 'Come to me, my earthstar!' she cackled.

Zak's breath caught and he jumped backwards.

'Spooked you! But that's not so difficult to do!' Iona jeered at the shocked expression on his face.

Red was immediately on her feet, alert for any sign of aggression between the two of them. There was a split second when Zak almost turned and stomped out of the shelter, but he decided that he wouldn't give Iona the satisfaction. *You don't suit your name. There's nothing blessed about you,* he thought.

'Spent the night with Elder, so I've got a picture of her in my head,' Iona explained as she continued working.

'I've only just managed to get away from her, and I'm not sure I want the old witch watching over me here too.' Zak shook his head as if to free himself from thoughts of Elder. 'Not that it looks like we've got much choice now.'

Iona shrugged and carried on working, carefully sketching the petals and leaves in Elder's hair. 'And you think *I'm* hard-hearted!'

'I didn't say that!'

'You didn't need to. You and your girlfriend have got it written all over your faces.'

'She's not my girlfriend,' Zak whispered.

'Whatever!'

Zak glanced down at Aisha's sleeping form and was relieved that she hadn't heard.

He remembered now the sketch he'd tried to do of Aisha, and how bad it had been compared to Iona's work. For some reason Aisha had stuck in his mind from the very first time he'd seen her. Was it possible that by focusing on someone strongly enough you could literally draw them to you? He had seen Iona too, and Elder in the wood. Why had they all come together in this place? He looked up at the giant image and shuddered as he remembered Elder forcing the bitter liquid into his mouth.

'I bet old Elder half scared you to death.' Iona laughed.

'And she doesn't frighten you?'

'Only when I think I might end up like her,' she sighed.

'Think you will?'

Iona set down her chalks and turned to Zak. 'I'll tell you what I know. You're in here playing dens, and the people that love you are going out of their minds with worry.'

'So why don't *you* go home then?' Zak asked.

'Haven't got one. I've not had one in years. You know the difference between you two and me?'

Zak shook his head and kicked at the ground.

'Perhaps you'll not want to hear the truth. It's not pretty. Nobody cares enough to look for me, not even my own mum, so now I'm just one of the great invisibles.'

'What do you mean by that?'

'It's something I've discovered. If you live on the

street, you wear an invisibility cloak. You don't know it at first, and you can't understand how people don't see you. Then you watch them and you see how they do it. It's a kind of trick, with no magic in it. They have this way of disappearing you, dissolving you with their eyes. If you're just sitting on the street, they can zone you out in a second.'

'But I've seen you selling your magazine and people stopping,' Zak said.

Iona shrugged. 'Sometimes I do all right, but even when you've got something to offer and they've got no excuse not to look at you, they can still make a split second decision whether to see you or not. I'll tell you how it is.' Iona sat down on the bench and faced Zak. 'They see you a way off, swerve out to the side as if they've suddenly got an appointment with the kerb, and then something happens to their eyes, like they've switched off inside – glazed over.' Iona searched Zak's expression as if challenging him to look away. He didn't. 'Suddenly they're passing you and looking off into the distance, like a white elephant's suddenly appeared on the horizon. Then *phew*! They're past! In the safe zone – I swear I've watched their shoulders relax, as if to say, *Thank God I'm off the hook . . .* – and those are the ones who at least know that they *should* care.'

Iona gestured towards Aisha and sucked her teeth. 'I wouldn't have minded being fostered if I could have been with someone like her carer. Still, at least I've got Red back.' Iona snuggled up to her dog. 'I don't know why, maybe it's the way she looks up at you with those trusting, pleading eyes, but she makes folk stop for just long enough to dip their hand in their pocket.' Iona leaned forward as if confiding in Zak. 'How sad is this? I've tried to study her look to copy it – what do you think?'

Iona peered up through her hair, softened her mouth and tilted her head to one side coyly.

That really is sad, Zak thought.

When the expression on his face didn't change, Iona laughed, a low, scathing laugh. 'See! Told you, not a heart-melt in sight! These are the facts. I haven't sold a single copy since she went missing.' Iona gathered Red close to her in a hug. 'You're my lucky mascot, aren't you, Red? My visibility cloak.'

'Maybe if you didn't look so . . .'

'So what?'

Zak hesitated. 'Tough.' He almost whispered the word, as if he thought it might come back to harpoon him.

'Maybe I *need* to look tough!' Iona said, sticking out her tongue to reveal her piercings, swishing her dreadlocks from side to side and opening her cat's eyes wide so that she resembled a tribal mask.

Aisha opened her own eyes just at this moment and looked alarmed, until Iona's face returned to its normal sullen expression. Aisha's gaze moved across to the wall, caught by the giant image of Elder looming over her.

'You're an artist?' Aisha asked.

'Maybe.' Iona began adding texture to Elder's hair. 'I'm sorry I was so angry with you,' she mumbled under her breath, without turning around.

'I was angry with you too,' Aisha admitted as the dog jumped up at her. 'Hello Red!'

At the sound of the dog's true name, Iona turned and smiled warmly at Aisha for the first time, and Aisha smiled back.

Chapter Forty-Eight

The low autumn sun had long faded in the sky and the air was now bitingly cold. Zak struck match after match but the flame kept blowing out. In the end Iona came out of the shelter and handed Zak her lighter. She cupped her palms around the damp leaves while he lit the tiny kindling sticks he'd placed on the fire floor. On the third attempt at clicking the lighter flint, the flame took.

'I've lit a few fires in my time,' Iona sighed as she watched her breath-mist float ahead of her. She drew closer to the heat, held out her hands and peered up through the trees. 'If you want to stay hidden, it's good camouflage in here. You'd have to build a pretty big fire for the smoke to be seen above this wood. Anyway, plenty of fires being burned this time of year.' She sniffed the air. 'I love that smoked burned-wood smell!'

The three of them stood around and watched the orange, red and purple sparks fly between the sticks as the flames zipped this way and that, searing into the wood. It took some time for the fire to give off any real heat, and when it did a sleepy, contented silence settled on them, as if the fire had warmed them through from the inside out. Red snuggled up between Iona and Aisha. It seemed that the world had shrunk to the three of them and the dog gathered together around this flame. They could be living in any time period. *How many people in generations before us have sat like this around a fire in a wood to keep warm?* Zak wondered as he looked up at Iona's face, noting that even she looked softer in the amber glow. At least she'd made an attempt to say sorry.

Aisha was staring into the fire, her mind miles away. She must have felt Zak looking at her and she glanced up, caught his eye briefly and then followed his embarrassed gaze up through the trees. The moon lit the high branches sending sliding shadows down towards them, though never quite reaching the earth.

A spark jumped out of the fire and landed on Aisha's jeans. Zak leaped up and swatted it out.

'You're quick on the draw!' Iona laughed.

Zak wished she wouldn't keep up this jeering, suggestive chat. It would have been so much better if Iona had never found them. They had been getting on fine on their own. Her constant hints that something was going on between them clearly embarrassed Aisha. The problem with Iona being here was that her eyes darted everywhere. She missed nothing. She was like a random spark: you never knew when she would leap out and singe you.

Iona rummaged in her bag and brought out a bar of chocolate. She unwrapped it and broke it into three. 'Treat!' she said, handing a chunk to Zak and Aisha.

'Thank you,' they chorused, both as surprised as the other at the girl's generosity.

After Aisha having a go at Iona about real starvation, Zak had attempted to stop himself thinking about the constant empty rumbling of his own belly. The thought had crossed his mind that he would only be able to stay in the wood as long as there was plenty of food. One of the feelings he hated most was being hungry and not knowing when he would next eat. He felt pathetic. These were the situations that his mum reported about. People having to uproot their lives because they could find no food or water, because of drought or famine or civil war that lasted, not hours or days or even weeks, but months and years. His stomach cramped in pain as he gulped the chocolate down too fast. What would it be like, day after day, to never know when you would eat again? The chocolate melted in his mouth and coated his throat in a velvety sweetness.

'If you could have anything you wanted to eat right now, what would it be?' Iona asked. 'It's a game I sometimes play to pass the time . . . You could call it torture!'

'Shalini's sambal curry and home-made naan.' Zak smiled as he summoned the smell of chilli, coriander and coconut.

'Spaghetti with tomato, basil and garlic sauce!' Aisha licked her lips as she imagined her favourite dish.

'Chocolate sponge pudding and custard!' laughed Iona, patting her stomach. 'Ooooh, that was good! I feel so full I can hardly move!'

Iona was licking her chocolate so that now it was just a tiny flat slither against the silver wrapping on the palm of her hand. 'Well, it's one way I have of getting by!

After she'd licked her hand clean of chocolate she started tapping her foot and clicking her fingers as if a music track was playing through her head.

'Now we've had our imaginary banquet, how about some entertainment? Shame I haven't got my guitar,' Iona said, then burst into song anyway. '*In this fair city, where the girls are so pretty, I first set my eyes on sweet Aishaaaaaa and Zak, as they wheeled their wheelbarrow . . .*'

She was mocking them, and Zak hated it. Iona was nothing like any girl he had ever met. Her voice was gravelly and strong, filled with a hard survival strength. Even her singing seemed like an act of protest. When she came to the end of her verse she turned to Zak.

'Your turn! It's not a campfire without a song!'

Zak shook his head. 'I can't sing!'

'Coward!' Iona laughed.

'No, really, I can't,' Zak insisted.

'Neither can I,' laughed Iona. 'But it's never stopped me. Except maybe that once when I was busking with a mate of mine and this bloke comes up to us and says he'll *pay* me to stop!'

Aisha laughed and Red wagged her tail and jumped at her in excitement.

'How about you, Aisha? Got any tunes?' Iona asked.

Aisha met Iona's eyes steadily; there was a definite challenge in their exchange. Then she bent her head forward and began to hum. It was as if she was drawing the music slowly up through the earth. *Is this the same song that drew me to the shelter,* Zak wondered. Then the words came. Red placed her head on Aisha's knee as her even voice rose up through the night. Zak was mesmerised. *How does this work? You listen to a song in a different language, and you don't understand a word, but the singer still manages to make you feel what they feel?* As Aisha sang she looked into the flames and her face turned golden in the fire's glow.

He would never have the guts to tell her but Zak thought she was beautiful. Not just her features and the way she looked, but in the way she held herself

262

with such pride and strength. He wished he could be more like that himself.

Red's eyes grew heavy, as she was lulled into a blissful sleep. When Aisha's song was over, the leaves swaying gently on the breeze seemed to be dancing still. Eventually it was Iona who spoke, and when she did, the hard edges had melted from her voice.

'What do the words mean?' she asked.

Aisha thought for a while and then began to translate, singing the lines again under her breath as she went. 'It tells of . . . a kind of deer . . . an antelope that's travelled a long way from home. Every person the animal meets on the way, they ask this antelope, "What are you looking for?" And he answers, "I am searching for my father and my mother." Then the passer-by asks, "But why have they left you all alone?" The antelope paws at the ground but cannot answer. For years the antelope searches, until the day it comes across an old woman walking with a stick. "Why are you always roaming?" the old woman asks the antelope. "Don't you think it's time to let your parents go?"'

There were tears in Aisha's eyes as she spoke, and she waved her hand across her face and laughed at the emotion that had caught her unawares. 'I don't know! It's hard to translate this sort of song-poem. It's just something my Aunt Lalu used to sing to me.'

As Aisha spoke Zak had the oddest sensation of having been here before and then he remembered his dream. How weird that both Aisha and Iona had appeared in that dream of the children fleeing and his mum had been the one leading them to safety.

'Where are your family anyway?' Iona asked Aisha.

Zak flinched at the memory of what Aisha had told him.

'I don't know,' Aisha whispered, but didn't offer any further explanation.

'Well, I like that about songs – how they can take you so far from where you are; sometimes it's good to get away.' Iona sighed.

Aisha nodded. 'Singing that song took me home.'

Zak pretended to be following the tiny bright flames that licked the fire, but he was listening intently to the girls talking.

He wondered whether Iona had got out of the habit of being with people, because now he was beginning to see glimpses of softness and kindness in her. She was not all bad, but he couldn't help feeling cautious, in case she ridiculed him again.

Iona leaned backwards and closed her eyes to listen as Aisha began to sing another song full of chords of longing and wishing. When she had finished, Iona whistled. 'Now there's a haunting song to wake the dead! I'll take you with me next time I go busking. We could make a fortune with your looks and your voice!'

Aisha laughed. 'Why did you say that, about waking the dead?'

'It's Halloween!'

Then it's my birthday, Aisha thought.

'Aye, the spooks will be out all over the place tonight!'

Iona jumped up and clapped her hands and Red leaped on to her back paws and danced with her around the fire. The older girl looked demented with her dreadlocks swirling and piercings glinting. Zak reached up to his neck and swallowed hard. His throat felt rough and sore. *Iona's not a devil, any more than Aisha's an angel. She's just a girl who's had a rough time.* Zak held his chilled hands closer to the fire to warm them.

'Cold hands, warm heart.' His mum's voice echoed through his mind as he remembered how she used to rub his hands together and place them inside her coat. Zak placed his own hand on his heart and felt its rhythmic beat. *Let her be alive, let her be alive, let her be alive.*

Chapter Forty-Nine

Aisha had lost track of how many days and nights she had spent in the wood since she'd scattered her day-counting conkers. So this had been her thirteenth birthday and she'd not even known it. She thought about telling Zak and Iona, but what would be the point? It had not exactly been a party, but it hadn't been a terrible birthday either and, if it felt different to other years, maybe, just maybe, tonight she would be granted the only thing she had ever wished for on this special day since arriving in this country.

No one had made the conscious decision to sleep under the moon, but the fire held them together – as long as it remained dry none of them wanted to leave its heat and comfort. Zak thought of the old house on Halloween, the warm glow of the lit pumpkin on the table. Of him and Lyndon trick-or-treating, greedily gathering sweets and then legging it home and storing their collection in giant jars. He thought of how he would gobble the whole lot down in one go while

Lyndon eked out his store, torturing him with it for the rest of the week. Zak smiled at the memory of his dad going so over the top dressing up for Halloween. It was a much bigger deal in the States.

Now Zak's mind tipped back to this same night only a year ago.

'Dad, it's embarrassing how much you're into this!'

'Keeping the ghosts from our doors is a serious business, Zak!'

'It's a load of rubbish. I don't believe in any of it, apart from the sweets!' Zak joked.

Then, as he walked out of the house, his dad sprang out at him wearing a plain, expressionless white mask. Zak had jumped practically out of his skin.

'Hah, got ya! You look mighty scared for a non-believer!'

Zak wondered if his dad was thinking of him tonight too in New York. As these thoughts filled Zak's mind he noticed Aisha's eyes grow heavy with the heat of the fire. Iona grabbed handfuls of the leaves that had dried out and stuffed them inside her sleeping bag for insulation. His own clothes had finally dried and he began to pile the layers back on, including his coat. Then he snuggled down inside his thick padded sleeping bag, lay on his back and stared up at the giant tree shadows.

The kind of spirits that hovered around this wood were entirely different from the fake ones trailing around the streets tonight. Zak closed his eyes and thought of the first time he'd seen Aisha, standing in a shaft of sunlight; of old Elder dropping breadcrumbs on their heads; of running away from her den and following Edwin to the air-raid shelter. Even though Zak was caught up in something he didn't understand, it felt as if real spirits had guided them all to the same place.

Red whined and came to sit by his side. Zak stroked the dog's silky coat over and over. He threw another big stump of wood on the fire and watched it smoulder and then catch into flames. He stared up at the moon as silvery wisps played over it. The more he stared, the more the shadows seemed to form into the shape of his mother's face.

Zak closed his eyes and felt the glow of the fire on his cheeks as he sank into a deep sleep.

Elder's face loomed out of the darkness.

'Elder knows where ivy grows, uncover the ivy, back through time, strip back the vine . . .'

She grabbed his hand and began pulling him through the wood. 'Cold hands, warm heart, cold heart, warm hands, isn't that what they say?' The reds and rusts of autumn blurred as she propelled him forward.

'Is this what you're looking for?' she asked.

He turned around, but he was alone again. Slumping to the ground, he felt in his pocket for a photograph. He took it out and looked at it. Heavy booted footsteps approached and a man in uniform called out to him.

'Here you are. I've been looking for you!'

Edwin placed a comforting hand on Zak's shoulder and peered at the photo in his hand. 'Oh, I remember that!' He sighed. 'A happy day. We didn't get so many together after that.'

'But yours is alive, isn't he?' Edwin asked.

Zak nodded.

'And your ma?

Zak shook his head. 'I don't know. She's gone missing.'

Edwin hugged Zak close to him. 'I tell you what, I'll make you a deal. You find where I'm rested, and I promise you your ma will come back safely.'

'What do you mean, where you're rested? Why do you want me to find you?'

Edwin picked up the photograph, smiled sadly and handed it back to Zak. 'Why do you think? You're not the only ones to shelter here from your battles. My ma, my sister Peggy and my pops and young Maisy and Eddie . . . Albert Bainbridge – he's not just a name in the plasterwork, you know. I gave my life, my brothers' too. Don't you think we deserve to be remembered?'

A woman appeared between the trees. She looked as if she had been crying forever. Edwin stood up and walked towards her, his arms flung open wide. Just before he reached her, he turned back to Zak. 'This is Hannah, my ma, you see, she can't rest until her boys are remembered!'

Edwin's voice seemed to fade away. Zak looked around but he was alone again. It was Elder's voice that now whispered through the trees.

'Hush now, Hannah. Rest yourself, rest. Let your spirit rest.'

Chapter Fifty

Iona closed her eyes before she was ready to sleep. She'd felt Zak watching her. *I'm well out of all the Halloween nonsense*, she thought. It was a bad joke that this was the only night of the year that she could appear on a stranger's doorstep and be offered a warm welcome and sweets. Last year she had knocked at someone's door and they had complimented her on her 'outfit'.

'Teenagers don't usually bother dressing up!' the woman had said cheerily as Iona took a handful of chocolates.

She had often wondered since what the woman would have said if she'd told her that she'd made no effort at all to look scary. Though her mates on the streets had found the story hilarious, the truth was that inside, every time she thought of it, Iona wanted to cry. *Am I becoming as wild and frightening as Elder?* She cast her mind back over the journey that she'd made from Elder's den to this place. She saw herself standing at the top of the slope screaming at Aisha and pictured her own face morphing into the Ogre's. She hated herself for becoming like him and hated the fact that Aisha and Zak had witnessed her like that. It was so long since she had spent any proper time with people younger than herself. Come to think of it, it was ages since she'd spent this amount of time with *anyone*. Zak and Aisha were probably more terrified of her than of any ghosts or ghouls wandering the wood.

Staying with Elder, watching her sleep, listening to her chanting, had given Iona the worst jolt of all. But no matter how mad Elder was, Iona still found it easier to be with her than these two, even though once or twice tonight she had started to feel that she could be friends with them. *But who am I kidding? Two's company, three's a crowd.*

The sound of the Ogre's voice came blasting into her mind as he hammered on her door bombarding her with insults: 'You're a waste of space . . . We'd be better off without you . . . The day you finish school is the day you're out of here, you little leech!' Iona packed her rucksack and walked out, past her mum sitting at the table with her head in her hands.

'It's better you go,' she'd whispered. 'But wait –' Her mum's hands shook as she unclasped her cross and handed it to Iona without meeting her eye. 'May God bless you.'

Two's company, three's a crowd, Iona reminded herself. If she hadn't learned that by now, she never would. If she could persuade Red to leave with her, she would head off in the morning. Iona lifted her face to the heat of the fire and breathed in the earthy wood scent.

The Ogre was sitting by her side. He took her elbow in his huge hands. She held her breath, her back tensed, every nerve in her recoiling as he loomed closer.

She felt a hot spark jump from her stomach and a flame begin to kindle inside her. It travelled up through her throat and out of her mouth and began to quicken and flare into the image of Elder; her flame-red hair formed an arching canopy over the whole woodland. The old woman reached out and took Iona's hand, pointing down to far below them where a thimble-sized Ogre cowered.

'He can't hurt you. He's nothing. Not worthy of the dust on your feet. No more fear, Elder's here. Rest now, dear, rest. Let your spirit rest.'

Chapter Fifty-One

Aisha's mind meandered between the branches, in and out of the saplings with their singing leaves, and travelled deep down among the labyrinthine roots of the ancient trees.

Elder blinked and stepped off the shelter wall. She carried with her an ancient stick which she raised, beckoning Aisha to follow. Aisha obeyed and climbed into a huge hollowed-out trunk almost large enough to walk through. Aisha took a step and then another and felt the heat on her face. She was standing on the red earth of home.

'Wait!' Elder called to her. She took her stick and swirled it around the base of the tree.

'Earthstars falling, death cap waiting, spirits calling, heat rising.'

Elder reached around her neck, took off her leather lace of amber beads and untied the knot. She rubbed one of the amber eggs in her hands. Aisha stared as smoke rose from it, then a spark, then a flame. Elder's skin was coated in a golden-coloured resin, sticky as honey.

'Watch. Watch her fly!' Elder whispered, as a ladybird began to stir to life and crawl across her wrinkled hand, finally breaking free of the sticky sap. It spread its wings and flew, landing on Aisha's forehead.

'Say the rhyme, speak the rhyme, follow me . . . Ladybird, ladybird, fly away home, your house is on fire, your children all roam.'

Aisha repeated the words.

'Close your eyes, make your wish and she will fly! Earthstars falling, death cap waiting, spirits calling, heat rising . . .'

Elder's voice faded into the distance and Aisha opened her eyes to find that her wish had been granted.

'Abo! My abo!' she called, and ran at her father, burying her head in his chest. She lay in his arms for the longest time as he sang her a birthday blessing. She was home.

Elder called and called to Aisha, but she could not hear her, so the old woman reached into the tree trunk, grabbed Aisha's hands and yanked her out with all her force.

'Difficult birth, difficult birth . . .' she whispered, rocking Aisha in her arms as if she was a baby. Then she raised Aisha's head and pointed back through the tree. In the distance a man and a woman walked together through a heat haze. They turned to her and waved.

'My hoyo and my abo, together now,' Aisha whispered, reaching out to them and struggling to release herself from Elder's grasp, but the old woman held her tight.

275

'Let your mother and your father rest now. If you love them, let them go.'

Aisha stopped fighting against Elder, raised her hands and waved until her hoyo and abo were no more than tiny dots in the vast landscape.

'Hush now, Aisha, don't you cry, Elder's singing you a lullaby. Rest now, let the spirit rest.'

Chapter Fifty-Two

Iona climbed up and over the shelter to the stream, where Red was whining. She called to her, but the dog continued sniffing the air as if deeply disturbed by something . . . or someone.

'I don't know what's up with her. There's no one there!' Iona said as she returned to the others and the dying embers of the fire.

Aisha shrank down inside her sleeping bag and wiped the tears from her eyes. She swallowed hard. She had never had a dream that felt so true. She had got her wish that her abo would appear to her on her birthday, but it was very far from how she had imagined their reunion. Somewhere deep in her gut she knew that she would never see him again and now she could hardly stand to open her eyes and face these strangers. But Red was pawing at her and forcing her to stir.

'Someone's been here all right,' Zak said.

Aisha opened her eyes to find Zak and Iona

crouching on the other side of the fire unpacking bags full of food.

'Treats from Elder!' Iona laughed. 'I *thought* I felt her around in the night. Maybe that's why I dreamed about her.'

Aisha shivered and her head felt tight with cold. She hugged herself and her eye was caught by a white paper flower pinned to her coat.

'Who put this here?' Aisha asked.

Iona pointed to identical flowers on her own coat and Zak's. 'Seems like we've all been given one.'

The thought of Elder stealing up on them, roaming amongst their dreams as they slept made Zak's skin crawl.

Iona smiled as she unpacked. 'She's so kind – it's not just food. She's brought a pan and a cup, spoons . . . all sorts. Even soap and a clean towel! She must have spent more than that tenner on us!'

'What tenner? Probably used the money she stole from me, along with my other things!' Zak grumbled. Now he felt sure that he'd placed his wallet in his rucksack with twenty pounds inside.

Iona rummaged in the bag, took out a wallet and opened it.

'Here.' She pulled out a twenty-pound note and threw it at Zak. 'Just because she's on the street, doesn't make her a thief.'

Chapter Fifty-Three

'Why do you think she gave us these?' Zak asked, inspecting the petals of the poppy. He'd felt like taking it off but something had stopped him. 'White poppies are for peace, I think. There's supposed to be a war memorial somewhere in this wood. I saw it on a map I found. But I just don't get why Elder would bring back my wallet and keep all my other things.'

Aisha bit her lip. 'Are you sure you didn't imagine the photo and the map after I told you about my dream? Finding that game was probably just some strange coincidence. Maybe I saw them before and didn't realize it . . . and you did hurt your head.'

'Believe what you want, but we dreamed about the same people.' Zak sighed and turned away. 'I didn't make up their names written on the wall, did I? I'm going to see if I can find Elder and get my things back.'

Aisha glanced towards the shelter. Iona had been inside snuggled up with Red for a while. Seeing how much Iona loved Red made Aisha feel guilty that she was the reason that the dog had strayed. It seemed right to leave them to enjoy their reunion in peace. Aisha turned back to Zak. 'I'll come with you, if you want.'

As they walked through the wood they carried their dreams with them, like burdens on their backs. Zak didn't blame Aisha for thinking that he was confused. She was right that he wasn't sure of anything. But she seemed caught up in all of this too with her dream of the wartime family, and there must be a reason why Edwin had led him to the air-raid shelter. He couldn't make any sense of it, but he couldn't ignore what Edwin had told him either . . . It felt as if he would be tempting fate if he didn't go looking for the memorial. Edwin's words haunted him. Iona talked of fair deals. Well this felt like a deal he couldn't afford to break – *find the memorial to give Edwin's mum peace and my mum will come home safe*, he repeated to himself as he kicked his way free of an ivy vine.

Aisha grabbed Zak's arm and pulled him back to stop him crushing something on the ground ahead of him.

Slung across arching branches of bracken were intricately woven spider's webs, sparkling like spun sugar with heavy drops of dew.

Aisha stopped and inspected them. 'How can such a delicate web carry something as heavy as morning tears?' she asked, pointing to a water droplet that threatened to dissolve the fine lace threads.

'You mean dew?' Zak asked, inspecting the webs more closely.

'No, I mean tears!' Aisha sighed. 'Liliana told me this story after one of my nightmares. Probably to make me feel better. She says these webs are dream-catchers. The weavers stay up all night, spinning webs to catch your dreams in, and when the sun heats the earth they all disappear, taking the bad feeling from your dreams with them and leaving only the good ones to dance free. Nice story, isn't it?'

Zak tried not to stare at her as she spoke. He loved listening to Aisha tell her stories. Her English was almost perfect with just a hint of an accent, but when she spoke she made the words sound fresh and new. Perhaps she thought that Edwin and Albert were some kind of fable too.

'You think all this stuff I've told you is made up?'

Aisha shrugged.

How can I get her to believe me? Zak remembered the questions that had run through his own mind when she'd told him her dream. 'How old was the Eddie you dreamed about?' he asked.

'Maybe nine or ten,' Aisha answered.

'And Albert?'

'I don't know, an old man.'

'So it could be the same Albert as the man in my photo.'

Aisha smiled kindly at him. 'I haven't seen a photo.'

Zak felt suddenly foolish. It was as if she pitied him. Why had Elder kept his things? What value could they be to her? If he could show Aisha the photo and map and the name in the plasterwork, then maybe she would believe him.

'Sometimes it's easier to think of strangers than the people you're really missing,' Aisha said breathlessly, and rested for a moment on a tree stump.

When he looked back at her, Zak was shocked to find that she was weeping. 'I had a dream last night . . .' She struggled to speak through her emotion. Zak took a step towards her, but she held up a hand as if to say, *I don't need you to comfort me.* Taking a few deep breaths she calmed herself.

'A dream about my father . . . he *was* an interpreter.' She spoke so quietly that Zak had to strain to hear her words.

'Was?'

'I think he's dead,' she whispered, letting the tears roll down her cheeks.

Zak moved closer to her but she waved him away again. He felt so awkward standing over her, seeing her this upset so he knelt on the ground to feel closer to her. Aisha was looking straight into his eyes now and seemed to be breathing more easily. 'In my country, you know, to be an interpreter is a very dangerous job. Sometimes you are not trusted by anyone – translating from one side to the other, people wonder what you might be adding or what you could be taking away from the truth.'

'But I don't understand. What's changed since yesterday? How can you know what's happened to him?'

Aisha made a fist and held it against her chest. 'In here, it feels different . . .'

Zak shook his head. It was his turn not to believe her now.

'You don't understand . . . I used to listen to BBC Somali service every week to see if my abo's name was spoken. Sometimes I used to think that even finding out that he is dead would be better than all the waiting and the never knowing. Every year on my birthday I've wished for him to come and find me, like he promised, and this year I think he did come, last night in my dream, to say goodbye. When I woke up I was sure he was gone.'

There was silence between them as Zak tried to take everything in. His dream last night had felt true too, but he couldn't tell her that. It was clear that she thought that he was still mixed up in his mind, but what Aisha was telling him about her father was just a feeling too. Yet she seemed so sure. Aisha wiped away her tears. Zak stood up and as he did she reached for his hand. He hardly dare to look at her as they walked on together but he wished that she would never let go as he felt the cool smoothness of her skin against his.

'It was your birthday yesterday? Why didn't you tell us?' Was all that he could think of to say.

Aisha shrugged.

Zak looked up between the great trees. This wood was full of dreams and dream-catchers and dappled light dancing on the earth like spirits from another world, another time, but it was also full of all that was real. It was not a place where you could hide from yourself or from the truth. He felt as if he had sleepwalked into the wood and only now was he beginning to wake up. Perhaps it was the same for Aisha too, finding a way to say goodbye to her father. Something inside him finally felt resolved. If it was the last thing he did, he would prove to Aisha that he was not following trails in the dark.

Chapter Fifty-Four

Breadcrumbs were scattered skyward then hundreds of pigeons rose in a flurry, pecking and flapping their wings in fighting flight and through this sea of fluttering grey Elder walked. The birds separated, creating a cooing corridor for her entrance. By instinct Aisha and Zak crouched out of sight. Elder turned towards their hiding place and gestured to a path on the far side of a fence. Zak and Aisha followed her gaze. A small white police van was making its way slowly into the wood, until the paths narrowed and it could go no further. A door slammed, and there were urgent voices and the sound of dogs barking and rummaging around in the undergrowth. Two Alsatians came sniffing towards them, but before they could get near, Elder intercepted them. She grabbed their collars and stroked between their eyes until the dogs turned over on their backs like docile puppies and let her tickle their bellies.

'Only the homeless woman!' one police officer called to the other.

'My name's Elder!' she corrected them.

'Are you all right in there, Elder? Need any help?' the policeman asked.

'Elder's fine, like good wine, the older the better!' She laughed at her own joke.

'Is that so? Well, you know we're always here to take you to the shelter if needs be. We're still looking for those missing children. You haven't come across them, have you?'

She shook her head and stopped stroking the dogs. They stood up, sniffed the air in Zak and Aisha's direction and then followed the policemen back to the van. It was as if they'd been hypnotized.

'I think she knows we're here,' Aisha whispered to Zak.

'She gives me the creeps.'

Elder started to walk in their direction.

Zak grabbed Aisha's arm and pulled her to the side as if he feared that the old woman was about to attack them, but Aisha tugged his arm away and stepped out of the thicket.

'Earthstars landing! Mustn't spring out at Elder, jumpy old heart, missed a beat.' Elder patted her chest but she didn't seem any more bothered by Aisha's appearance than of the presence of the pigeons that rested on her shoulders.

'You knew we were here!' Aisha whispered, and Zak came and stood by her side. Elder smiled at him, touched her own head and pointed at Zak where his wound had scabbed over completely.

'Come back to Elder's healing hands, have you?'

'Why didn't you tell them we're here?' Zak asked.

'None of my business! Elder's not a busybody. You want to stay, I'm not going to stop you. Free country – that's what they say anyway . . .'

'You brought us food,' Aisha said.

'Can't let my earthstars go hungry.'

'And these poppies,' Aisha added, indicating the one she wore.

'Poppies for peace, for rest, let the spirits rest, that's what I say.'

Elder held out her hand and released a scattering of leaves that floated on the breeze away from her. 'Little red leaves falling, falling everywhere, poor little mites, bleeding hearts, all Elder wants is peace, peace, peace.'

'Thanks for giving me my wallet back. Could I have my other things?' Zak asked, biting his lip as he spoke.

Without warning, Elder grabbed hold of her stick and started thrashing at the earth.

'Ungrateful boy, I made you well.'

Zak and Aisha began backing away from her. Now that her mood had changed she looked truly insane.

'I had a map . . . I'm looking for a memorial in the wood,' Zak pursued.

'Look low, low, lower!' As she spoke she knelt down to the ground.

Aisha and Zak followed her gaze and ducked down too.

Elder brandished her stick between the trees towards a thick mound of brambles. 'All overgrown now, all forgotten.'

'What is?' Zak asked and Elder spun around, her red hair swirling as the pigeons took flight.

'The dead – who do you think?'

Chapter Fifty-Five

Zak had grabbed hold of Aisha's hand and they'd run through the wood, half laughing, half petrified.

'I thought *last night* was supposed to be Halloween! I don't care what you say, she's not right in the head. I'll have to go back when she's not around,' Zak said as they stopped to catch their breath. 'But it seems like she's never that far away.'

Zak was beginning to feel that Elder was drawing them into something deeper than they could understand. *Why had she kept their presence in the wood a secret? Even going so far as to cover their tracks from the police?*

Red barked a welcome and ran up the slope to greet them and now she led them towards Iona, whose hoarse singing echoed from the direction of the shelter.

Zak slowed. The fire had been lit and blankets and clothes were hung around it. A pan had been placed over the flame.

'Where did you two go?' Iona said, appearing at the entrance.

'For a walk,' Aisha answered. Zak was grateful to her for not telling Iona about the memorial.

'A walk on the wild side?' Iona sang, laughing at her own joke. 'Whatever! You look happy anyway!'

'Just a walk,' Zak muttered.

'Well, thanks for the invite! But in case you were worrying about Red and me, we've had no problem keeping busy, have we girl?' Iona hugged Red to her and the dog snuggled in close. 'Want some tea?' Iona asked, pouring boiling water from the pan into a metal cup, then she spooned sugar into it, added milk and stirred. Iona had placed three logs around the fire, and they sat down and passed Elder's cup from one to the other. As Aisha sipped she felt her throat and stomach warm through. Now Iona grinned at Aisha, rummaged in one of the bags and lowered some spaghetti into the pan of bubbling water. When it was cooked, she drained it and stirred in some tomato sauce from a jar, before handing the pan to Aisha for the first taste.

Aisha twirled the spaghetti around the fork and ate a mouthful. 'Delicious!' she said. 'Dream food! Thank you!'

Iona shrugged as if she was so unused to receiving a compliment that she didn't know what to do with it. 'Don't thank me, thank Elder!'

When they had all swelled their stomachs with pasta, they stretched out beside the fire sleepily. It was incredible how content a full stomach could make you feel. Zak wondered if some of Iona's grouchiness came from being hungry so much of the time. When she'd pulled up her sleeves to cook, he'd noticed that she carried not a single ounce of fat.

Aisha sighed. 'I hope Elder's not insulted that we ran away from her.'

'I expect she's used to it. I think she likes having us here.' Iona took her turn to sip the tea and raised the cup in a toast. 'To crazy, kind old Elder.'

'It's the way she just appears out of nowhere that freaks me out,' Zak said, feeling the heat of the fire thaw his frozen toes.

'And you're supposed to be our great protector!' laughed Iona.

'Who said?' Zak joined in with the laughter.

'Close your eyes, you two,' Iona ordered, and placed her hands over Zak's eyes. He pulled away. 'Don't worry – I'm not going to eat you!'

Iona pushed them both towards the shelter and they stumbled. 'OK, OK, give me your hands.' She grabbed them and led them one at a time inside.

'Eyes closed,' Iona insisted, dancing around as she sat them down on one of the benches.

'Open sesame!'

The walls of one whole side of the shelter had been

covered in chalk drawings. Zak looked over to the door where the names of the wartime family had been left just as they were, except that Iona had drawn a suitcase around them as if the old names were about to take off on a new journey. There were pictures of Iona greeting Red, and Aisha in her blue scarf singing around the camp fire with Zak sitting next to her, and in the middle of them was Elder holding Crystal in her arms, surrounded by poppies and birds, conducting them all. The whole concrete wall had been transformed into a surreal impression, the chalk colours smudging into each other, but every scene that Iona had drawn was recognizable.

'You are very talented,' whispered Aisha.

Zak just stared and shook his head. 'I've never seen anything like this.'

Iona leaned against the bench opposite and grinned from ear to ear. Aisha smiled back, recognizing in Iona's face the joy she felt in her art. Aisha knew that feeling well; for her, she found that release in singing.

They sat around the fire all afternoon, keeping it burning, chatting easily to one another, singing songs – the girls laughing at Zak's gruff voice, and fussing over Red. Iona seemed to enjoy playing the host, offering around biscuits and heating the pot. Zak thought the hot, sweet tea might be the most delicious drink he had ever tasted as they shared the cup, passing it around the glowing fire.

Red was the first to sense a change as night fell. She sniffed the air suspiciously, whined and skulked into the far corner of the shelter. *Boom, boom, boom*, came the hollow sound above their heads. They ran outside to see the sky blasted by fountains of light, splashing rainbow colours across the night and cascading back down to earth. There were the deep hollow rumbles, and then the sprinkling showers raining down on them in white, blue and pink light. Zak and Aisha were transfixed as they stood in the middle of the wood, holding their breath. Iona studied their expressions. She had always loved to see people's faces transformed by fireworks, to watch all their worries ebb away. Even the oldest most cynical face relaxed into a child-like glow of wonder before these displays. Red whined and shivered again. Iona felt the animal's fear and stepped back inside to hold her dog close. She loved fireworks more than anything, but had never been able to enjoy them since Red had been given to her, because every year at the first sound of fireworks the dog's whole body trembled in fear and all Iona could think of was protecting her and making her feel safe. *That's what you should do if you love something, someone – not put yourself first.* She would never understand why her mum hadn't fought her corner against the Ogre.

Iona wound up the torch that Elder had brought

them, scanned the light around the walls and found herself settling on the names of the children who had come here for protection in wartime all those years ago.

Boom, boom, boom, went the fireworks.

What must it have felt like having to huddle inside this concrete shelter with bombs falling all around you, not knowing whether you would ever be able to get back out? Whether your home would be a pile of rubble when you returned? *What would I find*, Iona asked herself, *if I ever took myself back to the island to see what's happened to my home?*

The fireworks quietened and Red lifted her head. Aisha joined the two of them in the shelter and sat down next to the dog. Then after a pause the blasts started up again.

'Your turn!' Aisha said, pushing Iona outside.

'Happy Diwali!' Zak greeted her, as the sky exploded in a symphony of colour above their heads. Every year, for as long as he could remember, he had watched what Shalini called her 'Diwali sky'. She always insisted on them going together, and every year she cried. Now, feeling so far away from the people he loved, Zak felt as if he knew why Shalini was always so full of emotion on this night, thinking of her son who shared the same vast sky but was a whole world away in Sri Lanka.

Iona held her breath, felt for her mum's cross,

wrapped her arms around herself and swayed as her spirit briefly soared. When the last spark of light petered out of the sky, her body seemed to collapse inwards and she started to sob. Without thinking, Zak placed his arms around her shoulders and held her close. The emotion rose up in her, growing stronger and wracking her body.

Red appeared at the entrance to the shelter cowering low and still shaking with fear. Aisha followed her out. The dog went over and burrowed her head in Iona's side.

'I can't live like this anymore,' Iona held out a hand to comfort Red.

Aisha placed her arm around her too and the four of them huddled together around the embers of the fire.

Elder watched from between the trees, smiling at the warm glow from the bright little constellation of unlikely earthstars that shone before her, lighting up her wood.

Chapter Fifty-Six

The fire died to nothing but ashes halfway through the night. They were wearing every piece of clothing that they could find now, sharing them out, not caring who the items belonged to: gloves, hats, layers of socks, jumpers and coats. The two girls had taken the old bunk beds and Zak was resting on one of the benches. They did not speak but closed their eyes, each lost in thoughts of their own struggles. Sleep did not come easily to anyone that night. For each, the fireworks had ignited a longing for warmth and light.

'Zak! Zak! Zak! You can't go back till you've done that job!'

Sitting opposite him was an old man who looked vaguely familiar.

'Albert?' Zak whispered.

'Come off it! I'm not as old as all that! Albert was my grandpops! I'm Eddie.' The old man pointed to the child's name on the wall. 'That was me once upon a time! Thought I'd have a last look around the old haunts before I go!'

296

'Go where?' Zak asked.

'I don't know – where do we go? Knocking on heaven's door, underground, you tell me.'

Zak shrugged.

'See you've spruced the place up a bit though! I like the artwork.' Eddie nodded towards Iona's chalk drawings appreciatively.

Zak pointed at Iona on the top bunk. 'It's hers.'

'I used to sleep up there, until the night the bombs came down so hard I wet myself! Poor Maisy and Mummy on the bottom! Grandpops slept where you're sat, and sometimes I'd cuddle up with him. He never could sleep on his own after Nana died. Such a kind old man, always so sad about my Uncle Edwin and the others dying so young. It felt like whenever he said my name he thought of his son.'

Zak walked over to his bag and took out the game of jacks.

'Were these yours?' he asked the man.

Eddie clapped his hands on his knees. 'Hah! A last game of jacks!' He threw the ball up and attempted to gather all the pieces but ended up missing the ball.

'Bother. I used to be good at that game.' He turned his hands over and inspected them. 'See? Riddled with arthritis, veins sticking up everywhere. You need nice supple hands for jacks.'

The man patted Zak on the back.

'You can be the keeper of the jacks, if you want! Your turn now!'

Zak threw the ball in the air, scooped up all the jacks and caught the ball effortlessly.

'See!' The old man laughed and clapped him on the back. He took a red poppy he was wearing on his lapel and shakily pinned it on to Zak.

'You'll make sure they remember us all, won't you, son?' He winked at Zak.

Zak's head swirled as he attempted to join up all the information in his mind. For whatever reason, he had got himself caught up with this name from the plasterwork and the people had taken hold of him and would not let him go. It was as if they needed him as much as he needed them. What did it matter if Aisha didn't believe him? He had to do this for Edwin, for himself and for his mum, and afterwards he would go back home to see if Edwin had kept his promise. Maybe they could walk out of the wood together, he and Aisha. After her dream he sensed that she was ready to leave too. Zak imagined the scene of the two of them, carrying rucksacks, passing the redbrick houses with their neat tiled porches as they walked along Linden Road together towards number 22a and then number 48. Aisha would reach home first.

He glanced over at Iona in the top bunk and felt truly sorry for her. She was right to be bitter. *What would happen to her now?* He thought of Elder and how she had struggled through the wood to bring them food because she was lonely and wanted to keep them there. But maybe there was more to it than that. Perhaps she held the answers to other questions too?

At the first sign of light Zak climbed out of his sleeping bag as quietly as he could. His whole body shivered with the biting cold but he had no more clothes to wear. He pulled on his boots and stepped outside.

'You want to come with me, Red?' he whispered. 'Come on then, girl!' Red climbed to the top of the slope and sat looking down at the shelter as if unsure whether she should accompany him.

'Best stay here then!' Zak patted the dog on the head and she trotted back towards the shelter.

The smell of yesterday's spent fireworks filled the air as Zak set off in search of the memorial. The earth scrunched under his feet. This was the first hard frost.

Aisha heard Zak leave with Red and listened to Iona's faint sleep-sniffle. She thought about getting up and going with them, but she felt as if Zak needed to sort out whatever was troubling him on his own. Even through the thick sleeping bag she could not keep warm. Last night, standing watching the fireworks with Zak, she had felt completely happy for a moment. Seeing the sky light up had made her forget everything: where she had come from, where she now stood, what the future held . . . but now the world came spiralling back to her and Liliana's face filled her mind. *Surely*

299

she'll understand now how much I love her. Aisha listened to Iona's breathing change as she shifted in her sleep. *Today I will try to build Iona's trust and be her friend.* When Iona had been full of spite it had been hard to care for her, but now Aisha found herself thinking as much about Iona as about Zak or even herself. *What will Iona do when Zak and I go home? Who will care for her?*

Chapter Fifty-Seven

Aisha dozed for a while as a dust stream of sunshine pooled in the entrance of the shelter. She opened her eyes at last, feeling she needed to wash, to cleanse herself despite the cold. She rummaged in her bag for her toothbrush and toothpaste and the soap and the fresh towel that Elder had brought, then grabbed the tepee and the blanket off her bed that until now had doubled as a towel, and headed out to be dazzled by the brightness of the morning sun. The ground, the trees, the leaves were all coated in a silvery white frost that glistened making the earth feel fresh and new. Even in her trainers and double layer of socks Aisha's feet felt like ice blocks. She looked down at her watch and could not believe that it was already ten o'clock. Only a few days ago she had been waking at dawn. She wondered what time Zak had left. It had felt early.

A flock of woodland birds had gathered around the stream so at first she didn't see Elder crouching over the water washing her hands and face and dunking her hair. If it wasn't for the distinctive colour Aisha might not have recognized the shivering woman who had stripped down to an old-fashioned silky slip, her tiny body all jutting bones and hanging skin. Without her layers of petticoats and clothes, Elder was no bigger than a child. Aisha brought her hand to her mouth in shock to see someone so old and frail living outside at the mercy of the elements. Elder's whole body shook as she washed her doll, supporting its head as you would a new-born baby's.

'Clean as crystal, crystal-clean water,' she murmured, surveying the powder-blue sky. 'Crystal-clear day!'

Aisha looked up too at the single white sweep of an aeroplane track, as if the sky had been painted by an enormous white feather. She felt an urge to call out to Elder, but something stopped her. It was as if the woman was in her own world with an unwritten 'Do not disturb' sign surrounding her. At last Elder lifted her head. She seemed to look straight through Aisha, and yet she felt, as before, that the old woman knew that she was there.

'Time to cleanse away the sadness, time to let our loved ones go,' Elder was saying, as she wrapped the doll in a towel.

Are those words meant for me?

'I thought you'd all upped sticks and left me again,' Iona said, as she climbed up and over the shelter.

Aisha turned, placed her fingertips on her lips and signalled towards Elder. Iona tiptoed over to Aisha's side and they watched together as Elder dried her skeletal arms. She bent down to pick something up and tumbled forward. Iona grabbed the clean towel out of Aisha's arms, and hurried over to where Elder lay prone on the bank.

Elder nodded at Iona as she placed the towel over her shoulders. Then instinctively Iona took her feet in her hands as she'd seen Mrs Kalsi do so many times before. She dried between what looked more like knobbly twigs than toes, dabbing softly, half afraid that she would break them. Elder let her head drop back as if just this gentle human touch was comforting to her. The old woman was silent now and Aisha thought how peaceful she seemed without her incessant chanting. Aisha stepped forward to help but Iona shook her head, as if she wanted to care for Elder herself. When she was dry, Elder pointed over to her clothes. Aisha passed them to Iona and the older girl began to dress her, helping her on with layer after layer of odd assortments of cardigans, blouses, T-shirts, petticoats, skirts and tights . . . She realized as she piled on the mould-scented garments that it was not Elder who smelt so pungent but the clothes she wore. The old woman washed them, but was never able to dry them out properly, her clothes smelt exactly like the scratchy blanket they had used as a towel. Iona was aware that she had begun to smell that mouldy damp scent on all of their clothes. Finally, she helped Elder on with her shiny new wellies and eased her to standing. Elder shook her shoulders as if she herself was checking to see that everything was intact and then, without a word to either girl she turned and walked away.

Chapter Fifty-Eight

Iona sat on the banks of the stream, shoulders hunched and legs splayed unceremoniously before her. As Aisha drew close she noticed that her cheeks were streaked with tears again. Aisha knelt down by her side.

'I can't end up like her,' Iona wailed. 'That can't be me.'

Aisha was lost for words as Iona looked up at her for the first time with unguarded eyes. Instinctively she did what Liliana had done whenever she'd felt unutterably sad. She took Iona's head and lay it on her shoulder.

Iona pulled away. 'Don't be so nice to me, or I'll never stop crying!' She attempted to laugh through her tears. 'Where's Red anyway?' She peered around for her. Red was normally the first to come to her side when she was upset.

'Went out with Zak. I heard them go off together this morning.'

'Is he still going on about that war stuff?'

Aisha nodded.

'Well, I suppose we've all got to do what we've got to do. I'm telling you, I have to pull myself out of this state.' Iona peered into the wood as if looking for Elder, but there was no sign of her now. 'You know, she told me that her baby was taken away from her, and she never got over it. I keep thinking how sad it is that somewhere out there in the city there might be a woman called Crystal, who doesn't even know how much she's still loved by her mum. Tragic, isn't it? She's holding on to that baby they took off her so long ago, while my mum can't even be bothered to look for me!'

Aisha nodded slowly. She of all people understood what it meant for this girl to put her trust in her enough to speak of such things. Her own eyes glazed over as a huge wave of compassion for Iona rose up in her. She would have liked to reach out and give her a proper Liliana hug, but she sensed that Iona would push her away.

Instead Aisha took the blanket, walked over to the tepee and swiftly took off her coat, her oversized jumper and jeans and stepped inside.

Iona stared after her. She had not expected Aisha to be so unselfconscious. 'What are you doing?'

'Washing, cleansing!' Aisha called back, carefully unclasping her prayer beads. Then she untied her hijab, reaching her arm out of the tepee and hanging her scarf and beads on a stick next to the blanket. She gasped as she stepped into the icy water and her skin prickled with the cold. Her scalp felt tight and tingling. But as she washed, the smell of the rose soap Elder had brought entered her nostrils along with a memory of herself burrowing her nose in her Aunt Lalu's hair. Aisha breathed in the rich rose oil and began to sing. *Had Elder known that this was just the scent that would take her home?* Now she dunked her head under the water. Immediately her skull shrank with cold and she began to shiver and grabbed hold of the blanket.

'Would you mind lifting this up on to the ground so that I can get dressed?' Aisha called to Iona.

She moved the tepee on to the bank and Aisha shuffled over too and began to dress.

'You've got this all sorted. Mind if I copy you?' Iona asked. 'I could do with a wash!'

Aisha emerged still shivering as she dried a thick mane of wavy hair that reached down her back. Iona tried not to stare.

'Help yourself!' Aisha handed Iona the blanket.

'Keep it. I've got this!' Iona smiled holding on to the towel that she'd dried Elder with. 'You get undressed in there and I'll shift it over for you when you're done.'

'You shouldn't hide your hair like that!' Iona said

as she stepped inside the tepee to get undressed. 'Why do you cover it anyway?'

It was a question Aisha had been asked many times.

She remembered the day she had covered her hair for the first time. Feeling the scarf hold her securely under the chin. She'd looked at herself in the mirror and realized how much she looked like the pictures her aunt Lalu and abo had shown her of her mother as a girl. Just as she was about to attempt to answer, Iona screeched so loudly that Aisha thought she must have hurt herself.

'It's freezing in here!' An ice-cold spray splashed through the parting in the tepee screen as Iona washed her face.

Aisha smiled at the exaggerated shivering noises coming from inside the tepee as she smoothed her hands over her head. How could she explain it to Iona? Wearing the hijab made her feel as if she belonged, so that when she prayed she felt right. That first day she'd worn it to school, she and the Somali and other Muslim girls had stood together, chatting about the latest styles of wearing it, and she'd felt solid and strong and part of something beyond herself.

'You better not let Zak see you with your hair down! The way he looks at you!' Iona called out.

'He doesn't!' Aisha giggled.

She lifted the tepee up the bank so that Iona could get dressed under cover. Iona emerged with the towel draped over her head, hugging herself, rubbing her arms and jumping up and down to keep warm.

'Not that you don't look pretty enough with your head covered . . . I know I'd look a complete state if I had to wear one of those . . . What's it like in Somalia?' Iona asked as she finished dressing.

'You really want to know?' Aisha had not forgotten the insult that Iona had thrown at her when they'd passed on the street.

Iona nodded. 'I've never been anywhere else but here and Scotland.'

'I wrote a poem about my country at school, I learned it to read out . . .'

'Go on then . . .'

Aisha took a deep breath before she began to recite:

'It was beautiful my village before . . .
Taking water from the river,
Sapphire sky, turquoise sea, pale sand,
Green, lush mountains, red earth dust,
The smell of rose oil everywhere and myrrh
    incense on sun-warmed skin
But I don't know, now . . . what it looks like,
My country . . .
My country
Lives
Faraway in my memory
When I was still a child . . .'

309

'Where's *your* home?' Aisha asked Iona when she didn't respond.

Iona sat on the ground and hugged her legs close into her chest to hide the emotion in her face. Then she coughed to clear her throat. 'Iona's from Iona! The Scottish isle. Your poem took me back to our little cottage by the sea, building sandcastles. Well, that's what it was like before the Ogre came and smashed everything up!'

'Who's the ogre?' Aisha asked as she came to sit quietly next to Iona.

'My stepdad.' Iona clasped her elbow tight. 'But you don't want to know about any of that.' She prodded the ground violently with a stick . . . 'I'm sorry.'

The sorry came out as little more than a whisper.

'For what?'

'What I said to you when I saw you on the street.'

Aisha nodded slowly. 'Thank you,' she said quietly, then spotted something out of the corner of her eye and placed a finger to her lips, indicating the little blue-backed bird that was hopping close behind Iona.

She turned and smiled. 'Nuthatch! Looks like you!' she whispered, then held up her hand as if afraid that she had insulted Aisha again. 'I'm not being funny – Elder thought so too, what with their blue veils and big eyes . . .' At the sound of Iona's voice, the bird flew

away. 'Anyway, Elder said they were her favourites . . .
no offence meant.'

'None taken!' Aisha laughed.

'What is it about hair? Loads of religions seem to
have all these rules about it.'

'Well, you look like Mr Kalsi now, with your towel-
wrap!' Aisha joked.

'I'd like to see his hair under that turban. He says
he's never cut it, not in his whole life! Then there's
Elder with her dye . . .'

'And what about the way you have your hair!' Aisha
said. 'Is that religious or cultural?'

Iona laughed. 'Never really thought about it.'

The two girls sat by the stream for a while, as the
sunshine slowly thawed out everything from the iced
branches to the glistening hard earth.

'So, what's the story? Why did you run away?' Iona
asked gently.

Aisha liked Iona's directness. There was an honesty
about her that most people didn't have. She took a
deep breath. She had thought of little else since she'd
come into the wood.

'I just couldn't believe that Liliana would even
think of letting me go.'

'Sorry, I don't get you . . . She's looking for you all
over the place. She's frantic. The woman looks broken-
hearted,' Iona said.

'But she was willing to let me be adopted.'

'Lucky you!' Iona sighed. 'You're wanted by *two* families.' She squeezed Aisha's arm as if trying to lighten her mood.

'I just can't believe she's willing to let me go,' Aisha repeated, biting her lip to stop herself from tearing up. She felt the same raw feeling of rejection now as she had on the day that she'd packed her bags and left.

'It didn't look like that to me, when I saw her. It might not be what you think? You know that song . . . Iona hummed the tune for a moment until the words came to her . . . 'If you love someone, set them free?'

Aisha shook her head.

'Well, it's about giving people a choice. Maybe that's what she was doing.'

Aisha was amazed to hear Iona speaking like this. When she'd first met her, she'd done exactly what she hated others doing to her, and judged the girl. If enough people did that to you and you didn't have anyone to love, it would harden you up in time. *How would I be without Liliana?* Now, in the woods, she was seeing another Iona, and what she'd said was true. Maybe it wasn't as simple as feeling unloved by Liliana. Perhaps this was about accepting that her abo would not be coming back so that she could stop searching for him and step into her own future? The dream of Elder's amber egg igniting and the ladybird flying free flared in Aisha's mind. She knew now that she'd come to the wood to say goodbye to her abo once and for all so that she could begin her life without him.

'And what's going on with Zak? What's the story there?' Iona asked.

Aisha explained what she knew about Zak's mum being missing and that his parents had split. 'He was talking in his sleep about moving to a new house. He kept muttering about walls falling down. I'm not sure about the other stuff with the soldier, but he seems to be all caught up in thoughts of war. Maybe he's trying to understand something about his mum's work . . . I don't know – he's a bit mixed up.' Aisha shrugged.

'Aren't we all?' Iona laughed. 'I feel bad for giving him such a hard time now. I just hope he's looking after my Red.'

Chapter Fifty-Nine

Liliana and Shalini stood around the newly dug grave of Eddie Lowie. Liliana had placed a bunch of brightly coloured chrysanthemums in a vase and now set it on his grave.

'He loved our garden. Used to say to me that it gave him more pleasure than anything else, especially when he couldn't get out much.'

'What did he do?' Shalini asked.

'A carpenter. It was a family trade, he said. Went back generations. He seemed proud of it.'

'But he has no family now?'

'Seems not!' Liliana nodded to the gravestone next to Eddie's, which was engraved with the name 'Maisy Lowie'. 'She was his sister. I think I might have met her once,' she said, inspecting the other graves and reading out the names. '"Peggy Lowie" . . . Looks like she was the mother.'

Shalini sighed deeply. 'It makes me so sad when I hear of old people with no one to pass their stories on to, or to sit with them at the end. It doesn't happen so much back home.'

'I'm going to get a headstone made for him,' Liliana said. 'So if anyone ever comes looking, at least they'll find him here.' Liliana's voice wavered.

'You were a good neighbour to him.' Shalini linked arms with her as they walked away from the churchyard.

'I tried. No news of Zak's mother then?'

Shalini shook her head slowly. 'They're saying now that Zak might have been taken for political reasons, because of his ma's work. They're waiting for someone to come forward, making their demands.'

The longer time went on, the more hollow and hopeless they felt about everything.

Liliana looked back at the newly dug grave. 'The hardest thing would be never to know what's happened to them. Not to have somewhere to go to remember . . .'

Even after the search for Aisha had been ramped up because of the national press coverage, and the whole area scoured, there had not been a single sighting of either of the children. The two women walked on in silence over the frozen earth, asking themselves the question that neither of them could bear to speak. *When, and in what state, will Zak and Aisha be found?*

'This feels like proper winter now,' Shalini said,

shivering as the cold bit through her long woollen coat. Liliana took her friend's hand and squeezed it comfortingly. Coming together in this crisis was the only way to get through the agony of unknowing.

Chapter Sixty

Zak retraced his steps to the place in the wood where he and Aisha had last seen Elder. He bent down low, kneeling in the undergrowth, and sure enough, there, through a thicket of brambles, stood a tall stone structure covered in ivy.

Without thinking what he was doing, he began to trample the ground. When the undergrowth became too thick he hunted around for a fallen branch to beat his way through, thrashing at the earth, his warm breath blasting the chill morning air as he hacked out a passageway. He could feel the thorns entering his skin, but he didn't care, he had to get to the monument.

Now he felt the concrete slab beneath his feet, and grabbed at the ivy. It came away in great rope-like vines. He pulled and pulled until finally, underneath, he exposed a stone covered in lichen. Hunting around for a sharper stick, Zak began to scrape away at the moss until indents in the stone revealed themselves and he was able to read the words that must have lain covered for years. The borders of the stone were carved with ivy, acorns and leaves.

Zak held his breath in disbelief as he read:

FOR OUR FAMILY WHO GAVE THEIR LIVES

WORLD WAR I:
EDWIN BAINBRIDGE
JONNY BAINBRIDGE
STAN BAINBRIDGE
(SONS OF ALBERT AND HANNAH BAINBRIDGE,
BROTHERS OF PEGGY BAINBRIDGE)

WORLD WAR II:
PETER LOWIE
(HUSBAND OF PEGGY LOWIE,
FATHER OF MAISY AND EDDIE)

THIS STONE WAS COMMISSIONED BY ALBERT
BAINBRIDGE IN MEMORY OF HIS BELOVED WIFE
HANNAH, AND THEIR FAMILY LOST IN BOTH
WORLD WARS.

LEST WE FORGET

WE FOUND SHELTER IN THIS WOOD

Zak's stomach lurched as he read. He didn't know how it had come about, but these names written in stone were no longer just strangers to him. These were people that he felt as if he knew and cared about. Then he remembered his own dismissive words as he'd lashed out at Mr Slater – 'history is a pile of crap'. Now he knew that he had been chosen by the craftsmen of his new house to uncover this memorial. Reading the names over again, Zak tried to piece together the family tree. So Jonny and Stan were Edwin's brothers. They had probably all died in the trenches. Poor Albert and Hannah . . . his wife. When had she died and how? Zak wondered if it had been of a broken heart at losing all three of her sons. Only their daughter, Peggy, had survived. Thinking about the photo of Albert and Edwin, and counting forward in time to the war, Zak worked out that Edwin must have been about twenty-five or twenty-six when he died. The young soldier who had led him to the air-raid shelter would have been around that age too . . . Zak thought about the smiling faces in the photograph he'd printed off. In that happy moment Albert could have had no idea that his three sons would be taken from him so young.

Zak examined the names as he worked it all through in his mind. So the boy who had accompanied him to the shelter was the Edwin in the photograph, who had fought and died in the First World War along with his brothers. And the old man who had come to him in his dream was Eddie, the owner of the jacks, most likely named after his Uncle Edwin. He must have been the little boy who Aisha saw in her dream. Poor Eddie and Maisy – the children who had drawn on the shelter wall – had waited in vain all those nights and days for their dad to come home. *But I wonder why Aisha dreamed of Eddie as a little boy and he came to me as an old man.*

Zak could see it all laid out in front of him now, how this family of builders and carpenters who had made the house that he was living in had been . . .

'Felled, all felled.'

He swung around and there, following him down the path that he'd tunnelled out, was Elder, surrounded by a chaotic gathering of wings.

'Come out, come out! Where have all the words gone? Aisha's not the only one whose good at poetry, long tracts of verse . . . whole Odysseys were stored here once.' She knocked at her head in frustration and waved her arms around as if hacking her way through her own tangled memories until she finally caught hold of the thing she was searching for. 'This one's for you, Hannah. For all the mothers!'

> 'Felled, all felled,
> whose airy cages quelled,
> Quelled or quenched in leaves the leaping sun,
> All felled, felled, all are felled . . .'

Zak stared at Elder. Every time he looked at her, she seemed a little more haggard. Before he realized what she was doing, she had grabbed hold of his hand and squeezed it tight between her claw-like fingers.

'You unravelled the vine, but if you lay the stone bare, it's only fair, you need to care.'

With her back to the memorial Elder scattered crumbs for the birds and started chanting: 'Edwin Bainbridge, Jonny Bainbridge, Stan Bainbridge, Albert Bainbridge, Hannah Bainbridge, Peggy Lowie, Peter Lowie, Maisy Lowie, Eddie Lowie.'

'How come you know all their names?' Zak asked.

'Elder holds them in her head, all the children of Home Wood, every name has a leaf, every leaf has a name, golden for my precious ones, my hearts of gold.' She held her doll close and rocked her back and forth.

Chapter Sixty-One

Elder began digging at the ground in front of the memorial with her bare hands. As she dug, she sang to herself: 'For every season, turn, turn, turn, time to accept, time to forgive, but never, ever forget.'

Zak knelt down beside her to help and was shocked to see the hollow look of grief on the old woman's face.

'You'll help me say goodbye to my sweet Crystal, won't you?' she asked.

Zak nodded. He felt as if he had no choice, but maybe this was part of what he had come here to do.

Elder sat back and tried to catch her breath as Zak picked up a stick and continued to dig for her. 'I found you, Edwin,' Zak whispered to the memorial, 'so please, please, please, let Mum come home safe.'

'For every season, turn, turn, turn,' Elder sang again, crying as she rocked to and fro.

When Zak had dug the hole deep enough, Elder kissed her doll and pulled the blanket over its face and head. Zak placed a layer of leaves in the bottom of the hole and shuddered. To Elder at least, this really *was* her goodbye.

Elder kissed the doll's head, leaned forward and placed her bundle in the hole.

'Cover her with earth, earth to earth, earth to earth . . .' Elder chanted as Zak filled the little grave with soil and patted it down. She took off her poppy and laid it on top of the grave. Zak let his white poppy rest on the ground beside Elder's, then searched for his red poppy, until he remembered that it was the old man Eddie who had pinned that on him in his dream.

'Time to go home now,' Elder whispered. 'Time to heal these cuts and grazes.' She took Zak's arm and leaned on him heavily as they walked through the wood. She smelt sweeter than before, of mould and . . . roses. Zak looked around to try to find his bearings, but felt completely disorientated. The last time he had been in Elder's den the place had been shrouded in mist, but he must have walked miles and miles in circles, because it seemed that Elder's home was just beyond the stream, and only a little way beyond that was the air-raid shelter. From here the old woman must have been able to listen to them chatting and see them every day. So Iona was right – she *had* been looking over them. The smell of ripe apples wafted towards Zak as he helped Elder inside her den. She walked slowly over to the pram, got out a tube of antiseptic cream and handed it to Zak for his cuts. He thanked her then she felt around her neck, pulled a leather necklace of amber-coloured beads over her head and handed them to Zak. He peered through the clear surface to the treasures trapped inside.

'Untie them.' She ordered him. He did as he was told and unthreaded the egg-sized beads. Elder took them from him, inspected them and handed them over one at a time. 'The leaf family for you, to feel the bonded branches, tides of history, leaves scattered to the wind, the pain of war. Ladybird for Aisha – she knows, she knows. Butterfly for my Iona – not long now till she hatches out. Old pure wood goes way, way back in time, keeps you rooted. I can tell you something – old Elder's been around a few times.'

'Are you sure these are for us?' Zak asked her. It felt wrong to take them. They looked as if they might be the only precious things she owned.

'Who else but for my earthstars?' Elder nodded and eased herself to lying down and closed her eyes.

'Mother earth is cold and tired now, I need to rest.'

Zak looked around for a blanket and found one in the pram. He lifted it up but discovered that something had been folded inside. He unwrapped it and took out a photograph, a name carved in plasterwork and a map. Zak felt breathless at seeing them again. So he hadn't imagined any of it.

'Why did you take my stuff?' he asked sharply.

Elder's head rolled to the side and she opened her eyes.

'Elder needs to trust the ones who unravel the vine . . .' She pointed towards the entrance and Zak walked over to the wreath of dried leaves and began reading the golden names, some freshly written and some faded with time and age. There were many names he did not recognize, but plenty that he did.

'Crystal, Iona, Red, Aisha, Zak, Peggy, Eddie, Maisy, Albert, Edwin, Hannah, Kalsi, Abdi, Amina, Lalu, Liliana, Shalini . . . Jessica, Lucas . . .' Even Lyndon's name was there. Zak shuddered as he read the names aloud and Elder's eyes began to grow heavy.

'How did you know my family's names?' Zak demanded.

'Read them in Mrs Kalsi's newspaper,' Elder answered without opening her eyes. 'All my woodland children.' She pointed her finger in Zak's direction. 'Must remember, important to remember.' She continued chanting names of people he had never heard of, as if it was a mantra to send herself to sleep. 'Unravel the vine back through time . . . Ah, my sweet Crystal, I won't be long now, look for my light . . . look for my light.'

Zak lay the blanket over her body. Seeing his mum's, dad's and brother's names written there had filled him with a longing to see them again. He felt guilty now, for calling Elder a witch. What had she ever done except try to help him, in her own weird way? *But why would she write all these name on leaves? Did she think that these people were part of her life . . . her friends even?* Zak felt odd even thinking it, but it did seem as if the doll had kept her company and now she really was all alone.

Chapter Sixty-Two

Laughter rose up from the fireside as Aisha attempted to teach Iona a Somali song. Zak paused for a moment and listened to their conversation. It was hard to believe that these two girls had hated each other just a few days ago.

'I don't really do "soothing"!' Iona tried once more to follow Aisha's words and tune, before collapsing into giggles.

'It's hard to learn another language,' Aisha said, smiling. 'It's not just the words; that's just the surface of it.'

'But you can hardly tell you ever spoke another language.'

'I know but I still love speaking to my friends in Somali. When I was in Primary I used to run off to the toilets to look in the mirror to see if speaking English changed the way my face looked! Crazy isn't it?'

'I don't know. What language do you dream in?' Iona asked.

'Both now! But I remember the first time I dreamed in English how upset I was. It felt like a whole part of myself was drifting away. I told Liliana but she didn't understand why it upset me. She just said I should be proud that I can dream in two languages!'

'I'm with her there!' Iona laughed.

'I was afraid that I'd forget who I used to be. It's hard to explain but there are things you can say, ways of thinking and believing in one language that you can't catch the meaning of in another. Some ideas you just can't translate.'

'Deep! But I can't even speak another language except a few measly words in French. If you learned English, I don't see why I can't learn a little song in Somali. Let me try again.'

Aisha nodded and sang smiling at the intent way that Iona listened and then repeated the line, this time stumbling a little less over the unfamiliar sounds.

Zak walked across the mossy tree trunk that straddled the stream, scrunching leaves underfoot on purpose so that they would hear him coming.

'Where have you been?' Aisha called out as he clambered over the edge of the shelter.

He pointed back towards Elder's den. He still couldn't understand how it was possible that Elder had been living this close without them discovering her, however skilfully her den was hidden among the trees.

'With Elder at the war memorial,' he answered.

'You're not *still* going on about all that!' Iona laughed and ducked inside the shelter.

Zak smiled and took the photograph from his bag and showed it to Aisha. 'Is this the old man you saw in your dream?' he asked, pointing to Albert.

Aisha stared at the photo and frowned. 'He was older, but he did look a bit like that.'

'A bit?' Zak prodded.

'Well, I don't know. I only dreamed about him once!'

Zak ignored the note of doubt in Aisha's voice. '*This* man,' he said, pointing to Edwin, 'is the soldier who led me to the air-raid shelter.'

Aisha furrowed her brow, as if trying to work out a puzzle.

'Still don't believe me? Here! How do you explain this then?' Zak handed her the name in the plasterwork. 'Look, same people as on the shelter wall: Albert Bainbridge. Eddie and Maisy were Albert's grandchildren. Peggy was Edwin's sister and Eddie's mum. Convinced now?'

Aisha didn't answer, but took the piece of plaster from him and traced her fingers over the familiar name, then she picked up the map with the memorial stone circled in pen.

Now that she was faced with the evidence, the only way to explain all this was that somehow both she and

Zak had found a way to connect with the family who had sheltered here in an earlier era. Aisha cast her mind back to what Elder had said when she'd first come to the shelter. Something about her not being able to stay there among that family because there was too much 'longing' in the place. Maybe this wartime family had sensed their own longing and found a way to appear to them.

'I found these at Elder's place. She admitted she took them from me. I think she wanted to see if she could trust me before she showed me where the memorial was. She's got all our names written on leaves. Our names, our families' names and even Edwin and Albert's – all written in gold pen. She has this idea that she's looking after everyone who's been a part of this wood. Including us!'

'Maybe she is,' Aisha whispered.

'I was thinking we should ask her to come and sit by the fire.' Zak rubbed his hands together to keep warm. 'She's going to freeze up there tonight, and she's all alone.'

'You've changed your tune! She's always been alone,' Iona said as she joined them.

They stood around the fire for a moment then Zak remembered Elder's gift and took the amber beads from his pocket.

'Elder asked me to give each of you one of these.' Zak inspected the beads, shining a torch under the surface of the amber, to make sure he was handing them the right ones. 'She gave one to me too. She said the butterfly was for you, Iona, and the ladybird for Aisha; mine's got leaves inside. They're all different.' They each peered into the amber eggs, which were the colour of sunshine, honey and the autumn wood. The beads glowed warmly in the firelight.

'Why would she give these to us now?' Iona asked, inspecting the butterfly suspended in time.

'I don't know, but she buried her doll by the memorial today.' Zak found himself telling Iona.

'Why would she do that? She loves Crystal.' Iona began to pace up and down. 'Something's up with her. You're right – let's ask her to come over here to be with us.' She pointed a torch around the outskirts of the shelter.

'Where's Red, by the way?'

'Here with you,' Zak said, shrugging. 'Isn't she?' Both girls looked at him blankly. 'She got up with me this morning and came as far as the top of the slope, but I sent her back. I figured she headed back to the shelter!'

All three of them started hunting around, calling Red's name, but there was no sign of her.

Aisha looked down at the amber bead she held in her hand and felt for her own prayer beads under her clothes, suddenly needing their warmth against her skin. 'Elder showed me these before; she called them her inheritance.'

Without another word between them, they headed over the stream, following Zak and calling Red's name into the darkness as they went.

Chapter Sixty-Three

They stood outside Elder's den, not wishing to intrude. Since Zak had left her she had covered the low entrance with a piece of old wooden door, which they eventually pulled back. As they crawled inside they were relieved to find that Elder was sitting up on her bed of leaves. She placed her finger on her lips and beckoned them inside. Night lights had been lit in jam jars all around Elder's bed, as if she was setting up a vigil. She indicated for Zak to switch off his torch. In this light Elder's den was transformed into a painting; a warm glow fell across their faces, half in shadow, half in light, and everything was tinted with the soft colours of autumn.

'We've lost Red!' Iona whispered. 'Have you seen her?'

Elder grinned her gap-toothed grin and nodded towards her leaf bed. Nestled into Elder's side was Red, her tongue lolling. She was panting hard and great waves rippled across her tightening belly.

'What's wrong with her?' Iona knelt down next to her dog, a look of deep concern on her face.

'Nothing wrong, Red is strong, nothing wrong, sing a song.'

Red lifted her head and laid it on Iona's lap.

'I'm here now,' Iona murmured.

Then, as if she had been waiting for Iona's arrival, the dog's breathing seemed to ease, and she shifted her position on to her side and moaned, deep and low, as a tiny puppy slithered out of her. She licked away until the film that covered its body was cleared, then bit through the cord and the copper-coloured puppy let out a faint cry. No one spoke, not even Elder.

Then Red seemed to sleep for a while as she passed out of her the empty sack that the puppy had lived in. They were all entranced by the creature's tiny movements so it was hard to know how much time passed. An owl hooted somewhere close by, as if to welcome the puppy into the world. Then once again Red's stomach began to contract and roll, and they watched in amazement as another emerged. As before, Red seemed to know by instinct exactly what to do. Elder placed the two puppies by the dog's side and they began to suckle.

'How could we not have noticed?' Iona whispered. 'Maybe *this* is why she was hiding – she must have been trying to find somewhere safe to have her puppies.'

That night Red gave birth to three copper-red puppies – two girls and one boy. Red fussed over each of them.

'She'll be a good mother,' Elder predicted, and as she tended to Red the years seemed to fall away from her face. 'I used to dream of being a midwife,' she confided in Iona, and then she took the girl's hands in hers. 'You got your butterfly, didn't you?'

Iona nodded.

'Amber for love and happiness, for healing and sunshine. Time to fly free. You can take my wreath down now, unpin the leaves and let them go.' Elder was pointing towards the doorway. Iona hesitated, then walked over to the wreath, unhooked it and brought it back to the old woman. She knelt down and began to release the leaves one by one. There were hundreds or maybe thousands of names written on them.

'Lay them here on Elder's bed, by Elder's heart and Elder's head,' the old woman instructed.

When all the leaves were strewn around her, the golden writing shimmered in the candlelight.

'Did you find Lucy?' Elder whispered in Iona's ear. 'Look for Lucy Locket – she's not lost yet,' Elder murmured, prodding Iona's chest.

Iona began to search through the leaves as if her life depended on it, turning over leaf after leaf.

'What are you looking for?' Zak asked.

'Nothing!' Iona lied. She slowed her frantic searching as she came across the leaf on which Elder had taken it upon herself to write Iona's real name: Lucy. Her heart felt ready to burst as she placed the leaf carefully in her pocket.

'Did you find the little Lucy treasure?' Elder whispered in her ear.

'I did. Thank you,' Iona whispered back. It seemed to Iona that this was the kindest thing that anyone had ever done for her – maybe it was time to remember who she had once been.

'Good, good . . . then snuff out the candles and look for my light in the dark, my earthstars.' Elder glanced from Iona to Zak and Aisha and then to Red and her puppies and sighed with pleasure, drinking in the scene before her.

'A happy ending for Elder, full of light and life.'

'What do you mean?' Iona asked.

'Sleep now, go to sleep.' Elder sighed, attempting to blow out the candle closest to her but her breath was not strong enough. She gestured for Iona to help her. 'Time to let the spirits rest,' she whispered. Her voice was so weak now that she seemed unable to raise it above this wisp.

The three of them lay together on the carpet of leaves that covered the floor, in the pitch black of Elder's home listening to Elder's words echoing through their heads . . . 'Time to let the spirits rest.' Her words from their dreams fused with the small shifts and surprising little sounds that Red's puppies made in their sleep . . . and, as if under a spell, one by one they too drifted off into the deepest of sleeps.

Above them the breeze blew through the great trees of Home Wood. As the night went on it slowly built in force and began swirling around the den roof, whipping itself up into a storm.

Chapter Sixty-Four

Red whimpered loudly, making Iona jolt awake. She listened to the wind howling around the den and sat up. Now there was just enough light to see by. Her first thought was that Red might be in pain, but the puppies were snuggled contentedly into her, their tiny hearts beating visibly beneath their thin skins. Red's head lay on Elder's chest, as if protecting the old woman as well as her puppies. Elder's face looked puffy and her breathing had changed from a wheeze to a rattle. Iona placed a hand on Elder's forehead and felt the heat rise out of her. Iona turned to see Zak and Aisha sleeping and the puppies curled against Red like three little commas. It was as if they had all shrunk to the size of miniature models in a dolls house, so insignificant that the whole den could be picked up by the wind and lifted off the ground.

'What did you mean by a happy ending? Why did you bury Crystal?' Iona's voice woke Aisha and Zak. 'You can't die, Elder, not like this.' She clasped Elder's hands, but the old woman's breath was becoming more laboured by the second.

'We'll go for help,' Zak placed a hand on Iona's back, and Aisha nodded her agreement.

'Go to Mrs Kalsi, bring her here. But no one else. She'll know what to do.'

Red's hackles were raised as she nuzzled up to her puppies. She was whining constantly now.

'It's all right my girl, it'll be all right.' Iona stroked her dog's head to calm her. 'Please hurry, run!' she urged the others.

Zak pulled the door aside, and the storm ripped through Elder's den, raising her bed of leaves off the ground and propelling it outside. Hundreds of red leaves with golden writing swirled around their heads and out among the great trees of Home Wood. Outside the den it felt to Zak as if the whole wood was charged with Elder's magnetic energy, alive with a driving storm, the wind wheeling and wrenching through the branches. Aisha was blasted backwards by a powerful gust. Zak grabbed her arm and they held each other upright, bowing their faces against the force of the storm. Above them the great oaks creaked and groaned as their branches bent to the will of the wind. Zak and Aisha called out to each other as they tried to find their way out of the sealed-off area. No matter how hard they shouted to be heard above the storm, their voices were as light as the leaves being blasted and blown about the wood. It felt as if a million wild spirits had been released in flight.

Zak climbed over some low fencing and saw the conservation sign that he had not read since the day he'd entered the wood. They were now on the path that led back to the road. The overhanging trees were less dense here, but still the buffeted branches continued to shed their leaves. As soon as they reached the upper path Aisha and Zak began to run again, ducking away from the loosened debris of fallen branches that flew like furies around them. In the distance a deep groan rumbled from somewhere in the heart of the woodland. Zak and Aisha slowed their pace, stopped and listened to the sound of their own breath followed by a violent thud that made the earth shudder. Then a final last squall of wind before an eerie calm settled upon the wood as if all the strength had suddenly drained out of the storm. Zak took Aisha's hand and they walked slowly now as they approached the railings. The entrance to the wood was carpeted in a sea of red leaves and the metal gates were open.

The street lights shone through the dawn gloom and a lorry trundled past. How weird it felt to step out of the cocoon of the wood back into the early-morning city, as it rumbled into life.

'Do you think she's going to be all right?' Zak asked as they picked up their pace again.

'I don't know. I preferred the storm,' Aisha said, as they looked back into the wood that now felt still as death. Zak knew exactly what she meant.

Over their heads a raucous flight of geese crossed the sky in the perfect point of an arrow.

Chapter Sixty-Five

'Wild night. Still, no real damage done.' Mrs Kalsi surveyed the front of the shop and picked up the table and chair that had blown over in the wind. She paused and looked up to admire the stately journey of the geese crossing the silvery sky.

'How do they stay in such formation?'

Mr Kalsi came outside and wrapped his arms around his wife's waist, patting her ample tummy and peering sky-ward. 'In perfect shape! Like a Red Arrow fly-past!' He smiled.

'They sound like Elder! With her chanting!' Mrs Kalsi laughed, but then furrowed her forehead. 'I wonder where she spent last night.' She sighed, unaware that Zak and Aisha were even now making their way up the road towards them, with nothing but Elder on their minds.

'Mrs Kalsi!' Zak called out to her.

She paused on the pavement and her hand rose up to her mouth as if she was witnessing a mirage.

'Oh-hoh, oh-hoh. Quickly, Ashok, find my phone . . . our prayers have been answered! Don't be so slow. Call Liliana, call Shalini, tell them to come straight away – tell them children are safe!' Mrs Kalsi's feet were dancing with happiness. She hadn't run in years, but she was running now towards Zak and Aisha, her arms outstretched, shouting for joy. They slowed again as they saw her approach.

'Please, Mrs Kalsi, Elder's ill,' Zak explained urgently.

'What? What about Elder?' Mrs Kalsi asked, but didn't wait for a response. 'So you're OK, both of you safe, fine, not hurt? Where have you been all this time? We have all worried so much about you!' Her arms were flailing about and she struggled to catch her breath.

'Ashok, get food, some tea. You must be hungry. Look how thin they are, Ashok. We must give them food straight away.'

'Take a breath, Mala, be calm! My eardrums are going to burst with all these women screaming at me,' Mr Kalsi said, laughing as he came back out of the shop still on his mobile phone.

'We don't want any food. Please, call an ambulance,' Aisha begged. 'For Elder.'

'Why are they talking of Elder?' Mrs Kalsi was shouting in frustration now, but Mr Kalsi ignored her. He nodded at Aisha, dialled and waited.

Mrs Kalsi was looking from Zak to Aisha to Mr Kalsi in total confusion. 'But you *have* called Liliana and Shalini?' she asked him.

'That's what I'm trying to say. They screamed so loud, I think my eardrum is burst.'

'Stop talking about eardrums at a time like this . . .'

Mr Kalsi held up his hand to stop his wife saying another word while he spoke into his mobile.

'Yes, Home Wood Drive, by Kalsis Woodland Store. Homeless lady . . . Elder . . . I don't know details exactly . . . No you won't get an ambulance in there . . . and the missing children. Yes, yes, of course, police too.'

Now Zak and Aisha had taken hold of Mrs Kalsi's arm and were pulling her towards the wood despite her resistance.

'No, I can't. Liliana and Shalini are coming here now to find you. They'll never forgive me if I let you go again.'

Mr Kalsi took his wife by the shoulders and spoke in a calm, clear voice.

'No questions now. Just go. I'll stay here and wait for others. We know where you are. Take your phone. Go and find Elder – sounds like she needs you, Mala.'

She nodded to her husband, took a deep breath and followed Aisha and Zak into the wood.

*

Mrs Kalsi asked an endless stream of questions as they followed the paths that led to the conservation zone – questions to which they mostly answered, 'We're fine.' It seemed to take forever even to reach the closed-off area because every few minutes they had to stop for Mrs Kalsi to catch her breath. By the time they crossed the stream and approached Elder's den she was so out of breath that she could hardly speak a word.

'You have been . . . staying here . . . with Elder?' she managed to ask between gasps.

'Not really,' Aisha replied.

'This *can't* be where she lives.' Mrs Kalsi groaned and her hands began to shake as she bent down and pulled aside the wooden door that Iona must have replaced to shelter from the wind.

The girl was lying on what was left of the bed of leaves beside Elder, holding her hand. Red's head rested on Iona's stomach while her puppies were busy suckling. Mrs Kalsi clasped her chest tight as she attempted to take in the scene before her.

'Iona?' she whispered.

The girl lifted her head at the sound of Mrs Kalsi's voice. Her eyes were bloodshot, as if she'd been crying for a long time.

'It's too late,' she whispered, gently releasing Elder's hand from her grip. 'She's gone.'

Mrs Kalsi sat for a while with Elder's head in her

lap. 'I should have thought to bring a brush,' she said quietly, as she patiently untangled leaves and smoothed her fingers through Elder's hair, 'I came to you, Elder. Home visit. One last appointment,' she whispered.

Iona took charge of the arrangements, as if Elder had been a relative and she knew her needs better than anyone. Zak found the stretcher leaning against the side of the den, the same one that Elder had used to drag him into the wood. Iona took a blanket and lay it over the wooden structure. With great care Zak placed his hands under Elder's back and lifted her lifeless body on to the stretcher. She was no weight at all. Then Aisha lay Red's three squirming puppies wrapped in another blanket at the end of the stretcher and Iona helped Red to climb on beside them. The dog and her puppies together were almost as heavy as Elder.

It was a noisy dawn, as if the birds, sheltering from the wind, had been holding back their pent-up song and now began blasting the world with their chorus.

Elder's hessian pouch fell over the side of the stretcher as they carried her, slowly releasing a trail of breadcrumbs. Aisha turned and watched the birds fly in. The first to arrive were the two blue-backed birds, their delicate wings fluttering a farewell; then came the robins, sparrows and chaffinches, the screeching crows in their black dinner jackets and finally the pigeons with their titanium collars, pecking behind the stretcher like an unruly gathering of mourners.

The day was growing brighter and chill grey clouds scudded across the sky washing the morning with a silvery glow. The motley procession slowly bore Elder's body towards the gathering crowd of press, police, ambulances friends and family waiting on the pavement. Flashlights bombarded them as they left the wood. Mrs Kalsi was first to greet the deafening blare of the road, the blinding swirling lights, the sirens and all the questions.

Zak spotted Lucas first, then Lyndon and Shalini. He held his breath. *You promised me, Edwin. We had a deal.* Somebody turned him by the shoulders and he felt his mum's arms envelop him, grab a fistful of his tangled hair and pull him close. A strangled wail released from his mum's body that sounded like an animal's call. 'My Zak, my Zak,' she cried. Then he felt his whole family surround him in a tight embrace.

Shalini hung back a little and waited. Zak stretched out his arms and she too joined them in holding him close.

'I'm sorry,' he whispered to her.

Liliana was sitting in a police car with her daughter when Aisha walked out of the wood. She got out and staggered against the bonnet of the car, then opened her arms and Aisha walked into them. Liliana held her so tightly that the force of her emotion almost took the breath from Aisha's lungs.

A photographer pushed his way through the police barrier, came right up to Liliana and captured their embrace. The flash went off in their faces, but neither of them cared.

'Will you take Red and her puppies, just for a while?' Iona asked Mrs Kalsi, and she felt, under the circumstances, that she could hardly refuse.

'Sure you don't want me to come with you?' Mrs Kalsi asked Iona, but the girl shook her head as she watched Zak and Aisha being swept into the arms of their loved ones, and a sharp stab of sadness pierced her heart. For a while, in the wood, she had felt as if the three of them had become their own little family. Now it seemed that Zak and Aisha would go back to their old lives and she would be on her own once more. *Maybe I'm meant to replace Elder in the wood,* she thought to herself as she sat in the ambulance and studied the old woman's lifeless face that now seemed to wear all the scars of her hard life.

Chapter Sixty-Six

Of course, everybody wanted to know the strange story of what had happened to the missing children.

The press were hungry for each of their experiences, but were disappointed with the reports that they gave. Had the homeless old woman trapped them there? Did they believe she was a witch and why did they think she had kept them a secret? How had they survived? What did the three of them have in common? Had they made some sort of pact to stay together? Why had they chosen to stay in the air-raid shelter? What was the story behind the war memorial? Who would look after the puppies?

And as with all stories, Aisha, Iona and Zak each had their different ways of explaining events. Photographs of their emotional reunion on the street made it into all the major newspapers, along with one of Elder and the puppies on the stretcher. It seemed as if the news of their return had captured everybody's imagination. A picture of Aisha and Liliana embracing appeared everywhere for weeks afterwards. There was a lot of interest in Liliana's plan to officially adopt Aisha too. It sparked all sorts of debates about the pros and cons of adopting a child from a different culture and religion than your own, at Liliana's age as well.

Zak, Aisha and Iona were asked many times to speak of what had really happened to them in the wood. But in the telling each of them kept a little piece of their experience back. Without discussing it, none of them said a word about the amber eggs that had been Elder's parting gift – their inheritance.

'The truth is, I was only there because I was looking for my dog.' That was Iona's reply, but nobody was that interested in her story because she was not one of the officially missing children. As she herself said, no one had been looking for her or waiting at the gates of Home Wood to welcome her into their arms.

Zak was certain that there was no logical way to explain how he had been led by a soldier called Edwin to the air-raid shelter and then the war memorial, to follow the trail that now made him feel as if he was part of the bricks and mortar of his new house. So he simply said that he had run away as a kind of protest and come across the others by chance.

Now that Zak's belongings from the old house were unpacked, his mum was home for a while at least and Lyndon had come back to see him, it was starting to feel more like home. Zak often looked at the picture of Edwin and Albert he'd framed and placed on his desk and wondered whether they had been sending him some kind of message from beyond the grave. He had got his mum to agree that Albert's name in the plasterwork should be placed above the front door, so that every time he walked through it he thought of the wartime family and thanked them for helping him to make this place into a home. The only way he could explain to himself what had happened was that for a time a little crack had opened from the past and let him in.

Aisha told the reporters that she had run away because she was afraid of having to start again. She said she had made some unexpected friends in the wood, including a wise old woman who had looked after them all. Aisha felt for her mother's beads of jet. Thanks to Elder she knew that the spark of life burned on, that her father, her mother, her aunt and her home were still alive within her, no matter where she lived. And she had asked her social worker if she could meet the girl who would have been her sister if she'd been adopted. Her name was Ayan. Though the family had decided to adopt a baby in the end, Ayan and Aisha struck up a friendship of their own.

It seemed that Elder and her white poppies had bought them all a kind of peace . . . all except for Iona.

Chapter Sixty-Seven

Of the three of them, Iona found it the hardest to leave the wood and in fact, after Elder's simple funeral, she'd left Red and her puppies with Mrs Kalsi and wandered off again.

'This is my bad karma, for telling a lie,' Mrs Kalsi tutted to herself as she set up a dog duvet by the radiator in the shop. 'At least that girl could have stayed and helped look after her own dog and puppies!' she complained, but as she sat with Red and her pups watching their little exchanges of affection and annoyance, Mrs Kalsi couldn't help but fall in love with them.

'Just one, Ashok. Others we will find homes for . . . I have already thought up a name for this one! What do you think of Henna?'

Mr Kalsi smiled but shook his head. 'No, no, no, we can't take in any more strays!'

Iona was gone for two days. Aisha and Zak found her in the end. They felt guilty crossing over into the

352

conservation zone because they had promised they would never enter it again until the fencing came down in ten years' time.

'We'll be twenty three when this bit of the wood's opened up again! We should come back here together then and see the memorial and the shelter,' Zak said, as they traced their way back through the wood.

'Let's make a promise to do that, wherever we are, whatever we're doing,' Aisha suggested. She bent her head as Zak lifted up a low-lying branch for her to step underneath. It was impossible to imagine themselves that far into the future but it was also impossible to imagine a time when they would not know each other.

'Iona?'

'Iona?'

Zak and Aisha both called her name as they descended the familiar steep slope, and sure enough she appeared at the entrance to the air-raid shelter. Her face looked pinched and cold, and there were dark rings under her eyes. She smiled as if she'd been half expecting them, and they went inside. The back wall was now covered in chalk drawings of an island: sea, waves and rocks, and huge-winged seabirds flew around its surfaces. In one corner there was a tiny cottage and a little girl holding a woman's hand. In the girl's other hand she held an amber egg, and just appearing out of the top of the egg was a delicate pale green butterfly with yellow-tipped wings.

'Who's the girl?' Aisha asked.

'Her name was Lucy,' Iona said. 'All this is Iona, I told you . . . the island I come from. I changed my name when I ran away.'

'Lucy?' Aisha said the name slowly. 'It sounds sweet and young.'

'Well, I was once, believe it or not!'

'What are you going to do now?' Zak asked Iona.

'Not sure. I might go back up to the island for a bit,' she said.

'Do you know what Iona means?' Zak asked her.

She shrugged. 'No idea.'

'Blessed,' Zak told her.

'Not up till now!' She laughed grimly. 'These last few days in the wood, sometimes I've caught this little wisp of red between the trees, heard a chanting and followed it. I suppose it's just wishful thinking. I can't stay here forever, that's for sure . . . sometimes I think I'm losing my mind. I keep having this dream about that Eddie you kept going on about, Zak.' Iona reached into her pocket and took out the little purse of jacks. 'I've had the same dream every night I've been in here. This Eddie turns up, sits on that bench over there and goes on and on about you being the keeper of the jacks.' She handed the pouch over. 'Perhaps he'll get off my case now,' she laughed.

Zak smiled at Aisha as if to say, 'I told you so!' She

354

shook her head in disbelief, stood up and felt over the letters of Eddie's name on the wall.

'I have something I made for us all out there,' Iona led the way climbing up over the shelter to the place where a tree had fallen over the stream. 'I thought I might as well make use of it. I've turned it into a seat. Maybe we can come here one day and sit together with our feet in the stream!' Iona smiled at Zak as he read the crude lettering she'd carved on the back of the woodland bench . . . he could almost hear Elder speak the words, '*Look for my light.*'

It felt wrong sitting by the fire with Iona, now that they knew that tonight they would be safely home. They had been equals for a while when they had all sheltered here together, but now Iona was 'the homeless girl' again. There was so much that they could have spoken about and yet it was awkward between them. No songs were sung. They could not persuade her to come back with them, even when they told her that the Kalsis had invited her to stay for as long as she wanted.

When they left, Iona called after them, 'Thanks for coming to look for me!'

As they walked back out of the wood it felt to Aisha and Zak as if they were leaving a member of their own family out in the cold.

Chapter Sixty-Eight

Mr and Mrs Kalsi paid for Iona's travel back to her island. Mrs Kalsi offered to go with her, but Iona insisted that she had to make this particular trip on her own. She went straight to the cottage she had lived in when she had been the little girl Lucy, before the Ogre had entered her life. It was empty and derelict and everything seemed to have shrunk. For so long the place had been a giant in her imagination, but now she was standing here on the soft island sands, it seemed like a modest, delicate jewel.

Despite the cold, Iona stripped off and ran into the sea, as she had done so many times when she was still Lucy. She felt as if she was shedding all the grime of her street life as the ice-cold water seeped into her pores. When she stepped out of the waves she realized that the island had not shrunk at all; it was just that she had grown.

She had intended to spend one or two nights there, but she found that she had no wish to stay for longer;

to swim and feel free as she had in her childhood – and to know that she could again – was all that she had needed.

She waited at the little port for the ferry, watching the light dance on the water. 'Thank you, Elder,' she whispered to the breeze. The whole trip had lasted only a day, and yet it had taken her years to pluck up the courage to return.

'That's never little Lucy!' The ferry woman was staring at her now. 'I remember you when you were so high!'

Iona felt a sudden rush of warmth. She did not recognize this woman, but that didn't matter, because she was remembered, and it gave her a feeling that all the bits of her life were not carved up into little compartments that didn't join together. For the first time since she'd left the island she felt found. She reached around her neck for the cross her mum had given her and the leather tie she'd strung Elder's amber bead on and examined the delicate wings of the butterfly within.

Mr and Mrs Kalsi were delighted to receive Iona's call to say that she would be back earlier than expected. When she arrived they were dancing around their shop fighting over who should give her the good news. Mrs Kalsi won!

'I am delighted to inform you that your daughter's

beautiful portrait of her dog Red has been accepted into the Royal Academy Summer Exhibition!'

'Daughter?!' Iona laughed.

'Only a little untruth. You are living here after all, and who else but a mother would take in a girl, her dog and her puppies?'

There was an article about Iona in the *Big Issue*, and the front cover was a portrait of Elder that Iona had painted especially. At the bottom she had written: 'Homeless but not invisible'.

Aisha and Zak watched Iona's transformation day by day as Mrs Kalsi painstakingly combed out her matted dreads to unveil beautiful silken locks. She was putting on weight and her eyes and skin were bright with health and hope.

In return for living in the flat above the shop, Iona began working evenings for Mrs Kalsi, even after a long day at art college. In the daytime Mr Kalsi placed a copy of the *Big Issue* by his till and whatever small item he sold he couldn't help himself from telling Iona's story to his customers. He always ended with the same flourish. 'For Iona we think this is not a happy ending but a happy beginning.'

Chapter Sixty-Nine

Aisha found it. Well, strictly speaking, her puppy Conker found it. Aisha was walking through the churchyard when Conker, who was now six months old, started sniffing around a newish-looking gravestone, so Aisha stopped to read and her mouth fell open in shock.

'Eddie Lowie.'

This was the name of the little boy 'Eddie' on the shelter wall. The boy they had dreamed about – the original owner of the game of jacks!

Aisha read the gravestones of people she knew: Maisy Lowie, Peggy Lowie, Albert Bainbridge . . . all here under this earth.

She phoned Zak, but there was no answer, so she hung up and carried on home.

'But he was my neighbour!' Liliana said. 'He passed away while you were in the wood. It was only me and Shalini who went to the funeral . . . poor old thing. I didn't think to mention it – we were all so caught up with your homecoming celebrations.'

Aisha texted Zak:

U won't believe it. Found Eddie Lowie's grave, lived nxt door 2 Liliana. Died when we were in wood. Cd have met him in real life.

A message jumped straight into Aisha's phone.

Ask 4 date he died?

'Zak wants to know if you remember exactly when he died.'

'I do actually. It was on the night of Diwali. I remember because it made Shalini so sad.'

Diwali. Aisha texted back.

That was the night he came to say goodbye. I met him. You 2 in your dream. Iona 2. We all did.

Aisha read Zak's reply over and over.

'I bumped into Zak the other day. Hardly recognized him with his short hair.' Liliana smiled. 'He looks older too. What's his mum been feeding him? Shalini won't know him when she comes back. He's taller than you now. Handsome young man, isn't he?'

Aisha shrugged and felt the heat rush to her face. It seemed as if Liliana, Muna and Ayan had made a pact to mercilessly tease her about Zak. They were always trying to find out if something was going on between them.

'Has he asked you out yet? Come on, you can tell me,' Muna had pressed again today in school. 'I promise I won't tell my mum anything or she'll think you're leading me astray! It's bad enough that we're always out walking your dog!'

'As if!' Aisha laughed. 'We're friends, OK? Just friends! He's like a brother to me. I feel as if with you, Zak, Iona and Ayan, I've gained a brother and sisters.'

'Right on, sister!' Muna had raised her eyebrows incredulously and laughed.

Liliana stroked Conker's head thoughtfully. She had never imagined that she would feel such fondness for a dog. It had taken some time for Aisha to persuade her to take in the puppy, but now she couldn't imagine life without Conker around.

'Mrs Kalsi was saying we should all go for a walk through Home Wood, get Red and her pups together. She thinks it's time to let Elder's ashes go.'

361

Chapter Seventy

'Henna! This way,' cried Mrs Kalsi as her unruly puppy scrambled into the wood. 'I am going to have to send Mr Kalsi to dog-training school.'

'I think it's Henna that needs to go!' Iona joked.

'Ha ha, very funny, cheeky girl!' laughed Mrs Kalsi.

'Amber! Over here!' Zak called, and his dog came bounding straight over. 'Good . . . sit!' Zak handed the puppy a treat.

'Just showing off now. Maybe I should send Henna to Zak for training instead! Mr Kalsi is always spoiling her with treats, making her fat. See? OK, then, you can have a little treat too.' Mrs Kalsi relented, taking one out of her own pocket and holding it up for Henna.

'It's not for you, Conker!' Liliana said as Conker leaped up and stole Henna's treat mid-air.

'Feisty!' Liliana laughed, hugging Aisha to her.

*

'Just one last time!' Iona was saying as she stared into the conservation area. 'It wouldn't be right to scatter them anywhere else.'

Mrs Kalsi and Liliana reluctantly agreed, handed over Elder's ashes, and walked the paths around the closed-off area, hoping that they wouldn't have to explain themselves.

The floor of the wood was covered with a sea of bluebells and wild garlic and the air was perfumed by their bitter-sweet scent. It seemed as if the earth was finally springing back to life after the cold winter.

Aisha, Zak and Iona sat in the air-raid shelter, trying to take in all that had happened in the time that they had stayed here. Red lay across their knees as if she belonged to them all. The giant image of Elder with her wild leaf-threaded hair towered over them.

'It's a shame to think that no one's going to see this for another ten years,' Zak said.

'Maybe it'll have faded away by then.'

'Would you mind if it does?' Zak asked.

Iona shrugged. 'It was about us, our time here, wasn't it? Come on, let's do this thing.' She picked up the little wooden pot that contained Elder's ashes and led the way up and over the air-raid shelter to the stream.

They sat down on the seat that Iona had carved while she walked over the fallen trunk to a small upright tree with branches arching over the water. It was covered in clusters of large white flower heads made up of hundreds of tiny lace-like constellations.

'You know what these are, don't you?' She asked as she returned and placed the heads like delicate bouquets in Aisha and Zak's hands keeping one back for herself. 'Elder flowers!' Iona whispered.

Aisha smiled as she examined hers closely, 'or earthstars!'

Iona released the ashes slowly into the water then one by one Iona, Aisha and Zak scattered the flowers and watched them float away. Red lifted her head and sniffed the air as a gentle breeze whispered through the branches above them.

'I'm as light as the leaves that fall as I walk, as light as leaf rain . . .'

Q & A with Sita Brahmachari

Your characters are all very different. What inspired you to bring them all together in one story?

People use the word 'community' a lot, but sometimes I wonder what that word means. In London, where I live, it's possible for people from diverse backgrounds, hailing from all over the world, rich and poor, old and young, home dwellers and homeless, to be living in the same 'community' – they may pass in the street but never really get to know each other or have empathy for one another. By bringing such different characters together I wanted to explore what is meant by 'community'.

How has your own life inspired *Red Leaves*?

Being of mixed heritage myself I have thought a lot about belonging and identity. Sometimes when I was young the term 'half-caste' was used for someone with dual heritage like me. I hated that label . . . because I felt that my background gave me access to double, not half, a world. I always wanted to write a story about young people from different cultures, backgrounds and religions coming together. It's no coincidence that I've written *Red Leaves* now, when there is so much talk, lots of it negative, about migration that does not match with my experience of life in a vibrant, diverse city.

Where did the idea for the setting of *Red Leaves* come from?

I like to think up stories as I walk with my dog, Billie, and as I strolled through a city wood close to where I live the idea for *Red Leaves* began to emerge. Queen's Wood in London (where, in my imagination, the book is set) dates back to the Domesday Book and is part of the ancient forest that used to cover the whole of the UK. There's a wall plaque there inscribed with these words: 'This wood is gifted to the people of the city forever.' I like the idea of a place that is open to everyone who ever passes through the city, no matter where they are from or where they are going.

What is it about woodland that feeds your imagination?

When you live in a busy city, sometimes you feel the need to escape. The dense leaf canopies in woods can make you feel instantly cut off from the wider world . . . like stepping on to an island.

As well as writing novels I love writing for theatre. On the first day of rehearsals the designer presents a model box to the actors. It's a little like a doll's house except the box contains a miniature model of the theatre set and scenery, and little cut-out costumed characters of the actors, which are moved around to tell the story. This is the magical moment when I begin to see the play come to life. As I walked through Queen's Wood thinking about the characters in my story I realized that *Red Leaves* already had its model box – an urban wood. I thought to myself, *If this wood is 'Britain' now . . . it also contains Britain's past . . . And these ancient trees stand as witnesses to its history, its inhabitants and their wars and struggles.*

Why did you call the wood in Red Leaves 'Home Wood'?

Looking at the trees in the wood I wondered how deep their roots went underground. I wanted the roots of my characters' pasts to burrow out beyond the woodland, through the city and across the world as far as Syria, Sri Lanka, Somalia and America. Ask people where their roots lead to and you will find yourself travelling the world. As my characters entered Home Wood I noticed that each of them was struggling to find a sense of belonging. So I call my wood Home Wood because it becomes the home my three young characters are searching for. It is a city wood that offers shelter to anyone searching for a safe and loving home. It reflects a home I want to live in, an open place that inspires compassion and is not afraid of change. This wood belonging 'to the people of the city forever' could be in any cosmopolitan city in the world.

Acknowledgements

Thank you to my wonderful partner Leo and family, Maya, Keshin and Esha-Lily, for putting up with me disappearing into the woods of writing!

Thank you to Sophie Gorell Barnes of MBA Literary Agents for her constant support and sensitive readings of *Red Leaves*.

Thanks to my editor Venetia Gosling for our creative woodland editorial and the whole team at Macmillan Children's Books for supporting my work.

Special thanks to Helen Bray (Assistant Editor), Rachel Vale (Art Director), Talya Baker (Copy Editor) and Catherine Alport (Publicity Manager).

Thank you also to Nicky Parker, Publisher at Amnesty. I am very proud that Amnesty International has endorsed *Red Leaves* as a book that speaks of Human Rights both at home and abroad.

I would like to thank Annie Birch, Subject Leader for Language and Literacy at St Paul's Way Trust School, and the Somali Girl's Advisory Group: Sado Ali, Naima Omar, Mymona Noor and Jakia Parbeen, who read an early draft of *Red Leaves* and contributed cultural and religious details for the character of Aisha.

Thank you to Mary Mcilroy for sharing with me her contemporary knowledge and experience of being a foster carer. Thank you also to Christine Tyler, whose experience of adoption informed the relationship between Liliana and Aisha. The kindness and compassion of these women are at the heart of this book.

Thank you to my mum Freda and late dad Amal Krishna Brahmachari, who had such wonderful community spirit.

The idea for the painting of the dog submitted to the Royal Academy exhibition came from a painting entitled *Cassie* by Amie Douglas. Amie was in Year 6 of primary school when her painting of a dog was chosen for the RA Summer Exhibition 2012.

With thanks to the Queen's Wood Cafe for uncovering the memorial plaque and for holding the Elderflower Herbal Walk by The Handmade Apothecary, where I learned so much.

And last but not least I thank the beautiful red setter Nula and her pups, as well as our own lovely dogs, the late Ringo and our little dog Billie, for their loyal companionship and for inspiring the character of the beautiful dog Red and her puppies in *Red Leaves*.

Amnesty International

We are all born with human rights, no matter who we are or where we live. Sadly we are not always allowed to enjoy them.

Human rights are about justice, fairness, truth and freedom. We are all born with the right to an identity, for example, but also to equality, a home to belong to, freedom of movement and the entitlement to seek sanctuary. The three young characters in *Red Leaves* explore all these issues, and so do we as readers.

Our human rights are the bedrock of a healthy and diverse society. They help us to live good lives. But they are frequently under attack and we need to uphold them. Amnesty International is a movement of ordinary people from across the world standing up for humanity and human rights. We aim to protect individuals wherever justice, fairness, truth and freedom are denied.

If you're a young person you can find out more about human rights and how to stand up for them at www.amnesty.org.uk/youth

If you're a teacher you can find many free resources, including 'Using Fiction to Teach Human Rights', at www.amnesty.org.uk/education

Amnesty International UK
Human Rights Action Centre
17–25 New Inn Yard
London EC2A 3EA
020 7033 1500
www.amnesty.org.uk
@AmnestyUK
facebook.com/amnestyuk